THE ELECTRIFYING ANGELS FLIGHT

Joy Munson

Matchstick Literary
1-888-306-8885
orders@matchliterary.com

In Memory of James R. Munson

Special Thanks to Ram Wilson, Senior Literary Specialist
at Match Literary Publishing and staff members

Synopsis

The Electrifying Angel's Flight (sequel) to The Electrifying Demise

Six years have passed, and Angel Flight Gulf Stream medically equipped air transport plane fleet has added Angel Flight Four and Angel Flight Six.

The people in The Dalles, Oregon, are law-abiding citizens. The stories unfold, and new residents are welcomed, each having a fascinating history.

The Michael Murphy & Son Electrical Contractors business was the financier for the formation of Mike Murphy (the son) to realize his dream of becoming a MediVac service to people free of any charges.

Mike and Susan have their wedding anniversary evening without fanfare.

Mike is needing flight crews for additional planes, and the encounter with his first applicant for the pilot seat has a long story. He has a wife whose story is important as well. This passage covers conversation of general, getting acquainted subjects. It progresses to a short flight that involved teaching to achieve "smoothe" touchdowns for the comfort of ill or injured patients arrival at hospitals, etc. for urgent care.

The next encounter is a brawl with a thug at the local grocery store. This is exciting, and blow by blow narrative is action-packed!

The new pilot's lady and other women visit, and soon wedding plans are forming.

The tale continues when an attractive lady comes into Mike's office to apply for a pilot's position. She is a vibrant and robust character with issues; some immediate and others such as lodging, car parking, clothes. These are minor, and the significant problems are exciting, surprising, impressive and unusual.

Three guys from New Jersey came into the office. They were expected and looking to qualify for a job with Angel Flight. One of them is noticeably causing suspicion and distrust at first impressions. That was the correct impression for this guy.

There was a call for a copilot, and an available part-time pilot from Wyoming was hired for a one-time flight.

The Police of Chief in The Dalles is a Native American and has personality and fairness in his enforcement of legal statutes and sometimes affording competent counsel to wayward souls who go astray.

Along the way, many shadowy characters and policemen have encounters of different degrees and behaviors. In Chicago and in Atlantic City are battles of evil guy/right guy eye-opening events. Crime does not pay.

Romance, of course, is not missing from this book by any means, and there is no need to search for the scenes, although not to be alarmed by graphic explanations.

Many reverent scenes occur and are heartwarming and are good examples for any ready to notice. Brotherly love and counting are blessings are only two of many.

The emergency episode of a man injured by a bull is unique. He is a tough rancher and doesn't want sedation or any pampering. The part-time pilot was also a rancher, and a business deal was agreed by the two that will be a point of information to the average person. This copilot also shows a profound talent, none of which, his family nor friends were aware of.

A rickety truck parks in front of The Dalles police chief's office and a black confident, but obviously troubled young woman explains she is need of a job and has a son and mother for whom she is responsible. This episode is, again, human interest and does turn out for the best.

The plot thickens, and things begin to be apparent that dangerous criminal activity is about to be exposed, and the case can be closed.

Before and after the incidents and events there are picnics, casino activity, hand to hand contact of criminal vs. police, devotional scenes, and rarely does a problematic situation go unsolved.

The ending is quite violent but justified.

CHAPTER 1

Mike hung up the phone after a lengthy conversation with the girl at the greenhouse, leaned back in his chair, and stared at the picture on his office wall. It was the Lockheed SR-71. "What a magnificent bird," he said aloud.

"You are so right," echoed a voice behind him. Mike spun around to see to whom the voice belonged. "I'm John Schumann, and I understand you are looking for airplane drivers."

"I am," Mike answered, "What experience do you have, John?"

"Twenty years of electrifying feelings flying off carriers."

"Navy?"

"Marines," John answered. "I heard some retired top gunwas looking for drivers for his fleet of Med-Flies. I looked into it and decided I would like to be a part of something like that, and here I am."

"John," Mike said, extending his hand, "I'm the guy they're talking about. I was Top Gun, but that is history. I 'm just Mike Murphy now, trying to keep Angel Flight up and running. If you're serious, I'll have Heather get you an application and explain what we expect from you and what you will get in return. I was about to leave for the day when you got here, so if you don't mind coming back tomorrow at about tena.m., we will continue the interview. If you need to spend the night, we have an open account at the Marriott. Tell them you are with Angel Flight and just sign the tab. Enjoy your stay."

"I'll see you in the morning then, Mike. My wife is with me, and I'll pay her way."

"John, you now are part of our family, and that includes your wife and all dependents. Heather! Give this 'jarhead' an application and your orientation spiel. John, bring your wife inside. There is no reason she should sit in the car. We have a lounge area with fresh coffee, cold soda, iced tea, and if you ask sweetly, Heather will get a plate of just-baked applesauce cookies. I have to go. I am already late."

CHAPTER 2

Mike stepped into the kitchen with a puzzled look. Susan had a form-fitting, black, crepe fabric dress, cut just above the knees to show off her beautiful legs, three-inch heels, a simple strand of pearls and matching earrings. The table was ready for two with her good china and sterling silver flatware, and two candles cast a soft light on the scene. Mike could smell the steaks broiling and noticed the fresh green, tossed salad. "Where are the children?" he asked, "and what's going on?"

"It's our anniversary, you big dumb Irishman," Susan cried. "I can't believe you, of all people, would forget such an important event in our lives. Let's eat before everything else is spoiled."

"I'm sorry, sweetheart. I have no excuse for my forgetfulness except a total, out of this world, feeling as I enter this atmosphere of love and happiness."

Dinner was over when the doorbell rang. "Will you get that honey; I have to use the bathroom." While Susan answered the door, Mike put a black, velvet box at her place that contained a mother's ring with a half-carat diamond in the center.

Susan answered the door and received a dozen long-stemmed roses with a note. These long-stemmed roses pale in comparison to your long stems. Your beauty makes the most beautiful flowers envious. I love you. Your big, dumb Irish husband, Mike.'

After the shock wore off, she came to the table and noticed the black box. When she opened it, the dam broke, and she cried, not sobbed but cried like she hadn't cried in years. She put her arms around Mike's neck and sitting on his lap, let the tears of joy flow. Regaining her composure, she apologized for being so sensitive.

"Sweetheart," Mike said, "You don't need to apologize for anything. I hope you have some wine to top off this dinner. It was delicious, even though the atmosphere was a little chilly. I'm sure the wine will warm things up."

"I guarantee it will heat things up. The children are staying in their bunkhouse and will have breakfast with Grandma Romaine. We can make as much noise as we want," Susan purred into Mike's ear.

"Let's clear the table and have our wine," Mike suggested.

"I'm not in the mood for clearing the table," Susan responded. "The wine is on the bedside table; I'll meet you in the shower."

Susan had the shower head turned to a gentle spray with the temperature just below too hot. All the stress and tiredness seemed to run down the drain. Mike joined her, and they began their ritual of washing each other. Soon Mike embraced Susan, and she rested her head on his chest and moaned a sigh of contentment. After washing and drying, they slid into the bed. Susan wore "Windsong," and Mike wore "Brut." He kissed her and tenderly caressed her until they fell asleep in each other's arms. The cougar screamed, the owl hooted, and the Columbia River gurgled and splashed on its way to the Pacific. Soft pine-scented breezes wafted over the sleeping couple, but they didn't hear or feel anything.

CHAPTER 3

Mike awoke to the heady aroma of fresh coffee brewing and Susan singing-not softly humming as was her norm but singing, 'Oh What A Beautiful Morning.' Mike donned his robe and wrapping Susan in his arms and nuzzling her neck, whispered, *'I love you.'* I'm sorry I was such an insensitive ass last night. Who could forget our Las Vegas wedding night? You kicked the pants off an obnoxious drunk, and we got a new jet for Angel Flight."

"Darling, my PMS kicked in so let's forget the bad part, the rest isunforgettable, Thank you for my mother's ring and the special stone in the middle. Go dress and drink your coffee, or I'll make you late for work," Susan threatened.

"Any other day, I would challenge your threat, but today I have to finish an interview with a new pilot. A 'jarhead' named John Schumann came in just as I finished ordering your flowers. I put him and his wife up in the Marriott. I'm to meet him at ten o'clock."

After a quick breakfast, a kiss, and I love you, Mike was out the door.

John and his wife were waiting for him, even though he was early.

"This is my wife, Kim. I met her in Nam, and you can see why she captured my heart."

Kim was the "Asian" Susan; dark, flashing eyes that could investigate your soul or bore right through you, whichever was the feeling at the time. A smile that would melt steel and a beautiful body, clad in a lemon-colored sheath, slit to mid-calf. Her jet-black hair was bound in a matching yellow bow in the back and fell midway to her waist.

"I can see exactly why she captured your heart," Mike responded. "If you folks have the time, I would like you to come out to my ranch for dinner tonight. I want you to meet my wife, Susan."

"We have plenty of time. I just retired and wanted to see what you have to offer. It sounds to me like that is the kind of flying I want to do. I've had enough bomb runs and strafing, it's time I save lives rather than kill and destroy," John answered.

"John, you are just the kind of person we want to hire. We have so much in common we'll soon be finishing each other's sentences. While you and I are burning holes in the sky, Kim and Susan can get acquainted. If it's okay with you, I'll have Heather drive Kim out to the ranch, and you could bunk with us for a while. I have a feeling Kim misses her family, and we have a large family and plenty of room for you."

That sounds like a plan to me, Mike," John answered. "Is it okay with you, Kim?"

"If that's what you want, John, it's okay with me," she said nervously.

"Honey, it's what we both want that determines the decision. Remember, you are half the team, so your input is important. You are not submissive like the women are in Nam," John admonished.

"Okay, let's do it," Kim responded positively. "I feel daring, and I can take care of myself if you're not around."

Mike called Susan to let her know about Kim and John. "I could eat steak two nights in a row, anytime."

"I read you loud and clear. I'll take Kim with me to Bubb's. She might see something she would like."

"Good plan sweetheart, John and I are going to burn some holes in the sky. Dinner at six like always, I love you, bye. Heather! Take Mrs. Schumann over to the Marriott and help her pack up; they are moving out to the ranch for a few days. If you and Casey are free tonight, come on out and have dinner with us. Just tell Susan to butcher another cow, I've seen Casey eat. We eat at six. Come on, John, let's burn some holes in the sky."

CHAPTER 4

The latest addition to the fleet was all set and ready for immediate departure.

"John, it's your airplane, do what you would normally do, and I will critique your performance. We both know you are going to make a mistake or two. The time to learn is now. Remember, this is a passenger plane, and the rules and regulations arenot routine as they are on a cargo or fighter plane."

John made his walk-around inspection and entered the pilot's compartment. Mike was riding in the second seat.

"As I said, John, this your bird, and this is a training mission."

John turned to Mike and said, "Would you secure the aircraft for takeoff please and then start the preflight checklist."

"Yes, captain. The aircraft is secure for takeoff, checklist complete, ready to start engines. Captain, do you think it's hot in here?"

John blushed, "The APU isn't running."

"The switch is on your side, on your left," Mike explained.

"Okay, APU up and running, all gauges normal. Starting engine number one." The Rolls Royce whined, and engine number one was started, up and running, all gauges reading normal. "Starting number two." It also whined and started. "Engine number two up and running, all gauges reading normal captain."

"Thank you, Mike," now let's see if we can get this bird in the air. We are, Angel Six, right?" John asked.

"Roger, Angel Six," Mike responded.

"Angel Six to tower; request taxi clearance," John said like the professional he was.

"Roger, Angel Six. Cleared to taxi to runway 84. Do I hear a new voice?"

"I'm John Schumann. I hope to speak to you often."

"I'm Dale Matable, John. "Welcome aboard. Your boss is probably one of the most respected men in the area. Before he and Henderson started Angel Flight, this town was going nowhere. Since then, we've got new companies coming to town, creating good jobs, and increasing the tax base, so our property taxes stay low. Youare going to love the ride. Tower out."

"For just being Mike Murphy, you sure cut a wide swath," John said."You should run for Mayor or maybe Governor, hell! You might even be President."

"Maybe Mayor, and that's a big maybe. The people are going to council meetings and are demanding to be heard, and the council is responding. The reason most of them ran for the city council is not the pay but the insurance coverage the city provides. They don't want to lose that, so they do their best to satisfy their constituents," Mike answered.

John taxied to runway 84. "Angel Six to ground control, asking clearance for takeoff," he said.

"We have a Lear on its final, if you have time to wait, follow them," answered ground control.

"We've got time to wait since this is a training mission; if we had a patient on board, we would have been wheels up by now," John answered.

The Lear with the sign, 'Salmon and Sea Fresh,' painted on its side and vertical stabilizer, landed with a thump.

After checking both left and right for approaching aircraft and seeing none, he turned onto the runway, turned up the power, and was hurtling down the runway. At 150 MPH,John eased back on the yoke, the nose came up, and the rest of the Gulf Streamfollowed.

"I don't know what you've got under the hood, but I think the best the Corps has would, just to keep up,work hard," John commented.

"Just a couple of stock Rolls Royce juicedup. The latest and best they produce," Mike answered. "Call Troutdale and get clearance for some T and Gs (T=touchdowns and G=immediate takeoff goes). I'll make the first two to show you the first wasn't an accident. When we have patients on board, we don't want to cause them any more trauma, so we learn to make smooth landings."

Troutdale gave the okay for the T and Gs, and John got into the landing pattern. "It's your airplane, Mike, show me what you want."

It was a classic "Mike Murphy." No bump and only the scream of protest from the tires, as they went from 0 to 135 mph in an instant, indicating they were on the ground. Mike immediately applied full throttle, circled, and lined up for his second landing. "Let's get some coffee while we're here and go see Beaver Air," he suggested. "They are the ones who outfit our fleet."

"Sounds good to me, Mike, I need a potty break," John remarked. "What is the secret to your smoooooth landings?"

"Practice, practice, practice, and when you think you've got it, practice some more. Once you get used to your bird and know how it reacts, it gets easier. Remember, you have from 6 to 10,000 feet of runway to stop so that you could land hot in some places. I don't recommend it. I might add, an electrifying sensation comes with each success! Work at it, and it will come to you like it did to me, and the first time you get it right, you'll slap your head and wonder why it took so long to do it right. After your potty break and we have some coffee, you can fly solo and make a few T and Gs. I'll talk to Jensen, and youjust relax and get acquainted with your bird. As of this minute, you are Angel Six. Glad to have you aboard."

Mike watched John try to look nonchalant as he made his walk-around, but he couldn't hide the ear to ear grin. He almost ran around HIS airplane, climbed aboard, closed, and secured the door, and was soon airborne. His first attempt was not bad but could stand improvement. Troutdale was not real busy at that time of day, so John made five or six more. The last onewas exceptionally smooth, so he taxied to BeaverAir, where Mike was waiting with a Captain's uniform coat. It had the words embroidered on the right side above the pocket and John Schumann on the left. Mike held it for John to put on. It fit perfectly. John smiled broadly and walked proudly, not strutting arrogantly, but walking with pride and dignity.

"I don't know what to say, Mike, except thanks for your confidence in me. You will not be sorry," John said emotionally.

"There has never been a doubt in my mind. Now let's go home and show off your new work clothes," Mike suggested. "Park in the service area so Red can get you ready for immediate dispatch."

The landing at The Dalles was letter-perfect.

John slapped his head and said, "What took me so long? You're right about the electric thrill a perfect landing gives." That brought a roarof laughter fromboth.

Heather was back in the office when Mike and John returned. Red topped off the fuel tanks and made sure Angel Six was ready for immediate dispatch.

CHAPTER 5

"Heather, make sure the necessary paperwork is complete and have John sign them. We will take Kim the ones she needs to sign. Put John on the schedule as of now. Until you get your crew lined up,I will be the second seat, and Susan will bethe nurse if that's okay with you, John?"

"Suits me fine, but I don't understand me lining up a crew?"

"We want you to be comfortable with your new crew. If there is someone you would like to have, excluding Susan and myself, try to get them on board. There is no hurry, but we need it done as soon as possible. You may or may not have a female copilot or nurse, and you will be staying overnight in some cases, so we don't want any problems with jealous wives or husbands. I went through that for years, and trust me, it is pure hell. With a wife like Kim waiting for you at home, you would be insane to risk losing her over a one-nighter. You will be the person the crew is responsible to, so if you suspect something is going on that shouldn't be, they will be fired on the spot and will have to get home on their own. You call dispatch, and we will send you replacements or bring you home empty,whichever works the best for all of us. I realize you did not anticipate this when you applied, and I sure don't want to pressure you into a decision you will regret later. We do everything on a handshake, so what you decide, we shake on, and that binds us."

"Mike, here is my hand. "I would consider it an honor to represent and fly for such a company as Angel Flight. Let's tell Kim. By the way, you don't need to worry about me jumping the fence, Kim gives me everything I need, always. Sometimes,more.Sheis an incredible woman."

John continued to tell his Vietnam story in full: *"She risked her life to save me in Vietnam. My plane got shot down, but I survived. Kim's mother was murdered. She was protecting and hiding me. She risked her life to save me. Kim's mother was raped by some French low-life, and Kim is the result of the rape. Her mother was disgraced, and they lived in squalor or worse. When the Cong killed her mother, I knew I had to get Kim out of there, or the Cong would have used her for their pleasure. We got to a place where a chopper could pick us up. Kim found a 'friendly' who could radio for a helicopter. When the chopper came to pick us up, the lieutenant said, leave the bitch, I don't have room for her. I pulled my piece and said, lieutenant, I am Colonel John Schumann, United States Marine Corps. This bitch is my wife. If anybody stays here, guess who it will be. Get your ass over and make room or get out NOW. Do I make myself clear?"*

"I'll report this to my commander, Colonel Kopas, when we get back," the shavetail said.

Are you telling me 'Roly Poly Kopas' made Colonel?"

"Yes, sir. Do you know him?" the lieutenant asked.

"We went through flight school together, I was the best man at his wedding, and I am his oldest son's godfather, whose name, by the way, is, John Schumann Kopas. Yes, I'd say I know him. I'm also going to report this to our Colonel. I haven't seen him in a long time. If I know Roly Poly, when he finishes dressing you down, you'll want the floor to open upand swallow you. He will not raise his voice or swear at you, and he will calmly point out your mistakes and not miss a one; including those you made at OCS, put you on 'officer of the day' for thirty days and encouraged you to be civil to everyone and return all salutes. You will apologize to my wife here and now, and never refer to a woman as a bitch."

"Ma'am, I am truly sorry for disrespecting you, and I give you my word as an officer and a gentleman, even though my gentlemanly actions did not show very well, I will never make that mistake again."

"Lieutenant," John said, "you've been dressed down enough; let's shake hands, no salute, and start over as friends. After all, we are on the same side,"

"Thank you, Colonel," the shavetail said. "I appreciate that."

"Call me John, Lieutenant. What's your name?"

"Womak, sir, Wayne Womak," the Lieutenant replied.

Back at the Lieutenant's base, John asked him to tell the Colonel, "somebody wanted to see him, but don't tell him who I am."

The Lieutenant reported, "The Colonel is too busy to see anybody, sir. I mean, John."

"That's okay, Wayne; I know how to get his attention. John walked up to the Colonel's door, and in the worst baritone anyone ever heard, sang, "Roly Poly, daddy's little fatty."

"John Schumann, you kraut bastard, get in here. Lieutenant, why didn't youtell me who wanted to see me," Colonel Kopas demanded.

"Lay off him. I told him not to tell you who was waiting.He has already had his daily ration of ass-chewing. That's all you need to know," John answered.

"If you chewed him out, - nothing I can do to ease the pain, "Kopas said.

"I need you to cut through the red tape and bull shit so Kim and I can get married officially. She saved my life! The Cong murdered her mother for hiding me. They were saving Kim for their pleasure, so we got the hell out of there. That's when your Lieutenant and I had a 'come to Jesus session.' I've got to check into the hospital and get squared away. Kim would have no status as a single Vietnamese. As the wife of an officer, she can live in officers quarters, "John explained.

"Consider it done," Colonel Kopas replied. "I will testify that I witnessed your marriage, which will satisfy the 'Brass.' Lieutenant take this kraut to the hospital and get his wife suitable quarters. We don't have to know how long they will be with us, butif she has any trouble, even a run in her stockings, you will think the dressing down John gave was a walk in the park. Any question?"

"No, sir, I may be a little bit crazy but stupid, I'm not. The other wives are going to wonder what general she is married to," Wayne answered.

"I served two tours in Nam and enough time in, so they kicked me loose. I hadn't been doing much, and when you fly high-performance aircraftas I did, that's all you want to fly. The corporations are looking for someone twenty-five with a multi-jet ticket and several thousand hours, so I'm not even considered. I heard about you, and here I am, and that's my story Mike," John related. "Kim was working in the hospital as a nurse or as close to it as she could, with the limited education she had, but she pulled me through. She has seen and treated all kinds of wounds, from gunshots and stabbings to only plain beatings.Do you think she would pass the test to be part of my crew?"

"John," Mike said. "Your story is historic now and heroic. Thanks for giving me your and Kim's background. Like I told you, John, you are Angel Six. The crew is your responsibility. If you would be comfortable with Kim as your nurse, we have no objections. Now we must find someone to fill the second seat. Do you have anyone in mind, or should we run an ad?"

"Don't run the ad yet. Kim cuts a wide swath. She may know or has heard of someone. Let's ask her first," John answered.

"Heather! Are you and Casey coming tonight?"Mike asked.

"Yes, we are," Heather answered. "Susan said dinner at six."

Chapter 6

"John, you follow me, and let's go out to the ranch," Mike directed.

As Mike turned off the highway, he saw Hawk's police car, the TV station's news truck, Bubb's pickup, and a lot of strangers. He saw Susan, Kim and Bubb talking to the reporter while the TV camera was filming everything.

"What's going on, Hawk?" Mike asked.

"It seems Susan and her little sister went into Bubb's for groceries. Two would-be holdup men came in, stuck a gun in Bubb's face, and demanded the money, then, noticing the sisters, decided to take them with them. The little sister tried to talk them out of it, but they wouldn't hear of it. The little sister walked up to the guntoter and, according to Bubb, took the gun away, tossed it to Susan, kicked the gun toter in the face, bloodied his nose, cut his lip, then a backhand judo chop to the throat put him down. The other headed for the little sister, so Susan put a thirty-eight slug in his kneecap. I'm here to write up the report on the attempted robbery. Bubb says you can't buy groceries from him because your money is no good. He said he saw the gunman squeezing the trigger and was praying when the sister did her thing. What's Susan's sister's name?"

"Kim Schumann," Mike answered. "That's her husband there in the flight coat. I didn't realize how much they resemble each other. They

"

are not sisters, Hawk, but from what you just told me, they went to the same school.Get your wife and come out for steaks. We eat at six."

"I'll do it. I can finish my report without a lot of people around," Hawk said as he climbed into his squad car and left.

Bubb came over and shook Mike's hand.

"The Lord blessed this town and especially me, when you decided to stay here. I'm sure had it not been for Susan and her sister, I would be dead."

"Mr. Bubb, although they look enough alike to be sisters, they are not related, and please let me pay for our groceries. If you want to throw in some soda or ice cream for the children once in a while, that's fine, but I want to pay for my groceries because if I ever got something that was bad I could bring it back but if I hadn't paid for it, I couldn't."

"That makes a lot of sense to me, Mike. A steak now and then would be okay, wouldn't it? Especially if it was over-aged," Bubb quirked, "I've got to get back to the store." He gave Susan and Kim hugs and kisses, got in his pickup, and drove to town.

The TV crew left the crowd, and at last, the two couples were alone.

Mike made the introductions. "Susan, this is John Schumann, John, Susan, my wife. You two could almost be twins. John is Angel Six and believes Kim has the stuff to be his nurse, so all we need now is someone in the second seat."

"Do you folks want coffee or milk while Kim and I unwind?" Susan asked.

"I'm fine," John said. "Are you ladies, okay? You don't seem to be the worse for wear."

"We are fine, but those two gunmen are in bad shape," Susan commented. "Mike, you should have seen her in action, I've been around the block a time or two, and she is the fastest with her hands that I have ever seen. It was almost a blur. She had the gun in her hand, tossed it to me, and had the thug on the ground so quick you can't believe it. When the other one made a move towards Kim, I was sure words wouldn't stop him, so I gave him a shot in his knee. Poor Bubb, he was terrified and speechless. His wife came in and took care of him,and we just picked up our groceries and came home. Somebody heard the gunshot and called Hawk. Bubb filled him in. He came here to make his report then, the TV crew showed up and made a circus out of it. Bubb brought us a bunch of steaks and couldn't thank us enough."

"I discussed that with him." Mike said. "I invited Hawk and his wife for dinner tonight, and since we have plenty and a new addition to our family, let's have Bear and Faun, Grandma Romaine, Mom and Dad, Julie and Howard. I'll cook the steaks and some brats and hot dogs."

"I'll make an Asian salad," Kim volunteered.

"I passed some sweet corn on the way out here," John said. "Kim will need some things from the store, so we'll pick up the corn on the way."

"Sounds to me like we're going to have a party," Susan said.

Mike had the coals exactly right for grilling when Heather and Casey arrived.The rest of the family was showing affection; meanwhile,the Chief was completing his report.

With tears flowing, Kim thanked everyone. " I miss my mother very much. She was all the family I had. When John rescued me, I was grateful. He told me he married me so I could live in the Officers' Quarters and when we got to America, if I wanted my freedom, he would understand. One day when I was visiting him in the hospital, he told me he owed me his life and said he wanted to spend the rest of his life with me. I told him I owed my life to him and wanted to spend the rest of my life with him. He said he didn't know how love was supposed to feel but was sure he was in love with me. I fell in love with him as I heard himshouting at the Lieutenant, "this bitch is my wife, and if anybody is going to be left behind, It's the Lieutenant. I believe he would have shot him, but fortunately, it wasn't necessary. As it turned out, the Lieutenant is one of our best friends. Your wonderful people here have made me feel the love I have missed for so long, and I thank you."

That brought a round of applause and more hugs, kisses, and tears.

Dinner was over when John suddenly spoke up. "In all the excitement, I forgot that this is Kim's birthday."

Heather quickly got up from the table and went into the kitchen, returning with a beautiful cake that had a single candle in the center.

Everybody joined in singing Happy Birthday to Kim, who turned to her adoring husband and said, "I love you; John Schumann and I don't want to live anywhere but in this town. I also want a real wedding."

John arose, with a slight bow to Kim, and said, "I love you too, and I also want to live here. We have finally come home, and we will have a real wedding. Mike, would you be my best man?"

"I would consider it an honor," Mike answered.

Kim asked Susan to beher matron of honor.

"Of course, we sisters have to stick together," Susan joked. "Mike and I were married right here, and if you think it would work for you, set the date and leave the details to us. You worry about your dress and John's suit. We can take care of everything else. Mike wore his dress whites."

"I can't imagine a more beautiful place for a wedding," Kim said. "Is it alright with you, John?" she asked.

"Yes, it is. It is more than alright. It's perfect. Do you have a date in mind?" John inquired.

"How about the Fourth of July. It will make it easier for you to remember our anniversary," Kim teased.

"July Fourth it is," John agreed. "How about I wear my Dress Blues; Mike, you wear your Dress Whites."

"I'll have to lose a few pounds, but I should anyway," Mike answered.

The sun had dropped behind Mt. Hood, and darkness was fast approaching. The party broke up with hugs, etc. for Kim.

Winnie approached Kim and said, "I can never take the place of your mother, but I would like to have you call on me when you need mothering. That's a universal language."

Kim hugged Winnie and, with more tears, said, "Oh, Momma, I miss you so much. Thank you for being here for me when I needed you. Will you help me with my wedding dress and sit in my mother's place when I'm married." That brought tears from Winnie.

"I've always wanted to help my daughter with her wedding dress and where else would I sit. If you ask Murph, he will walk you down the aisle," Winnie continued.

"That would be wonderful," Kim wept. "I've never had a real father."

Murph overheard the conversation between Winnie and Kim and said. "I can't be your father but, I can be a real Dad, so come over here and give your Daddy a kiss."

"The Schumanns slept in the spare bedroom at the duplex.

"You will hear a woman scream tonight, but it is only our neighborhood cougar," Faun told the guest couple. "I won't try to guess what your normal mornings are, so you are on your own. I've made the coffee, and breakfast fixings are in the fridge. Good night and welcome home."

The cougar did scream, startling Kim. She cuddled John for protection and comfort. The cougar screamed, the owl hooted, the wolf howled, and the Columbia River gurgled and splashed on its way to the Pacific. God's voice was a lullaby to the happy couple who slept like they hadn't slept in a long time. A cool breeze blowing over the sleeping couple bringing the sweet smell of pine and the far-off rumble of thunder heralding an upcoming rain roused them from their deep, restful sleep. John slipped out of bed and brought Kim, who was deep in thought, her morning coffee.

"Honey, I don't ever want to leave this place. I never realized what a home was until yesterday. I lived in poverty, where every day was a constant struggle for just the basics. I realize now, Momma and I just existed; she never had two hours of peace in her life. She was content because everyone else was in the same situation. Can we buy a house and stay here, please?"

"I don't see any reason, why not. I'll talk to Mike's friend, Howard Morrison, today and see what he has available. I'm going to shower and shave, and if you want, I'll fix breakfast."

"I want to fix it for us, John. You shower, and I'll cook."

CHAPTER 7

Mike was on the phone with Hawk when John arrived. John went into Heather's office and complimented her on her cake. "It was delicious," he commented. "If you have the recipe for that cake, I would like to have one for my birthday on June 20th. I'll pay you for it, of course."

"No, you won't," Mike said, entering the office. "You are part of our family, and you don't buy your own cake. If you want to buy cakes, buy them for the "Cake Walk." The Senior class must raise funds for their Prom. They work hard to come up with enough money to have a nice dinner and live music. They don't ask for donations; they have car washes, slave auctions, and most anything else to raise the money."

"Kim says Susan has talked to her and is sure she can handle the nursing duties, so we've got two of the three we need for the crew. We want to buy a house here and make this our home. Kim said she didn't know what home felt like until yesterday. She said, "Home is when you feel you are loved and cared for from those around you. She never had that before."

"Excuse me," a soft sensual voice said from behind them, "Which one of you gentleman is Mike Murphy?"

"That would be me," Mike said as he stood and extended his hand to face a beautiful blonde, about five foot nine in her bare feet, but with her four-inch heels, she was almost as tall as Mike and John. "What can I do for you?"

"My name is Veronica Lane. I understand you are looking for pilots. I graduated from the Air Force Academy fourth in a class of one hundred, ahead of all the other females. I have checked out in F15s and all the other high performance the Air Force has in its arsenal. I am 30 years old, divorced, and not looking, I am by nature, a caregiver, as are most women, and the thoughts of killing people, including women and children, was appalling to me so I resigned my commission and here I am. I understand you primarily fly critical patients, especially children, to the best hospital for their particular needs at no charge."

"That's correct, "Mike said. "This is John Schumann, Mrs. Lane. He is the commander of Angel Six. His wife is the flight nurse. You are lovely. There are times you will be spending a night in a hotel, and an attractive, unattached lady is going to draw considerable attention, many times aggressive. Do you think you can handle those conditions?"

"As I said, I'm not looking. I am a mature woman who knows her way around the block. Four years at the academy prepared me for most situations, so, in answer to your question, yes, I can handle the situation. If the man is attractive and attached, I will leave him alone but, if he makes a move on me and I am in the mood, I'll be all over him like bees on honey."

"Heather," Cut the paperwork on Mrs. Lane. She starts today," John said. "Are you ready to poke holes in the clouds," Mrs. Lane?"

While Ronni was changing clothes, John and Mike were talking about housing for him and Kim.

"There's a thirty-acre piece just NW of our house I've been thinking about buying," Mike said. "You have just made up my mind for me. I'm going to buy it and divide it into five three-acre lots and leave the other fifteen acres as common ground for horses, etc. Get a house plan, John. Mike Murphy and Son Electrical and Engineering will build it at cost. Our bank will finance the loan at 4.5%, no points or early pay-off penalty. What do you think of that idea.?"

"Too good to be true, Mike. The big boss upstairs has watched over me since I turned my life around and gave my heart to Jesus. I'm going to see if she flies as good as she looks."

Ronni wore an Air Force jumpsuit with her name on the pocket and captain's bars on the collar. She walked up to Red and introduced herself to him, thenturning on her heel did the walk- around, not missing anything. She mounted the steps, closed, and secured the door, and strapped herself into the copilot's seat. Ronni went through the preflight checkoff list,touching each dial and switch, being sureeverything was in order. Completing the check, she started each engine, and when everything was as it should be, gave the signal to the ground crew to pull the chocks. When she sawthe chocks were gone, she said firmly," Captain, your aircraft is ready for flight."

"Thank you, Ronni, would you like to take a test drive?" John asked.

"Yes, I would, sir. Thank you." Getting all the clearances required, she turned onto runway 84, and easing the power to maximum was quickly airborne.

"What's under the hood, sir? The thrust is powerful. I was surprised, not prepared!" Ronni exclaimed.

"Only the latest and best Rolls Royce power plants juiced up by a mechanic in Troutdale. I agree with your position on women in combat. Killing is against all their instincts. I prayed every time I dropped a load in Nam for forgiveness, and for the safety of the innocent victims, the politicians call collateral damage. You are a first-class airplane driver, Ronni. Vector over to Troutdale for some T and Gs. I'll make the first two, and then you will know the first wasn't luck."

Two perfect, electrifying landings later, he turned theyoke over to Ronni. "We will have patients on board, so we are particular about our landings. We don't want to jar them off the gurney. You shouldn't have much trouble getting the hang of it since you are used to seven thousand feet or more runway. I was a carrier pilot and had to land and stop quickly, and I had the hook and cable for a braking system. Put us on the ground, and we'll have lunch. I'll stay on the ground and watch from here. When you're ready to call it a day, pick me up."

Ronni's first landing was right for her first try.

"Taxi over to Beaver Air and park in front of the office. They might be busy. Try to turn us so that we don't need their mule to get away," John explained.

After lunch, Ronni made her walk-around, pulled the chocks herself, and made ready to take off. Giving her a thumbs up and getting one back, John took a seat by the window to watch. The third and fourth were close enough to what they wanted, and she could get away without bothering Beaver Air. She shut down the port side engine and welcomed John aboard.

"That last approach was perfect,Ronni. Do you want to keep control, or are you tired?" John asked.

"I'm on a roll and not the least bit tired. I'd like to fly us back home," Ronni replied.

"It's your airplane, Ronni. Take us home," John ordered.

Back at Angel Flight headquarters, Ronni executed a picture-perfect landing, taxied up to Red, who already had the fuel truck in position. Mike greeted them with coffee and spice cake.

"Heather baked it for you on her lunch break," Mike announced. "That was a beautiful landing, Mrs. Lane, - - Okay, Ronni, it is. How does she fly, John?" Mike asked.

"Do I fly as good as I look," Ronni laughed.*"I knew Ihad it made when that instant electrical thrill came to me,"* she said to herself.

An embarrassed John answered, "I'm sorry for the crude comment, and I apologize for it. As I said earlier, you are a first-class pilot. Mike, Angel Six has a full crew, and as soon as we complete orientation, and the necessaryRed tape, we will be ready for dispatch. I must properly thank Heather. I'll see you at the ranch."

CHAPTER 8

"Did you come prepared to stay, or do you need time totie up loose ends," Mike asked.

"I don't have any loose ends to tie up. Everything I own is in my Town and Country parked out front. I have a limited amount of cash to get by on, but I can and have managed to get by. I came to stay," Ronni stated positively.

"You can stay at the Marriott and just sign the tab. Dinner includes wine and a limited amount of alcohol. You must be ready to depart on a moment's notice."We have no schedule."Mike continued, "My folks have room at their house and would welcome you as a daughter. I just had another thought. Murph, that's my Pop, has his fifth-wheel set up out at the ranch. You or the Schumanns can stay there. Ifyou 've become part of the family, you might as well live with us. Check into the Marriott while I get things sorted out, and you decide what's best for you. Come with me over to Mary's café. I want you to meet someone."

Hawk was sitting at his regular spot and motioned for Mike to join him.

"Who is your lady friend, Mike, and does Susan know about her?" Hawk joked.

"Hawk, this is Ronni, the latest addition to the family. She just joined us today and will be at the Marriott for a few days," Mike said.

Hawk said, "There is a small reward for those two that Susan and Kim corralled yesterday. They are entitled to it, so have them come in and sign for it." Turning to Ronni, he asked, "You're not a martial arts expert or anything like that, are you? What is your name?"

"My name is Veronica Lane, and I do pack iron and have a federal permit for it."

"Ronni," Hawk said, "We treat everybody the same, so if you would bring your piece to the station, we can get a spent round, check the serial number and record your fingerprints."

"I have no problem at all with that Chief, I'll see you in the morning," Ronni responded.

"Be here at seven-thirty, and I'll buy breakfast," Hawk added.

"How can a girl refuse an invitation like that," Ronnisaid. "I'll see you in the morning. Bye now."

"There goes a woman who knows what the score is," Hawk commented. "What do you know about her, Mike?"

"She is a graduate from the Air Force Academy, finished fourth in her class of one hundred and is one fine pilot. Divorced, not looking, and no family. That's all I know," Mike answered.

At seven-thirty on the dot, Ronni breezed into Mary's in worn jeans, a denim shirt, turquoise earrings and, cowboy boots with dogging heels. Her long, blonde hair in a braid held by a turquoise-studded crunchie. Spotting Hawk, she sat in the booth opposite him.

"Good morning, Chief. What a beautifulday," Ronni commented. "Too bad the rain missed us. "It looks like the crops are a little dry," she added.

"Good morning, Ronni. It is a beautiful day. We do need the rain, but how could you tell," Hawk questioned.

"I'm a farm girl from the Midwest," Ronni answered. "I was active in Four-H and raised Quarter Horses. Don't let the soft voice and blonde hair fool you. I've had several encounters where the guy wrote a check with his mouth that his body couldn't cash. I'll have a western omelet, wheat toast, toasted, not just dried out, OJ, coffee and, a glass of cold milk, please."

"That sounds good to me," Hawk echoed, "I'll have the same."

At the 'cop shop,' Ronni gave the Chief her gun so he could record the serial number, then he took her fingerprints. Handing her thirty-eight caliber Berretta back to her, he asked, "Would you like to use our pistol range, Agent Lane?"

"Yes, I would, Chief. How did you know?" Ronni asked.

"I had an undercover agent call on me a few years back," Hawk explained. "I was working on a local drug case here, and he told me they were working on an international counterfeiting case. We were to be onthe watch for an agent. You don't look like a G-man or person, whichever you prefer, so I figured you must be one. You came across personally like you had rehearsed your speech many times. You can fire whenever you are ready."

"I'll fire into the water barrel first, then I'll finish that clip and use two more," Ronni commented.

"The Chief watched with interest. *She knows how and when to use a weapon,*" Hawk said to himself. "Good shooting agent Lane, if you would like to clean and oil your piece, you can use my cleaning kit," Hawk offered.

"Thank you, I will. You know you are the only person that knows. What I am and my undercover status is protected. We are close to breaking this case, and it goesextremely high." Ronni said.

"I know better than to blow your cover, Ronni," Hawk commented, "If you need to talk to me, tell me you need to get some shooting in. If I see you and take my hat off and brush my hair, that's a signal; brush off, stay-away. I'll call you for coffee; It seems I am teaching you sign language." Hawk laughed.

"That wouldn't be too bad an idea, Chief. Very few people would know what we would be saying. Let's think about it." Ronni said.

"If you go out to the ranch, ask my dad, Bear, to teach you; he is a better teacher than I am," Hawk suggested.

CHAPTER 9

Mike was on the phone, talking to Howard about the thirty acres he wanted to buy.

John was reading the Angel Flight Manual outlining the duties of the crew and how the payroll management was structured.

Heather announced, "a new, New Jersey Casino crew was coming for orientation and the other necessary red tape, and so, we will wait until they get here to go through orientation. It works better when you have more than one crew. You get more questions, which clarifies more issues; thus, we all are better informed."

On hearing the news about the new crew from Jersey, Ronni smiled and asked for a manual like John was reading. Heather produced one, and Ronni was soon deep into it, making notes for the question and answer part of orientation.

"When is orientation scheduled?" John asked.

"Thursday morning at eight-thirty here. Coffee and sweets, as well as soda and fresh fruit, will be furnished. Lunch at Mary's. The meeting room is all set up, and you will order off the menu; Are there any questions?" Heather asked.

"Mike, if you could find room for me at the ranch, I would like to stay out there," Ronni inquired.

"No problem. The boys are using the bunkhouse, so if you don't mind a single bed, you can use Carl's room." Mike offered. "I'll be working late tonight. You can follow John, or if you want to leave now, and get acquainted, just follow old highway thirty west, and when you see the sign, "Ferry," hook a right, and you are there."

"That sounds easy enough; I think I'll do it," Ronni responded. "I want to meet Hawk's dad. From what Hawk told me about him, he is an interesting individual."

"Individual is correct, there can't be another Bear Claw in the world, and he is interesting," Mike told her.

Heather announced over the intercom:

"Hawk is on the phone, Mike; he said it is important."

"Hello, chief," Mike answered, "What can I do for you?"

"I need to talk to you in my office I've got some important information I think you ought to have," Hawk reported. "That's all I'm going to say, so get your Irish butt over here."

"I'm out the door now," Mike stated.

Hawk was waiting for him with a puzzled look.

"What's bothering you, my redskin brother?" Mike said lightly. "What's this important information I should have," he continued.

"What I am going to tell you does not leave this room. As far as I know, you and I and the person involved, and that person's boss are the only people on the planet that are aware of this. Ronni is an undercover Fed. They have been working on an international counterfeiting case for some time and are about to bust it. If she asks for time off or a change of assignment, don't question her, just do what she asks. She doesn't and won't know I told you unless you tell her. I don't think you should tell anybody, including Susan."

" Thanks for the tip, Hawk. I'll see you for our shoot-off on Thursday." Mike left.

The New Jersey crew landed the next morning and arrived at the office looking like hoods. They seated themselves across from Mike and presented their papers. Heather came in with some checks for Mike to sign. When she was gone, Gino, the copilot said, "How about you tell that broad we need some coffee."

Mike was instantly on his feet, temper raging. Trying to control himself, he said through clenched teeth, "That is no broad, her name is Mrs. Carey, and if you want some coffee, there is a restaurant about five thousand feet East of here, and before you ask; no, we don't have a courtesy car and they don't deliver. You will treat all my people with dignity and respect. Your manner may be acceptable under the rock you crawled out from under, but it is not, I repeat not, acceptable here. Do you understand? If there are no questions, and you still want coffee, start walking. I'll be here when you get back."

Ronni rode in with John, and were in the lounge when the trio from, Jersey got back from their coffee break.

Ronni had her Air Force flight suit on; John wore jeans, a western shirt, and boots. Gino asked John, "Is blondie your old lady?"

"No, she's just a good friend,"

"Oh, someone to sleep with when your old lady ain't around. Is she any good? Yea-aah!. How about it, honey, do you want to see a real man in action."

Before John could react, Ronni was on her feet, putting her finger in Gino's chest, she said, "Listen, you piece of dirt. I grew up on a farm, and I have three older brothers You can't show me anything I haven't seen before, and probably in better condition, so before you write a check with your mouth, make sure you've got funds to cover it." She immediately delivered a straight right to the nose and followed with an uppercut that lifted him off his feet and put him on the floor with a bloody nose and loose teeth.

"If you would like to continue this discussion further, my name is Veronica Lane, Mrs. Lane, to you. John, honey, let's go 'aviate' in that cute little, Cessna 310, and look at Mt Hood."

Mike came into his office and faced the rest of the crew.

"Do you have a problem with what just happened?"

"No,sir," they answered in unison. "We told him his mouth was going to get him in trouble. What do we do for a copilot?"

CHAPTER 10

"I can find one for you unless you have someone in mind," Mike said. "Wait here until I get back from getting him a room at the motel."

Mike drove past Mary's to show Gino where he could eat until time for him to leave. He noticed Hawk was there, and after getting Gino checked in, he went to talk to the chief.

"Hawk, check this guy out. I'm betting he has a record, and maybe an outstanding warrant.

"He got Ronni and, everyone pissed off. Ronni knocked the shit out of him. He's staying at Motel Eight. I fired him on the spot, and he is in a bad mood. You got my okay to harass him all you want. See you tomorrow."

Hawk was having an afternoon donut break at Mary's.

Gino came in with his face puffed up, and Hawk could see that his lips were bleeding. He paid the tab and sat at the table with Gino.

"What happened to you?" Hawk said, "and don't tell me you fell. Someone beat the crap out of you and, I don't tolerate that. I'll take you to my office; you can swear out a complaint and, I'll arrest the perpetrator, put him in jail for a day or two and, if he has a record of this kind of behavior, then it's a repeat offense and could carry six months as a guest of the city."

Gino thought to himself, *'I'll cook up some story that she Sunday punched me. I'll show that bitch nobody messes with Gino Consiglio'.*

At headquarters, Hawk got the complaint form and asked Miss Johnson to come in to be a witness.

"Tell me exactly what happened and don't leave anything out." Winking at Miss Johnson, Hawk said, "Is this the third or fourth one this month? We are going to stopthese beatings."

"It's the sixth. You forgot the one at Bubb's, when the woman beat the hell out of one guy, and another woman shot some guy in the kneecap," Miss Johnson said, hiding a grin.

Gino spoke up, "It must be the same broad that done this job on me. I was just sitting in the office of Angel Flight, reading their manual, when this blonde broad started beating on me. I was just sitting there, and she threw a right that rang my bell, then a left that put my lights out. Then, when I came around, she said her name was Veronica Lane. She and her squeeze were going to 'aviate,' she said and look at some damn mountain. That's the whole story, just as it happened."

"I've known Mrs. Lane for some time, and that just doesn't sound like her but, I guess PMS can strike any time, and you never can tell when or what the consequences will be. If you just sign your name right where the X is and alsogive your social security number, I'll have Miss Johnson witness it and make a copy for you. Wait here, and I'll take you wherever you are staying,"Hawk said, "then wait for Mrs. Lane to finish her practice flight."

As soon as Mike had given Hawk the story on Gino, the Chief called his office and had them call New Jersey to run a check on Gino Consiglio.

The officer who called New Jersey reported that, "Gino Consiglio has a long rap sheet but nothing outstanding. He has Jersey Mafia ties but nothing we can hold himon,"

"I'm sorry, Mr. Consiglio, but I must detain you for a day or two," Hawk said. "I'll take you to where you are staying, and you are free to walk around and do anything legal you want to do. Just don't even think about leaving town until I say it's okay. If you have a gun, I must have a spent round and the serial number. Your fingerprints are already on file in New Jersey."

"I ain'tpackin' heat," Gino protested.

"Be sure of what you say, sir," Hawk spat back. "If you are packing heat and I don't have the information I asked for, it's a felony in this jurisdiction, and that is a mandatory one-year as a guest of the State of Oregon. We are liberal with our gun laws, but we do enforce the laws we have with no exceptions. A former senator thought he had enough clout to beat the rap; one year later, he was a free man. Again, I say, be careful what you say. Now reach behind you and carefully hand me that forty-five you're carrying in your belt; I may be a 'hick' cop, but I can read signs."

Red-faced Gino did as Hawk requested. After getting the information he wanted, Hawk delivered Gino to Motel Eight. "Remember, don't even think about leaving town without my permission. Good evening."

CHAPTER 11

John and Ronni returned from their 'aviating.' Mike announced he had to fire a New Jersey copilot and would be away for a few days. He announced that he would be flying second seat until there is areplacement.

Ronni said, "You have enough on your plate as it is. I'm single," and looking directly at the two remaining crew members, she continued, not looking. "You leave me alone, and I'll leave you alone; do we understand each other?"

"Yes, ma'am. I'm Marco Bataglio, the pilot, and this is Gerald Hudson, the medic. I'm sure I speak for both of us when I say, 'Welcome Aboard.' Turning to Mike, he asked, "What is our flight number?"

"You are Angel Flight Four. Your landing was a little rough. We have patients with serious problems on board, and we don't want to bounce them off the gurney on landing. Ronni will show you how we want it done, and I suggest that until you have a smooooth landing, you let her make the landings. That feeling of electric excitement will race through your veins at the realization you have made the perfect landing! When you have a chance, make some T and Gs to get to perfection. It just takes practice. We will see you here at eight-thirty in the morning for orientation. Marriott's courtesy car is waiting outside; just sign the tab. All arrangementshave been made. Everything is on us."

"What am I going to do for a copilot?" John asked.

"Just East of Cheyenne, there is a seven-thousand-foot runway. A tall, redhead, named Yale Yocum is there. He is qualified and knows how to land. He has a wife and kids and doesn't like to be gone too long. After orientation, you and Kim fly over there and pick him up but be ready to eat the best steak you ever had. Ray and Virginia Bodie own the ranch where the runway is. He had it built so he could land a jet but had a heart attack, and the FAA pulled his ticket. I got the Cessna from him. The copilot you are going to pick up is their son-in-law. They raise Angus beef and butcher and age their own, and it is the best you'll ever eat. Just thinking about it makes me hungry. I'll call the Bodies and let them know what is going on so they can throw a loop around Yale and get him ready to 'aviate.'" Mike explained. "Heather,we are done for the day, close the office and go home," he added.

Orientation went smoothly. Ronni and John took copious notes while Marco and Gerry paid attention but looked bored. A 'pop-quiz' at the end brought them to focus, and they asked questions. Heather explained the subject of their questions had been covered extensively in the video and gave them one to view at the hotel.

"Bring it back in the morning, and we'll take the test over again. If you are successful, you can leave." Heather said.

Ronni called and said, "she needed to get some shooting in."

"Fine, I was coming to pick you up," Hawk said. "Gino Consiglio filed assault charges against you. I have him under house arrest until we can check him out.At this time, there is nothing I can legally hold him on. I'm just harassing him like Mike asked me to do. After I pick you up, we'll swing by the motel so he can identify you. You will be in the back seat with your hands behind your back."

Ronni sat in the back seat as Hawk instructed while he went to find Gino.

"Is this the person who beat you up?" Hawk asked.

"That's the bitch, sir, that's her," Gino said.

"If you weren't such a weak specimen and been able to stand up, I'd have put you out of service for a while, and if I ever see you again and can get my hands on you, I'll do just that." Ronni said. "and that is no threat, that is a one hundred percent guarantee!"

"That's enough, lady," Hawk said. "Let's get you booked and in jail so I can go home."

At headquarters, Hawk and Ronni had a good laugh, and then she told him she was the new copilot on Angel Four and thanked him for his cooperation in her investigation.

"Ronni, please be careful. Those people play rough, and murder is just a part of their job. It makes no difference to them who or what you are if you are in their way, you die. In your case, it wouldn't be quick. They would all have their turn on you then dump your naked body someplace," Hawk cautioned.

"I understood that when I signed on with the FBI," Ronni answered.

"I would like to have you on my police force," Hawk said, "If you have a mind to settle down to a slower pace, you have a job here."

"Thank you, chief, I'll remember that, but for now I have to get back to the ranch and get ready to leave tomorrow," Ronni said.

When they got to the office of "Angel Flight, everybody was gone.

"I'll have Sgt. Watkins take you to the ranch," Hawk apologized. "He patrols that district in his line of duty. Sgt. Watkins, what's your 20?"

"I'm at Mary's about to eat supper."

"I need you to deliver an important package to Mike's ranch. I'll drop it off. It's perishable but not very fragile."

"How will I recognize him, chief," Ronni asked.

"He will be in uniform and be the biggest man in the place," Hawk told her.

CHAPTER 12

Ronni went into Mary's, and sitting at a table was a man in uniform. Walking up to him, she said, "If you are Sgt. Watkins, I'm the package your chief asked you to deliver."

Sgt. Watkins stood up, removed his hat, and said, "Yes, Ma'am. I am Sgt. Bill Watkins, at your service. I have just ordered supper, if it's okay, I'll eat first. Could I buy you supper? It would please me a lot. I don't like to eat alone, but since my wife died a year ago, I eat alone a lot, and it's a lonesome time."

"Thank you, Sgt. I would be delighted to have supper with you. I, too, hate to eat alone, but since my divorce three years ago, like you, I have eaten many meals alone, and I know that lonely feeling," Ronni said. "My name is Veronica Lane. My friends call me Ronni. I'm the new copilot for Angel Four, and we are leaving tomorrow."

"Mrs. Lane, please call me Bill," he asked.

"If you are buying my supper, we must be friends, Ronni laughed."Call me, Ronni. "Tell me about yourself, Bill. Where were you born, and just how big are you?"

"I was born in Chicago; my folks ran a small grocery store and could barely keep food on the table, so college was out of the question. I enlisted into the Marines, and my size was what the FMF (Fleet Marine Force) was wanting. The Navy drives the boats, but we do the shooting. We can wear both Navy and Marine insignias. While I was away, the folks missed a couple of protection payments, and the mob used them as an example to the rest of the small merchants and shot my folks and burned down the store. When I got home, I started looking, and I guess you would call it investigating, and found the ones that did the job. I had positive proof and took it to the authorities, but they just turned their back. Less than ten percent of the murderers ever went to prison. I explained to the chief that I took care of the hoodlums my way and came out here. He conducted his investigation, sent me to the Oregon State Police Academy, and hired me. That was ten years ago. I met Roselyn Caldwell at the Police Benefit Ball, and we were married a year later. I have a five-year-old daughter named Lucinda and a seven-year-old son named after me, but we call him WJ or Willy, never junior. I'm 6 feet 4 inches tall, weigh 285 pounds, and have a thirty-eight-inch waist. Susan Murphy has taught the police department a lot of martial arts. I have a black belt in Karate and TiKwonDo. Now it's your turn."

"What a fascinating but sad story," Ronni began, but what happened to the ones who killed your folks?"

"Rumor had it that they got too hot for the mob, and it's not too hard to guess that they had someone cool them off in Lake Michigan," Bill smiled, "But I wouldn't know anything about that."

"I was raised on a farm in the Midwest. I am the little sister of three brothers. I raised and rode horses and was active. My brothers put a damper on my social life. They felt nobody was good enough for me. My application at the Air Force Academy was accepted. I graduated fourth in a class of one hundred. I am qualified to fly all the Air Force has in their arsenal. Not having much experience with men because of my sheltering brothers, I married the second guy I dated, After three years, I realized we were never on the same page, and he was seeing any girl he could get to go to bed with him. I divorced him, put my belongings in my Town and Country, and came to apply for a job with Angel Flight. They hired me, and I leave for New Jersey tomorrow. Things have moved so fast I haven't had time to think about what to do with my car, etc. All I need is clothing and makeup."

"You could leave your things in your car, and I can put your car in my garage," Bill offered. "I have the space, it would not bother me at all, and you would have to come here to retrieve it, and I would have a chance tobuy your supper. Again. I haven't enjoyed eating like this in a long time. Thank you, Ronni."

"Just so we understand each other, Bill. I'm not looking for a husband or a relationship. This evening has been a most pleasant time, one that I'll always look back on with fond memories. With that said, if you still want to park my car in your garage, I would appreciate it a lot."

"Ronni, I didn't mean to imply that since I fed you, you must sleep with me. I'm not that kind of a guy. I'm not looking, and since we understand each other, we can be good friends. I better get you to the ranch."

"I'll have my car in front of the office and give Heather the keys. I'll explain the situation," Ronni stated as she said good-night to Bill.

"I got so wrapped up in Angel Flight and buying more land I forgot you needed a ride," Mike apologized.

"No problem," Ronni answered. "Sgt. Watkins bought me supper and brought me out. He is going to put my car in his garage until I can make other arrangements. He is one big man," she added.

"As big as he is, he doesn't use his size to intimidate people. He is quiet and gentle," Susan remarked, "and a particularly good student of the Martial Arts. Did he tell you about his black belts?"

"Yes, he did. We had an enjoyableevening and are understanding friends. Neither of us is looking for a relationship at this time," Ronni commented. "I've got to shower and pack for my adventure with Angel Four. Good night everybody. I'll see you in the morning."

Ronni lay under the covers reflecting on the events of the last two days. She had never felt so secure. Her job was dangerous, but she had the training needed to get her out of most situations, for the others, she would have to rely on instinct and her faith. The soft breeze wafting through the cedars brought a fragrance you can't buy at any price, the distant rumble of thunder suggesting a rain but promising nothing. The neighborhood owl hooted, the horses snorted, the cougar screamed, and the river gurgled and splashed on its way to the Pacific. An Oregon lullaby, and Ronni was soon restfully sleeping.

It had rained during the night, and the aroma of the cedars blended with freshly brewed coffee was overwhelming. Nobody could stay in bed with those tempting aromas. Ronni dressed and went to greet the day, and whatever it would bring, Mike and John had already left for the office. Susan and Kim were sipping their after-breakfast coffee when Ronni came to the table. A few minutes of girl talk, a quick glass of juice, and a slice of toast and Ronni was out the door and on the way to work.

Chapter 13

On the way to Angel Flight, Ronni thought to herself, *'If I ever decided to settle down, this is the* kind *of place I would choose.'*

The crew of Angel Four had just arrived. She put herluggage in the lounge and went to find Heather. Ronni gave Heather the keys to her car and told her, "Bill Watkins will be by to pick it up. He's going to put it in his garage until I can get back to it or whatever. Everything I own except what I have packed in my suitcase is in my car. I'm glad it will be in good hands. He and I had supper together last night and decided we are going to have a friendly relationship, nothing more."

Marco and Gerryhad completed their retest and passed it with respectable, if not perfect, scores.

"Mrs.Lane, if you are ready to leave, we are," Gerry said.

"You two go on, I have to talk to Ronni," Mike said. "I'll bring her out in a minute or two. Ronni, if things get out of hand, and you need or want out of there, call me, and you will be on the next flight. You are already the little sister I've always wanted and never had. I can't help being concerned for your safety."

"Thank you," Mike," Ronni said with a tear in her eye, "I've never had so many people care about me. I want to settle down here someday, but for now,I've got a job to do."

With a warm embrace and a kiss on the cheek, Mike whispered, *"Be careful, Agent Lane. The chief told me,and if you ask for a sudden transfer of assignments, I wouldn't question you. I haven't told anyone, not Susan or John, nobody."*

Ronni climbed aboard and watched as Marco was finishing his preflight walk-around. He seemed calmand competent. He took his seat; Gerry closed and secured the door.

"Mrs. Lane! Would you prepare for takeoff, please?"

"Gerry, Marco. We are a crew and will be spending a lot of time together. Let's be friends and begin calling each other by our first names. I'm Ronni. I want to make one thing abundantly clear, if either of you have any ideas about getting too friendly with me, forget it, especially that you are both married. If you want to cheat on your wives, that's up to you, but I will have no part of it. Now let's see if I remember how to start this machine!"

After going through the preflight checklist, she started the engines. After both were running well and all gauges and dials read normal, she said, "Captain Marco, the aircraft is ready for immediate takeoff."

"Thank you, Ronni. Would you like to get us airborne? I've flown this bird, but you haven't. It might be a good idea for you to get the feel of it. I appreciate your honesty, and I promise I will not make any moves on you and will do my best to prevent anyone else from doing so," Marco stated.

"That goes for me too!" Gerry chimed in.

"Angel Four, you are cleared for immediate departure."

"Thank you, ground control. Didn't you see that UPS about to touch down? If we had followed your okay, we would be all over the runway, and the UPS freight would be a mess. Please be more observant. Angel Four, we are rolling." Ronni stated.

Applying maximum power to Angel Four, Ronni noticed a decided difference in the thrust. It took longer to reach flying speed than it did in Angel Six.

"What do you have under the hood?" Ronni asked.

"I don't know, Marco said. "Some company in Philly did the job. Gino and I picked it up, flew back to the office in Atlantic City, picked up Gerry, and made a few more trips.At last, all was ready with Angel Flight. That took about two weeks, just burning fuel. We flew to Chi-Town, Frisco, LA, Diego, Vegas, and Saint Louie. We need to stop there on the way back to Atlantic City; if you can set that course, I would appreciate it."

"Did you file a flight plan?" Ronni asked.

"No, I didn't," Marco said. "I didn't think it was necessary."

"The reason it is necessary is in the event we don't arrive at our scheduled destination, the authorities will have some idea as to where to look for us. It is one of your important responsibilities as a flight commander. I will do it for you if that's okay with you. I don't want to appear bossy or try to undermine your authority, but I would feel better if we followed proper procedure." Ronni stated.

"That's okay with me, Ronni. You're more experienced than I. If you want to run first seat, that's okay too." Marco said.

"Marco," Ronni said, "My flying experience has been military aircraft. The flight plan, etc., is SOP with everyone. You earned first seat, and I will help you keep it. Remember this. I will be teaching, not bossing you. I am a damned good pilot and instructor and will train you so you can fly for any pilot job you might happen to receive. Lindberg Field just ahead. Ask if we can make a Touch and Go. I'll make two landings; the second will be to show you the first was no accident," she added.

Landing at Lindberg Field, Ronni taxied to Cardinal Air Park. She retrieved her overnight case from the cargo hold and went to the ladies' room to freshen up. The trio had lunch using the Angel Flight credit card. Those were the two smoothest touchdowns I have ever experienced," Marco said over coffee.

"Yeah, I didn't even wake up until you shut down and the silence woke me," Gerry said.

"Landings should be smooth each and every time. No sense in jarring our patients any more than necessary", Ronni said. "When we get to Atlantic City, I'll show you how I do it, but you can develop your method. It is not that difficult. You just need to make the first one, remember how you did it, and practice, practice, practice. You will know you have made a perfect landing when an electric current seems to give you the sense of a job done to perfection."

"Let's go to Atlantic City," Marco said. "Do you want to continue to 'drive,' Ronni?" he asked.

"Yes, I do. I need to get to know this airplane," Ronni answered.

Putting her overnight case in the cargo hold, she noticed a large case strapped in. It had Oriental signs and labels on it. She couldn't see who the receiver was, but she made a mental note to check it out the first chance she got. After they got into the air and leveled off, the plane was tail-heavy. She adjusted the trim to compensate for it but said nothing to Gerry or Marco.

"I've set the course for Atlantic City and filed a flight plan, Marco. It's your airplane," said Ronni. "Let's see how you land," she continued.

Chapter 14

Hawk had sent all the information he had on Gino's gun to the Atlantic City Police Dept., and the New Jersey state police. The report came back the next day.

"Ballistics has a decisive match with a slug removed from an NYC undercover officer. We never could find the weapon. Gino Consiglio was a person of interest, but we didn't have enough on him, and we had to kick him loose. The DA is issuing an Arrest Warrant that he will have to have in his hands before he can be released."

Hawk reported back that Gino was under house arrest and wasn't going anywhere. "We may be a hick town, but we have as good a police force as there is anywhere. Send the warrant, and I'll serve it and deliver the prisoner to you in Atlantic City."

Fed-Ex delivered the warrant early the next morning. Hawk called Sgt. Watkins and said, "I know this is your day off. I have an arrest warrant for Gino Consiglio, that grease ball at Motel Eight. If you would like to serve it and deliver him to the police dept, in Atlantic City, you would get some overtime, and I have Ronni's cell phone number. I'm not trying to be a matchmaker, but you two seem to enjoy each other, and if you are away from here, you can relax and be yourselves."

"Since you put it that way chief, I can't refuse. Book the flight, and I'll pick him up," Bill said.

"You leave Troutdale tomorrow morning at nine-thirty. Mike will fly you over in his Cessna." Hawk said. "He could hear the pleasure in Bill's voice at the chance of seeing Ronni again."

Bill knocked on Gino's motel room door. A voice from inside asked, "Who is it, and what do you want?"

"Sgt. Bill Watkins, I have a warrant for your arrest for the murder of a New York City police officer. I'm to deliver you to the Atlantic City police dept."

"Come on in officer. The door is unlocked," the voice said.

Bill walked in and came face to face with Gino's Forty-Five.

"Is that the gun you used on the policeman?" Bill asked.

"Yeah! You will never live to see me in the slammer. You are as dumb as you are big, and you are big."Gino snarled.

"What is your next move, Mr. Consiglio?"

"We are going to get in your squad car and head for Portland, somewhere along the way I'm going to blow you away like I did that cop from New York. When I get to Portland, I'll call the boss for some cash and lay low for a while," Gino said.

"And what do you think I'm going to be doing all this time?" Bill asked

"You'll be just sitting there like the dumb cop you are," Gino said

"I may not be as smart as you, Mr. Consiglio, but I am smart enough to make sure my gun was loaded before I pulled it on anyone. Now just hand it to me, and let's go. We have a plane to catch."

"If you want it that bad, come and get it, cop, as he pulled the trigger, twice!

Bill walked across the room and closed his large hand over Gino's, who was still hanging on to his gun. Bill squeezed Gino's hand, and fingers, and Gino screamed in pain as the bones broke. "Would you like another try?"

"You broke my hand and finger, you big @#!....!"

Bill whirled aroudnd to face Gino and said, "Before you continue with what you were going to say, you little slimeball, I'm tired of your mouth and arrogance. Shut up and get in the car before I get thoroughly pissed off and save the State of New Jersey the cost of a trial and the expense of keeping you. You have a better chance with a jury and the shyster lawyer our boss will hire, than you have with me. When you get to Atlantic City, they will have someone look at your hand; in the meantime, show me how tough you are and swallow the pain. After all, you brought it on yourself."

Noticing Gino nursing his hand, Hawk asked Bill to explain.

"He pulled an empty gun on me and wouldn't let go of it. I had to take it away from him. That's all there is to it chief," Bill explained.

"Mr. Consiglio," Hawk said. "This has not been one of your best weeks; remember us if you should make the unwise decision to return - If you beat the rap."

"He can't beat this one; He confessed to me while he had his gun on me."

"It's just your word against mine. My mouthpiece will tear your testimony apart like the trash it is. I'll come back to even the score."

"I may be a hick cop in a hick town and dumber than a box of rocks, but I have it all on this tape," taking it out of his shirt pocket. "I'll make a copy of it for us and one for the Atlantic City Police. Here is your ticket verification and travel voucher, Bill. Mike is ready when you are."

Chapter 15

The flight to Troutdale was uneventful.

Mike asked Bill, "What happened to Gino's hand?"

"Mr. Smart ass pulled his gun on me, and in the struggle to take it away from him, his hand and trigger finger got broke," Bill explained.

Bill sat Gino in the window seat to his left.

"Give me your left hand. I'm going to cuff you to my left wrist. That won't be very comfortable because of your swollenleft hand. I would have used your right wrist, but like I told you earlier, you brought it on yourself."

They had a two-hour layover in Chicago. Bill took the cuffs off so they could use the men's room. Bill had never been to Chicago's O'Hare Airport and was noticing everything like some backwoods tourist. He couldn't help but see the blonde with ample cleavage and the rugged man near her.She caught Gino's eye and blew him a kiss. Gino waved at the pair with the cuff still on his left wrist.

"You must be proud of the fact that you are under arrest, to be showing your bracelets," Bill said.

"That's Joe Pistillo, a friend of mine. I didn't think you noticed, you weren't paying much attention to me," Gino said.

"This place has a lot of mirrors, Gino," Bill commented.

Joe Pistillo trailed them into the men's room. Bill, anticipating a problem, snapped Gino's other cuff to the urinal. Gino protested, but

Bill told him, I'll take the handcuffs off when we are finished and ready to go out," Turning to Joe Pistillo, he said, "You need a new tailor. That thirty-eight you've got in your left shoulder clip is obvious."

Pistillo's right hand moved snakelike under his $750 tailor-made suit. He was much too slow. Bill's martial arts training kicked in. Before Pistillo's gun cleared his shoulder holster, his wrist was in Bill's vise-like grip. Stripping the gun from the thug and tossing it in the urinal away from Gino, Bill gave Pistllo a right jab to the nose and a left hook to the jaw that put the thug on the floor with a bloody nose and broken jaw. Taking some paper towels, he fished the gun from the urinal and washed it off in the lavatory. Gino is screaming for help from the onlookers who just stared in disbelief of what they just witnessed. A Chicago police officer hearing the commotion came running in with his gun out!

"Freeze," he commanded.

Bill raised his hands and identified himself.

"Officer," he said. "There is a thirty-eight in the lavatory. It belongs to this man who I believe is Joe Pistillo. The one handcuffed to the urinal is Gino Consiglio.He is under arrest for the murder of a New York City police officer, and I'm taking him to Atlantic City. You will find all of the necessary red tape in my right inside pocket. Mr. Pistillo was trying to release my prisoner, but he was too slow on the draw."

Airport security arrived and helped the police officer sort out the facts; Gino was telling a different story. Joe Pistillo had another version.

"We will call Hawk in The Dalles, and the police department in Atlantic City," Bill said.

"No need for that, Sgt. Watkins. My name is Paul Jacobson. My friends call me Jake. The control in this hassle, and your physical strength allows you to call me Jake or anything you like! Your Chief wired us that you were on your way, and if you needed any help, he would consider it a personal favor. He also said he doubted you would need any help unless they sent seven or eight thugs to springyour prisoner. We'll take care of Pistillo. We are not the most efficient police department in the country, and we do have a lot of unsolved murders, but in Pistillostype of case, we don't fool around. He will be in the state pen for at least ten years for assaulting a police officer, carrying an unlicensed gun, and a few other things."

"Thanks, Jake, " Bill said. "They're calling our flight. We've got to go."

"Come on," Bill said, " uncuffing Gino from the urinal. I should leave you there for people to be able to harass you, but it wouldn't be fair to them."

The buxom blonde they had seen earlier had already made a new connection, and upon seeing Bill and Gino heading for their flight, gave the one-finger salute.

Atlantic City police were waiting at the gate when Bill and Gino walked through.

"Welcome home, Gino," they said. "What happened to your hand?"

"I want to file a police brutality lawsuit against that hick cop," Gino whispered *"He deliberately broke my hand and finger when I was surrendering my piece."*

Winking at Bill, the Atlantic City police officer said, "I'm Lt. James Walker. Did you deliberately break his hand and finger?Is that right, Sgt Watkins?"

"No, sir," I was trying to break his neck and got his hand instead. It was an accident."

"You can release him into our custody, and we will take over from here. We'll sign the necessary forms," Lt Walker said.

"I would prefer to do this at your headquarters, if you gentlemen don't mind. I'm sure you are who and what you say you are, but I'm just a dumb hick cop from a hick town, and there has already been one attempt to break him out. He is part of a mob with long arms. I will surrender him at your Police Headquarters."

The denial of Lt. Walker's request annoyed him. "If that's the way you want it, Sgt. Watkins, that's the way it will be," he stated. "I came out to meet you, thinking you could get back home as soon as possible. My car is waiting out front. Shall we go?"

"Gino and I will take a cab, if it's all the same to you," Bill stated. "The longer I'm in police work, the more suspicious I am. I'm not used to the big city. Where I'm from, we know everybody and never lock our doors or cars. We sleep well at night, knowing everyone is watching out for everyone else. We have a crime or two now and then, but when we eliminate those, we know it narrows the field considerably. On the Fourth of July weekend, our local grocery store was left unlocked. When the owner came in on Monday, there was over $200 cash and some checks; also, a note from one person who said she couldn't make change for what she bought, but she would come back Tuesday to pay. She signed her name and left her phone number. Those are the kind of hick town people I know. I can't trust anybody here because I don't know anybody here. I'll see you at the station. Come on, guy," and headed for the cab stand.

When Bill got to the police station and turned Gino over to the detectives, he said, "I hope Lt. Walker is not too ticked off, because I wouldn't release Gino to him."

"What Lt. Walker?" the detective demanded. "I'm Lt. James Walker, and I have been here all day building a case against this scum bag."

Bill told the real Lt. Walker about the reception at the airport and the incident in Chicago.

Lt. Walker stared in amazement after hearing Bill's story.

"You're telling me that you held Gino in custody and disarmed Joe Pistilloby yourself." He said.

"Yes sir, that's what happened," Bill said. " I accidentally broke Gino's hand and finger, getting his gun away from him. Sometimes I forget how strong I am. I'd like to check in somewhere. Where do you recommend? I need to shave, shower, change my clothes, and relax. I'd like to go someplace quiet with good food, reasonably priced. Remember, I'm only a hick cop from a small hick town, not very sophisticated."

"I have read these reports, and if what you say about yourself is right, don't ever change. I would like to have you and ten others, just like you, on our police force. As far as a place to stay is concerned, the casino area is going to have what you want, with the possible exception of quiet; but, if you stay on the upper floors, it will be reasonably calm. I'll drop you off at Trump Plaza and go with you when you register."

"Thanks, but no thanks. Can I call you Jim?" Bill said.

"Of course, call me, Jim."

"I would prefer not having any ties with the police. You are probably already suspicious of something big going on here. I would prefer not to have any contact with the police until we have reliable sources to confirm the activities. I'll check with you before I do anything. I don't want to blow anyone's cover."

"Okay, Bill. I'm proud to know a hick cop from a hick town with no sophistication. You are one smart fellow!"

CHAPTER 16

Bill took a cab to Trump Plaza, checked in, and asked for a room on one of the upper floors.

"I'm sorry, sir, without a reservation, you will have to stay on the first or second floor." The desk clerk said.

"Okay, second floor, non-smoking room with a queen-size bed," Bill said.

"Yes, sir, I can see you need a large bed. My name is Marilyn. I'll be here all night, if you want anything, I mean anything. Just call me," she said suggestively.

"Thanks for the information. I'll put it in my memory bank," Bill replied.

He showered, shaved, and dressed in typical western garb; cowboy boots, with high dogging heels, plaid western cut shirt, soft denim jeans that showed some wear, held by a wide, tan, leather belt with a large buckle that said 1994 National Steer Wrestling Champion. A turquoise-studded bolo on rawhide thongs served as a neckpiece and topped off with a flat crowned Stetson. He called Ronni's cell phone to leave a message, but to his pleasure, she answered.

"Veronica Lane."

"What a beautiful sounding name, and a voice that goes with it," Bill replied. "Ronni, this is Bill Watkins. I'm in town, and if you haven't had supper yet, I would like to take you out."

"I don't know when I've been so glad to hear from a friend. It's a rat race here, and the rats are winning. I would love to have supper with you, but I insist on buying yours. Where are you staying?"

"I'm at the Trump Plaza, room 210."

"I'll be there in twenty minutes. I'll call you from the lobby."

Twenty minutes later, there was a knock on Bill's door. He opened it to a surprised Ronni.

"We have almost identical clothes on. A crunchie captured Ronni's long, blond hair loosely falling past her shoulders. "May I leave my jacket here?" she asked.

They settled at the table, each ordered steak, baked potato with sour cream and chives, salad with Vidalia onion dressing, and coffee.

"We would like to have our coffee now, please, and later a bottle of Sangria," Ronni said to the waiter. "What brings you here, Sgt.?"

"Please don't call me, Sgt. Call me, Bill. I brought Gino back. The slug from his gun matches the slug that killed a New York City cop. Gino was a person of interest, but they couldn't build a solid case and had to kick him loose. This time they have his gun and the slug. He's toast. Hawk got wind several years ago about something going on back here, and he sent me to look around, more or less undercover. I cleared it with Jim Walker and told him I would check with him before I did anything. I didn't want to blow anyone's cover."

Supper was over, and dessert was Cherries Jubilee. Ronni and Bill were enjoying their wine and watching people when a drunk stumbled and spilled Ronni's wine all over her shirt.

"I'm sorry, honey," the drunk said. "Let me take your shirt off and wash it out,Bill saw trouble, and as the drunk tried to unbutton her blouse, Bill grabbed his wrist.

"Why don't you go sober up and leave the lady alone?" Bill asked quietly.

"If I don't, and I decide I want to see what she has, what are you going to do about it?"

"I honestly don't know. I could break your arm. I could break your leg or just punch your lights out. I haven't decided. Are you sure you want to do this?" Bill said.

"You can bet your cowboy life we do," one of the other three said.

Bill jumped up and kicked the first drunk in the mouth, knocking several teeth loose or out, and putting him out of commission, gave the closest one a solid kick in the groin with his pointed-toe boots, laid a hard right hand to the wind of the third, causing him to lose all he had to drink or eat. The remaining one put his hands in the air!

"I don't want any more," I'm sorry," he said.

"Smart move," Bill said. "I was saving my best for last. Get a mop and clean that mess up and make your friends help you; don't even think about ever laying your hands on my wife. Is there any part of that you don't understand? Come on, Honey, I've had about as much excitement today as I can stand." They took the half-full wine bottle and went upstairs.

"Oh, Bill, I was so scared. I could just see me laid out buck naked while they took turns on me. I had no idea what would happen to me. Did you realize you told them I was your wife?"

"It was a natural reaction," Bill said. "We had just finished a good meal and were enjoying each other's company like a happy couple."

Bill suddenly shed a tear. "I miss those happy times, and you are the first to fill that void."

They kissed each other's tears away. Bill unbuttoned Ronni's blouse.

"Take it off, and I'll rinse it out," he said.

"Throw it on the floor with my bra," Ronni ordered...........

Sometime later, Bill said, "Ronni, I didn't plan for this to happen. I apologize for my behavior. I feel like a heel for taking advantage of you. I haven't had sex since my wife died, and I just got carried away."

"I'm going to shower and wash my blouse," Ronni said. "Let's finish the wine."

"I'll shower when you finish and join you for wine.".

"Haven't you ever heard, save water, shower with a friend."

"Yes, I have, but I don't trust myself."

"My blouse is soaking wet, and it's past midnight. Where am I going to sleep?" Ronni demanded.

"You take the bed, and I'll sleep on the floor."

"I'm trying to seduce you, Bill. I want you to make love to me. I don't have any PJs, but I sleep nude sometimes anyway."

Ronni came out of the shower, wrapped in a towel. "I feel so good."

"Yes, it does. I'll be out in ten minutes, and we'll have our wine."

Ronni had the lights low, soft romantic ballads coming from the stereo, and the wine poured. She was sitting on the couch and beckoned for Bill to join her.

Bill was wearing a soft, wine-colored sweatsuit. He sat back on the couch and stretched his left arm across the back. Ronni moved close and nestled herself against him. They sat and listened to the music until the wine was gone. ....

"I made love to Veronica Lane, but I call her Ronni. My late wife and I had a great marriage and a good sex life, but it was never like this. You are lovely, Ronni."

"Who seduced who, last night?" Ronni demanded over breakfast.

"I'd say it was a dead heat," Bill answered. "I don't believe in one night stands. I do want to see more of you, and I want this to turn into something permanent."

"I couldn't agree more, Bill. We can build a relationship on solid ground, and it will develop into something permanent."

"I'm going to stay around for a few days and see what crawls out of the woodwork," Bill said.

CHAPTER 17

John and Kim had gone to pick up their co-pilot, Yale Yocum, at the Bodies' ranch near Cheyenne. Ray and Virginia Bodie rolled out their usual red carpet for the newcomers. Kim stared in amazement at the vastness of the view and how far she could see. "I'm not used to all this space, she commented to Virginia. My country was small, but it had a lot of forests and mountains. When John brought me to the U.S., we lived on base, and there isn't much to see there. The other wives shunned me because I am Vietnamese, and we had no social life. We came here, and the people have been so friendly. I feel like I have a family again. The Cong murdered my mother and father, raped and murdered my sister. I only escaped because John would not leave me behind. I don't know what love feels like, and I don't know if I love John or feel indebted to him, but I do know I want to stay with him forever."

"That sounds like love to me," Virginia said. "Let's go see what the men have cooked up."

Kim looked at the abundance and variety of food on the table. She bowed her head, closed her eyes, and in her native tongue, prayed.

She slowly raised her head; told the folks she was giving thanks for John being able to save her. She was sure her family was in heaven, looking down on her. They were in the arms of Jesus, not because of anything they did, but because they, as a family, admitted to being sinners and asked to be forgiven and gave their lives to serving others, and had paid the ultimate price. Tears were streaming down her face.

Ray was the first to speak, "You said you were sure they were in heaven just because they asked to be forgiven, not because of anything they did? That's all it takes, just ask for forgiveness?"

"That's all," Kim responded and related the parable of the rich young man.

"Virginia and I go to church regularly and give generously, but according to what you just said, that doesn't make any difference. Our priest has never said anything about admitting being sinners and asking for forgiveness. I'm going to ask him about that on Sunday."

"If that's all it takes, why don't we all do it right now," John said.

"It sure as hell… oops," Ray said, "can't hurt anything. Kim, since you have made the trip, would you lead the way?"

"I would be happy to," she answered, "It isn't necessary, but since we are a family, why don't we join hands?"

In her native tongue, holding firmly to John and Ray's hands, she said, "Father God, Brother Christ, we come before you with bowed heads and admit we are sinners. We give our lives to You and ask for forgiveness. We dedicate our lives to serving You in any way we are able. I thank You again for John and my new family. Bless us, Amen."

Hugs and kisses all around. It was an entirely different party that sat down to enjoy the abundance.

"Kim," Yale said. "I will never take for granted my many blessings. I don't know how it happened, but I feel like a different person than I did earlier today. I feel like a weight has lifted from my shoulders."

"It's probably the man upstairs taking your load. Did I say that?" Ray asked, shocked at his comment.

"Yes, you did, Honey," Virginia said. "I now believe in miracles."

John and Kim slept in Bodie's guest room. They lay in the darkness listening to the coyotes howl, the horses snorting, and the far-off call of a mother cow calling her calf.

Kim rolled up next to John and whispered, "I love you, John. I want to spend the rest of my life with you."

"Kim," John answered, "I owe my life to you and would never leave you. I love you more than any man has a right to love a woman, and at supper, you showed a depth of soul I have never seen. We lay here listening to God's voice, and feeling his love as the comforting breeze brings the sweet smell of new-mown hay over us. God is in His Heaven, and all is right with the world."

"I have never known such peace," Kim stated. "My life in Vietnam was a constant struggle for existence. I never knew anything but war and fear until you rescued me. Now, when I see people, here in the land of plenty, complaining and protesting about every little thing, I get irritated. If they lived one week, like I lived most of my life, they would kiss the ground where they stand."

Coffee was ready. Ray and Virginia were doing the morning chores when John and Kim came into the kitchen. There was a note on the fridge: 'Don't know what your usual breakfast is, help yourself. Ray's homemade bread, fresh eggs, juice, bacon, and homemade sausage are in the fridge. Don't leave before we have a chance to have a cup of coffee together. R.& V.

John and Kim had finished washing their breakfast dishes, when Virginia and Ray came in after doing their chores. Virginia filled four cups and suggested they have their coffee on the patio.

"This is one of the thirty perfect days of the year. We shouldn't waste it by spending time indoors unnecessarily." She commented. "Kim, thank you for your prayer. Yes, like Yale, it has made a difference in my life."

"The important thing to remember is God loves you. He not only forgives you for your sins, but forgets them as well." Kim said.

CHAPTER 18

John answered his cell phone. He listened intently, then said, "There's been an accident. An ambulance is bringing a rancher who lost the battle with a bull. He is in serious, not critical condition. When you get here, our dispatch is to take him to New Orleans. I'll get the bird (plane) ready. Kim, you pack our uniforms and be prepared to load the patient."

"I'll call Yale," Ray said. "He is eager to fly, and I will say, he is damned, oops, darned good."

The sound of a wailing siren, in the distance, heralded the approach of their patient. He was a good-sized man about six-foot-tall, broad shoulders, large callused hands, face tanned from years working in the outdoors that had already worn out two bodies. He would not consent to any sedation.

"My name is Anthony Hroch, pronounced, rock. People call me Tony. I ain't never ridden anything I couldn't control. I want to talk to Laramie and her husband about improving my herd using that new-fangled artificial insemination. My bulls will be unhappy, but that's their problem. I'll pasture a few cows with them for natural mating, but I will need Laramie."

"You can talk to Yale, or as we call him, Eli, now. He's the copilot," Ray said, "now shut up and get out of here."

John asked Yale, "What shall I call you, and do you want to drive?"

"Eli is fine with me, that's what I'm most used to, and yes, sir, I like to drive a plane."

Eli went through the checklist and turned to John, "Did you make the walk-around, and is everything okay?"

"Yes, to both questions. Ray will pull the chocks when you give the signal."

Eli expertly started both engines, and when he was satisfied with the readings of the gauges and dials, he gave Ray the signal to pull the chocks. Ray pulled the chocks and held them up for Eli to see. Eli gave him a thumbs up, eased the throttles to the firewall, lined up on the runway, and was wheels up when John spoke.

"I have been around pilots for a lot of years, and have seen good ones and bad ones. You are one of the best I've ever seen. If you wanted to, you could get a ticket on almost any airline."

"I confess, I love to fly, and I'm not afraid of leaving Ami a widow. We make a comfortable living by working smart and hard. I'm not needing the size of payroll checks and perks that the airline pilots get. I want to tuck my kids in every night. Ami and I learned about loving together. There is probably a lot we don't know about it, but we're satisfied with what we have. I thank you for the compliment on my 'aviating.' That's what my Uncle Red calls it. He taught me not only how to fly, but the importance of the details, like flight plans, etc. You did file a flight plan, didn't you?"

"Yes, and the weather in New Orleans; temperature 89 degrees, humidity75%, wind from the south at 15 miles per hour," John answered.

Air traffic control reporting to John, "Somebody identifying themselves as Angel Four has asked me to tell you to go to your private line."

"Thank you, ATC. I'll report back to you when I return, Angel Six out. I made the trip, Angel Four. What's on your mind?"

"This is Ronni, John. Who is your copilot?".

"His name is Yale Yocum. He is the nephew of Red Kely, the Service Department Supervisor. He is not as cute or pretty as you, but he is an excellent pilot. One of the best I've ever seen. Where are you, and where are you heading?"

"We just cleared Oak City airspace deadheading to Frisco. How about you?"

"We picked up a rancher in Cheyenne that lost a fight with a bull. We are taking him to New Orleans. I'll see you tonight. If you ever layover in Cheyenne, don't hesitate to stay with the Bodies. Good luck, Ronni. Kim and I hope to see you soon. Looking forward to getting better acquainted. Angel Six to ATC, over and out."

Kim came forward and said to Yale, "Mr. Hroch is awake and alert and wants to talk. Why don't you go visit with him, and I'll sit here with John."

"Okay, Mrs. Schumann. My name is Yale, but folks call me Eli."

"Please call me, Kim, Eli, Mrs. Schumann is so old-fashioned."

"It is a sign of respect and courtesy, Ma'am." Eli took a seat where he and Tony could talk.

"Young feller," Tony said. "I couldn't help hear your conversation with the nurse. It is such a pleasure to see and hear respect and courtesy, especially in young people. You set a standard most people fall short of, mostly men, and particularly young men. When I get back on my feet, I want you and your wife to take full control of my herd. Cull out the bad ones and replace them with some of your stock. Your stock is as good or better than I've seen. I've been watching you two since you were married, and I was there when you put the brakes on that charging steer. Any man would be proud to have you for a son or son-in-law, or friend. We have just made a deal. Here's my hand on it. When I said full control, I meant just that. Nobody is going to question your decisions. I want to develop a herd as good asyours."

"Thank you, sir. You have given Ami; that's what I call Laramie, and I an awesome responsibility, and we won't let you down. We can't do the job overnight, it will taketime. I guarantee you will have the best possible bloodlines, and here is my hand on that. I'm going to call her and give her the news soon. She and Ray can go over to your place and see where and what we need to do to start this new job. Virginia can watch the kids, and everybody will be happy."

Tony said, "I'll call my foreman and tell him about the change in management and that he is to cooperate one-hundred percent."

Kim sat with John and watched interestingly and asked, "What that dial meant, or what is that gauge measuring? There are so many things to watch, and she said, "How do you keep track of everything?"

"Honey, I've been doing this for years. There were just a few instruments at the beginning of my training, making it easy to learn, but each aircraft has not the same technology. I had the basics but, the advancement of aviation itself is ongoing, and the learning process for pilots becomes more detailed and 'in the air piloting' is an important skill, hand in hand with classroom instruction as well as textbooks. This Angel Flight occupation has introduced another aspect of training. It is crucial to learn to make perfect landings for the comfort of the patients on board. You will know when you have made a smoooooth landing when you have a moment's sensation of electricity racing through your body!

"I'm going to love working with you, John. It's going to be hard to adjust, but when we get settled in the routine, it will seem like a permanent vacation."

John said, "We've just entered New Orleans air space. You should make sure our patient is secure."

Eli came to the cockpit and buckled himself into his seat.

"Do you want to take over and put us on the ground?" John asked.

"Yes sir," Captain, I'm not a smart ass, sir, that is your title, and unless you say otherwise, that is the way I will address you," Eli said.

"I appreciate your respect, Eli. Why not save the formality for when there are others around, when it's just three of us, John is fine."

"Okay, John, " Eli said, "Would you prepare the aircraft for landing?"

"Yes, sir." John chuckled as he went through the checklist. "Checklist now complete, see if you know how to land."

"Landing. That's the most natural part. An airplane can land itself. It's what to do when I am on the ground that confuses me."

Eli had learned well. No bump, just the scream of the tires, and the roar of the engines when he reversed the thrust to slow down. A follow-me pickup led them to the ambulance. Eli shut the engines down, the door opened, and Tony was in the ambulance, when John said, "I know it's not going to happen, Elli, but I would love to have you as my permanent copilot."

Delta Park had hooked their mule to Angel Six. Kim, John, and Eli gathered their suitcases and hailed a cab to the hospital tovisit their patient.

They had taken Tony's clothes off, and he was in a hospital gown. The doctors and nurses gasped at what they saw. Tony was one huge bruise.

The doctor said. "We will need X-rays and other tests to see the extent of the injuries, and the nurse will give you something for the pain."

"Pain. Who the hell is in pain? That damned bull is the one that needs a pain shot!"

"You have broken ribs, possibly a concussion, cuts and bruises over most of your body. You've lost a lot of blood. You must be in pain or shock."

"Sonny. Three years ago, that same damned bull gave me a compound fracture of my left leg. That hurt some, but I didn't take a pain pill or shot then, and I ain't a-gonna take one now. Is there any part of that statement you don't understand? Tomorrow that bull will be dog food."

Satisfied that their patient was in good hands, the trio from Angel Six checked in at the Holiday Inn.

"It has been an interesting and exciting day," Eli commented. "I would like to clean up, change clothes, and have supper in the dining room."

"Oh, yes," Kim echoed. "I am tired. A quiet supper and early to bed sounds good to me. I didn't do much today, but the change of pace I'm not used to."

"We'll meet you in the dining room, Eli," John said. "We will be a little late. You know how long it takes a woman to dress."

"Yes, I do, John."

Eli called Ami to tell her about the contract with Tony Hroch. "It's going to take a lot to do what he wants, and we should begin as soon as possible. This job might last a long time. I'd like you and your Dad to go over and see how much work is going to be involved. Tony told his foreman to cooperate with us. I love you, Ami, and I miss you and the kids. I'll be home as soon as possible."

"I love you too, Honey, We miss you. The kids all prayed for you tonight, voluntarily. Dad and I will check on Tony's herd soon. Dad has been going nuts with nothing to do except chores, and Mom will have the kids spoiled when I get back, but that's nothing we can't handle Good-night, Honey."

Eli was sipping coffee and doing one of his favorite things, 'people watching,' when the Schumanns came in to join him.

"It's amazing how a hot shower not only washes your body, but also relieves the stress and rejuvenates you too," Kim commented."

They finished dinner and were enjoying a bottle of fine wine when the band started playing.

"Good evening, ladies and gentlemen. My name is not MacNamara, but I am the leader of the band. My name is Paul Hayes. We are a small band, but we try our best to make big band music, the kind where you hold your partner and follow the music. We'll start with 'Moon River.' Let's dance."

"Dance with me, John,' Kim asked. "We have been to many Officer's Club dances, but we never danced."

"I'm not a good dancer, and believe it or not; I'm self-conscious."

"I've watched you box, John Honey, and the moves in the ring are just like dancing. Please give it a try."

"Okay, I owe you at least a try," John agreed.

It took a while, but each step came a little easier. By the time "Moon River" was over, they were in sync. "Ebb Tide" followed, and John was enjoying himself. They were moving as one.

Kim looked up at John, dreamily eyed, and said, "I love you, John, and I want to spend the rest of my life with you, no matter where." They held each other closer and just followed the music. They danced as long as there was music and a few steps more.

"This next set will be a change of pace. Some country swing. Grab your partners and dance." Paul announced.

Eli left the table and walked across the floor to the bandleader and said something to him. The band leader looked surprised and nodded his head. Eli stepped to the mike and started to yodel. I mean, he could yodel! The dancers stopped to watch and listen. The band played 'The Tennessee Waltz', and Eli sang in a deep baritone voice; "I was dancing, with my darling, to the "Tennessee Waltz," when an old friend, I happened to see."

John gave him a big thumbs up, picked up the wine bottle, and waved good-night.

Eli continued entertaining; tunes of Johnny Cash, Sonny James, and a few others. The music stopped, but the dancers wanted more from Eli. He held up his hand for silence, and when they quieted down, he thanked them. "I only sing for pleasure, not money, and I'm a rancher from Cheyenne, and I sometimes fly for Angel Flight. We brought a neighbor who lost a fight with one of his bulls, to your hospital. I don't think he did lose the fight. He's in the hospital, but the bull is dog food. I'm going to close with one of my favorites. Marty Robbin's, My woman, My Wife. I love you, Ami."

The Schumann's went to their room, happy the evening had been so pleasant and confessed their love for each other, freely and honestly.

CHAPTER 19

"Dispatch called this morning. They haven't found a pilot yet, but you can go back to ranching," John said. "I'll miss you, Eli, you are a damn good pilot, and a joy to be around. How many people know you can yodel?"

"I think Ami knew, but she has never said anything, and only those people we saw last night."

Kim came bouncing into the coffee shop, humming. She gave John a big kiss on the mouth. "It's a beautiful day, and dancing is such a pleasure. Aren't you glad you tried, Honey."

"Yes." He blushed as he answered. "It is a real pleasure, and we are going to do more of it. We are going to deadhead home, but will stop and let Eli off in Cheyenne. You and I will go on alone, Honey."

"I'll miss you, Eli," Kim said. "We haven't known each other very long, but I feel I have known you for years."

"We westerners make friends fast. We depend on our neighbors when they are in need. We may have no use for the person that needs help, but that makes no difference. He needs help, and we help him, and he would do the same. I didn't mean to digress like that. I wanted to say, we are more like family than friends, and our latch-string is always out. Let's go home, I've got kids and a wife that need loving, and a ranch to help run."

Three hours later, Eli greased the Gulf Stream onto the runway on Bodie's ranch. John and Kim stayed just long enough for coffee, and a pit stop. Eli's wife and kids were all over him, like an old shirt. It was hard to tell who was the happiest to be together again. It was a dead heat.

"Remember, Eli," John said. "The second seat is yours whenever you want it."

"And give all this up?" Eli said. "I don't think so."

"Why don't you come upfront with me?" John asked Kim. "It's a better view, and we can talk about our new house."

"I'd like that."

John put the plane on autopilot and sat back to relax.

Out of the blue, Kim asked, "What is the mile-high club?"

John sputtered and stammered and asked, "Where did you hear about the mile high club?"

"I overheard some girls in the ladies room in New Orleans talking about being initiated into the mile-high club. They sounded like it was something special."

"It's just sex in most cases. Love doesn't enter into the picture. To belong, you have sex in an airplane while flying a mile high. We don't need to be uncomfortable in an airplane. We can make love at home, anytime. Agreed."

John landed in The Dalles in mid-afternoon. He made his report to Red about maintenance problems, gave Heather his log, and went into Mike's office to see if there was any news on finding a pilot.

"Nothing's happening right now, but one will turn up, like always thirty seconds before it's too late," Mike laughed. "How was your trip, and how do you like Eli?"

"Good trip. Kim likes her job and is very good at it. Eli is one of the best I've ever seen. He is professional, and his landings are the smoothest. He can fly with me anytime. Kim and I want to buy a lot when they are available. Two or three acres is enough space for privacy. See you at the ranch."

Chapter 20

A battered pickup with California plates pulled up at the police station, A black lady got out and went inside looking for the Chief. Miss Johnson ushered her into Hawk's office. She stood nervously and waited for him to notice her. He was on the phone with Sgt. Watkins.

"Stay as long as you need, and watch her back. This thing can bust wide open any minute, and she will need backup whether she admits it or not. Be careful, Bill, I want you both back here. Good-bye."

"Yes, miss. Please have a seat. Is there anything I can get for you, coffee, ice tea, soda, anything at all?"

"A glass of water please, I've been driving almost non-stop for two days. My name is Victoria Parks. They call me Vicki. I have a long story to tell, and I will answer any question honestly."

"Miss Parks, I was about to have supper. Will you join me? My treat and no strings attached. Okay?"

"Okay, and call me, Vicki. Do you have a place where I could clean up and change clothes? I smell bad and feelgritty. I do have a clean change of clothes."

"Miss Johnson! Please take Vicki to the ladies shower and make sure there are towels, washcloths, and soap. Give her a plastic bag to put her dirty clothes in," Hawk said. "Thank you, Miss Johnson. Vicki, you take all the time you need. I'll be waiting right here, and you know us red skins have patience," he laughed.

"Here is my driver's license, sir. Please check me out. I don't believe I have any wants or warrants."

Vicki came from the shower into Hawk's office. She wore jeans and a UCLA sweatshirt.

"I feel so much better, and I know I smell better." She said.

"You can leave your truck here and ride with me, up in front. I think you told me you have ridden in the back of a squad car a time or two." Hawk said.

"More times than I can count. I hope that's all behind me now. I need a job, and I'm willing to do anything. I'm not here looking for a handout; I just want a legup."

"You've come to the right place, Vicki, and call me Hawk, or chief. Everybody else does until they cross the line, then it's sir."

Hawk drove out to Mary's Supper Club.

"Good evening, Hawk. Your usual table?" Barbara asked.

"Yes, please. Our newest resident, Vicki Parks, is looking for a job. Keep your eyes and ears open, okay? We will be here a while, Vicki has a long story to tell."

"Honey, you tell him everything, don't leave anything out. He will never tell a soul what you tell him. Sometime I'll tell you what he and Mike Murphy did for me. What can I get you?"

"I'll have the fresh salmon with baked potato, sour cream, and soup, Hawk ordered.

I'll have the same with a salad instead of soup, ranch dressing on the side," Vicki ordered.

"We'll both have coffee," Hawk continued. "Now, Vicki, tell me your story, from the beginning."

"My Dad was killed in a drive-by shooting when I was twelve. It seems like yesterday, but it was eighteen years ago. My Mom worked two jobs to keep us fed and clothed, but that wasn't good enough for me. I fell in with the wrong crowd and started smoking cigarettes and later, weed. I became a prostitute to get money to pay for the weed. I rose to the 'hard stuff' and couldn't sell enough prostituting and started dealing. I was so down. I found myself pregnant by someJohn. I tried to go straight, but the lure of money kept drawing me back. The baby came, and I looked down at my son, and made the promise to him, and me. I will turn my life around. You are going to have a home where you are safe. My son and I dried out together. My eight-pound baby son gave me the strength to make it. I got my GED and worked in the housekeeping department in the same hospital where my son was born. One day I thought to myself, this is as good as it is ever going to be for you unless you get more schooling. I started looking at the high-paying jobs. I've always wanted to travel. I learned what pilots earn and decided that was for me. The next part of my story, nobody knows except Blacky Harmon and me. He was a big-time drug dealer, and I knew where he kept his money, and when the box would be full. I waited in the shadows, watching for him to leave, I opened the door with a locksmith's gun and took the cash box. My heart was pounding so hard I thought sure he would hear it, but I got away clean. My mother was working. I took it home and counted it; there was $250,000. He was about to make a buy. The cartel showed up to collect the drugs, and he didn't have the money! The fight was noisy, shots fired, and the police came and arrested everyone still breathing. Blacky got twenty years. I took the money and went to Cal Aero Tech and learned how to fly airplanes. I am qualified for multi-jets, but if you hadn't noticed, I'm black, I'm a woman. I have not found an airline that will hire me. I met a pair of Latino brothers who told me about your town and how they escaped. Blacky was released early for good behavior. I decided I'd come and check you out."

"Vicki!" the chief said. "Not that it makes any difference, are you a church-going person?"

"No, sir, I'm not a church-goer. I've heard most churches aren't preaching from the Gospel and don't talk about salvation. I know, when I die, I'm going straight to Heaven. And when you have led the life I've led, that is a huge gift. Why do you ask?"

"This building and everything else, including the airport, is owned by my best friend and blood brother. I know he is looking for a pilot. He's gone home for the night. I'll drive you there, and you can find it in the morning. I have to ask this question. How much do you have left out of the $250,000, and where is it?"

"I have about $100.000, and it's under the seat of my pickup."

"Vicki, I'm going to place you in custody for your protection, and put the money in the safe overnight. We will open an account in the morning when the bank opens. Nobody needs to know anything about it. You are our guest and treated as such. You willbe in a cell by yourself and have clean sheets. Is that okay, or would you rather stay in a motel?"

"It sounds strange, Chief, but I'll rest easier locked up.'

"Rise and shine you sleeping beauties," Hawk called into the cell block. "You drunks get cleaned up. You are to appear in court at ten. The judge hates beards and slovenly appearances. Miss Parks, I have a special treat for you. Get your black ass out here.

That comment brought a roar of catcalls and whistles and a very shaken, Vicki Parks. Hawk shut the cellblock door. I apologize for that, but the prison grapevine is very efficient, and if they had a clue as to what is going on, we would be in trouble. The special treat is breakfast at Mary's Café. I'll come back and retrieve your cash and deliver it to the bank, andafter breakfast, I'll introduce you to Mike Murphy."

Vicki's pickup was in the bank's parking lot when the Chief pulled up. He took Vicki by the arm and led her to the Manager, Marian Ward.

"Mrs. Ward, this is Vicki Parks, our newest resident. So new, she doesn't have an address yet. She has a sizeable amount of cash, all legally obtained, and would like to open some accounts, checking, and a savings plan. I'll leave you two to talk business. I've got some crooks to catch."

Mike was sitting at his desk when Hawk came in.

"Good morning, brother," Mike said. "What's on your mind?"

"You're not going to believe me; I'll let her explain. Here she comes now. Mike Murphy, meet Victoria Parks. She is a certified multi-jet airplane driver looking for a job," Hawk grinned.

"Heather," Mike called. "I'm sending Miss Victoria Parks in to see you. She is our new pilot. Assign her to Angel Six and call John and tell him to bring Kim and come and meet their new crew member. She is on the payroll starting today, hold the paperwork for now!"

"Sir, you don't know anything about me."

"Hawk said you were a certified multi-jet driver. What else is there to know?"

"How about checking into my past. I've not lived an exemplary lifestyle."

"We don't care about your past, and call me, Mike. We are only concerned about your future. We will dump you in a heartbeat if you go back to your old ways. The ball is in your court."

"What kind of business are you in, Mike?" Vicki asked. "I want no part of anything illegal."

"We transport critical patients to a hospital where they can get the best possible care; This is an essential part of our business. We charge nothing for the service. If a person of means needs our service, we treat them the same as those who don't have a dime. We expect and sometimes ask for a donation, which is tax-deductible. Usually, they come through with a generous amount. Do you have any specialties you can share? Your pilot held the heavyweight boxing champion of the entire Pacific, and his wife is a master of several of the Martial Arts."

"I know street fighting and can hold my own in most cases. A swift kick in the crotch and a sharp fingernail in the eye usually does the trick." Vicki answered.

"That would do it for me," Hawk said. "Good luck, Vicki. You have a friend if you ever need me."

Chapter 21

"Where are you living?" Mike asked.

"Laughing, Vicki said, "I spent my first night, that was last night, in jail. I had a bunch of money, and the Chief thought it best to lock it and me in the jail. He helped me open an account at the bank this morning. I have no idea where I will live. I don't want an apartment. I want a house for us. My son and Mom are in L.A. now."

"You can stay at the Marriott until you find permanent quarters. We will take care of the room and meals. Booze is limited to minimal quantities, a beer or a glass of wine with dinner, etc. When you go on flight status, you must be sober and ready to leave immediately. I'll call my friend Harold. He's an honest realtor, and knows what is available for rent or to buy. I'll leave you to fill out your employee paperwork."

Vicki, after she finished her paperwork, was studying the Angel Flight Manual orientation rules when Mike came to tell her of his visit with Harold Morrison, the realtor. He has a house you may think suitable for you and your family. He will be here at one o'clock to pick you up and show the house, Mike told her. "If you want to buy property and need or want a loan, we will give you what you need at four percent, fixed thirty years, no points. Let's go to lunch. Your crew is waiting at Mary's Café."

"May I, at least, buy my lunch?" Vicki pleaded. "I feel like a kept woman, and I am used to being independent."

"Yes, if you insist, and you can pick up the tab for your crew, if it won't run you short," Mike stated.

"I've got enough; I'll buy lunch."

When they got to Mary's, Hawk was sitting in his usual spot. He took off his hat, and carelessly brushed his hair back. Before Vicki could say anything to him, Mike ushered her to the round table where John and Kim were waiting.

"When Hawk brushes his hair back, it's a brush off, don't come over, don't speak to me, I'm working on something," Mike explained.

"John and Kim Schumann, this is Miss Victoria Parks, the last member of your crew. She would like us to call her Vicki. Vicki, this is John and Kim. She is buying lunch. Her day is tied up, so you will have to check out her flying tomorrow. "You three are going to be working closely together. You could spend the day getting acquainted."

"I'd like that a lot," Vicki said. "I'm not used to being alone, and I have no real friends."

John suggested that Kim spend the rest of the day with Vicki and 'girl talk' while he went to see about Angel Six.

"Good idea, John," Kim said. "If Vicki and I are going to work together, we should be well acquainted with each other, like sisters. What do you think, Vicki?"

"I think that sounds like a plan." She replied. "I'm supposed to meet with a realtor at one in Mike's office. He has a property I might be interested in renting or buying. I've lived in a ghetto long enough, I'm going to have a house. Where were you raised, Kim?"

"In a little village in Vietnam. I'm the result of a rape by some French bastard. John was a Marine pilot and got shot down." Kim said. She paused and tried to control her emotions, but with tears and sobs, she continued. "My mother and I hid him from the Cong. Finally, the Cong killed all the men and children, then raped the women and then killed them. John and I witnessed the whole terror. They must have thought they had killed everybody because they walked away. I have the face of the one who murdered my mother burned into my brain. If I ever see him, I will take pleasure in exacting my kind of justice."

Vicki handed Kim a tissue, put her arms around her and held her close, comforting her.

"I had a walk in the park, compared to that," Vicki said.

"I never tell that story. It brings back horrible memories."

"Kim, I'm glad you told me. My story is not as violent, but if you have read the newspapers, you know what goes on in the ghetto.

I was a whore and a drug addict at fourteen, and a mother at sixteen. I was pregnant by one of my Johns. I was as far down as a person can get. I promised my son when he was only three days old that he would have a better life. He gave me the strength to turn my life around. It's almost one; I'd better get to Mike's office."

"May I come with you? I want to see the house my sister might buy."

The house was in an older neighborhood on a quiet street. There was an extra lot and several full-grown Bing Cherry trees for shade. The kitchen was functional, and it had a snack bar that would seat four adults and room for a kitchen table. The combination living/dining room and a wood-burning fireplace that showed signs of use were beautiful. They entered the hallway and looked it over; three bedrooms, a bath and a half, and laundry facilities in the hallway near the bedrooms and bathrooms. The oak floors so shiny you could almost see yourself in them. The basement was dry. A new 50 gal. water heater was in the corner, and electric baseboard heat was satisfactory.

Vicki told Mr. Morrison, "I don't need to look any further. I want to live here with my mother and son. Will there be a problem because we're African Americans?"

"We do have a few misinformed souls in town, but by and large everybody is friendly, We just try to be good neighbors."

"That's all I want. I just want to be a good neighbor. Is the house for sale or rent, and what are the terms and conditions?"

The rent is $750 per month with $1500 damage and security deposit and a one-year lease. The deposit will earn 4% interest. The asking price to purchase is $125,000. It is part of an estate, and the heirs want to sell it quickly," Harold said.

"I noticed some loose roofing material on the west side. Also, the gutters and downspouts need repair or replacement, and the house could use a coat of paint. I haven't looked at the garage yet, but I'm sure it needs some repairs. I would assume it was roofed at the same time as the house and needs a roof, gutter, and downspout repairs, also. I'll get estimates on the work that I think needs to be done, whether I rent or buy, I'll call you no later than noon tomorrow. Would you hold it for me, and do you want a deposit?"

"No, a deposit isn't necessary, Miss Parks. You are an intelligent woman. Few men I know would have noticed those defects and called my attention to them."

Mike said, "I'll wait for your callback at the Angel Flight office. Now might be a good time to do a shake-down flight. You are a full crew now. Things are different when you are in your working environment than on the ground in a relaxed atmosphere."

"Good idea, Mike," Vicki said. "I haven't flown in a while, and I should practice. I have no experience other than flight school. I'm nervous and excited at the same time. The house Mr. Morrison took me through is perfect, and there are a few items that need attention; roof and gutters, downspouts, exterior paint, etc. I will get estimates and call Mr. Morrison."

"I'll call Harold for the address and try to have some estimates for you when you get back from 'aviating.'"

CHAPTER 22

The Angel Six crew walked over to where it was parked. Vicki looked at it with a wide-eyed expression and commented, "She is beautiful. Are you telling me the three of us are going to work together, and I get to fly her? Angel Six is beautiful! How much time will I get to fly?"

"Yes, Vicki," John answered. "You are the pilot hired to fly this bird, and you can drive almost as much as you want. One thing we are particular about is the touchdowns. The patients are always in pain and suffering severely. We practice landings every chance we have and strive for the smoothest landings possible. The patient's comfort is our concern. We practice until there are no bumps at the touchdown! We all keep in mind that we feel a small shock of electricity affirming success when we execute a perfect touchdown. I'll make the first two. The second is to show you the first one wasn't just a lucky one. Okay?"

"Okay, shall I call you captain or John or what?" Vicki asked. "You are the one in command."

"Call me John only when there are no patients or strangers near. Captain is the professional title. It's my job, as captain, to see that all checklist and maintenance defects are corrected. It is also my job to assign tasks to people.who trained in specific areas of expertise. I will show you how to file a flight plan. There are times when I will ask you to do that. We always make a walk-around inspection. We touch all the control surfaces and make sure there is nothing to hinder the functions.

The last thing is to remove the sleeve from the pitot tube. Always finish in making sure the wheel chocks are in place. Some hangars keep the wheels chocked until you signal to pull them; others remove them as you board. It sounds like a lot, but I will be involved, too. Are there any questions?"

"Not that I can think of," Vicki answered. "I'm smart enough to know I don't know all the answers. I will not hesitate to ask questions."

"Let's 'aviate,' John said. "We don't need a flight plan today. We'll just be doing, Touch and Go" (smooth landings practice). Remember to recognize the small electric shock that happens when your landing is perfect. You make the walk-around, and I'll watch and critique when you are finished."

Vicki strolled around the plane. She touched each control surface, double-checked for any hindrances, pulled the sleeve from the pitot tube, and triumphantly carried it aboard.

"Letter perfect," John commented. "Next, you or Kim will raise the steps and close and lock the door by just pushing the button with the door symbol on it, and hydraulics will do the rest. While you do that, I would be going through the checklist and getting ready to start the engines. Strap yourself in and go through the preflight checklist. Touch each gauge and dial, and when you finish, start the engines. It makes no difference which one you start first. When that engine is up and running, and all dials and gauges read what they are supposed to, start the second engine, and follow the same routine. If you are satisfied that everything is right and the 'fasten your seatbelt' sign is on, you say, IT'S YOUR AIRPLANE. I'll either take control and get us off the ground or let you do it. I think it would be good for you to get us off the ground. It will relieve the tension your under, right now. I will only have my hands on the yoke in case there is something I don't like. I will say, let me have it, and you take your hands off the yoke. I don't expect it will happen, but I want you to be ready to obey instantly."

Vicki eased the power up until they were rolling and taxied to the take-off zone. She looked both left and right, and then looked again. She released the brakes, slowly and called Mr. Rolls and Mr. Royce for full power and expertly put Angel Six into the air.

"Oh, wow." She said. "I never got that kind of a high on drugs, and I know drug highs. Thank you, John. I was so nervous I was going to screw up, by the way, the walkthrough calmed me down a lot. Now show me how to land, and explain everything you are doing, while you are doing it."

"Vicki, I think the airline industry lost an excellent pilot, and Angel Flight gained one. You will be running the first seat before long." John said.

"About the landings: First, you must know your airplane. Angel Six reacts differently than any other. Each plane has it's own personality. You have to feel your way to the ground. We'll look at the landing checklist and go through it step by step. Do not even think about memorizing it because one day, you will be distracted and forget something, and it could be fatal. In WWII, a pilot tried to take-off from a carrier with his wings folded. He got airborne, but the Marines lost a Corsair and a pilot. How can you miss not having your wings spread?"

John put his plane on the ground without the thumps and bumps most pilots create. Pushing the power to full thrust, they were airborne again. The second landing was a carbon copy of the first. Once in the air, he turned to Vicki and said, "It's your airplane, Vicki. Relax and do the best you can. I'll take care of the checklist; you just land and takeoff."

The first touchdown was a little rough, which brought a look of dismay on her face. She powered up and was airborne when John said, "For your first try in a strange airplane, you did well. We would have all walked away, which is the definition of a good landing. Now go around and try it again. Nobody expected you to get it right the first time. That would have been just lucky."

"You make it look so easy, John, like anybody, can do it."

"I can't tell you how many times I had landed before I came to Angel Flight, and it took me many tries to get it right, don't worry about it. It will come with practice. I can tell you, at your first perfect landing, you will have an electrifying moment of success, and you will know your landing was perfect!"

Each touchdown became a little better than the first, and after three hours of T and Gs, John said.

"You are all tensed up. Taxi up to maintenance. We'll continue another day."

Red was waiting for them as they taxied into the service area.

"Young lady, you have the makings of a fine pilot, and a good instructor. If ye listen to him, and relax, it will all come together for ye." He said.

CHAPTER 23

Mike had the estimates as promised. Vicki looked them over and called Harold.

"I'm ready to make an offer to buy," she stated. I'm offering $115,000 cash; $25,000 upfront and the balance on closing if the repairs are completed. My offer when I must bear the expense of the repairs is $100,000 and $25,000 upfront.

"I think you've bought a house, but don't call the movers yet, Miss Parks," Harold said. "I'll call the owners in the morning and get back to you with an answer as soon as I get their decision."

"Well, Mr. Mike Murpy," Vicki smiled. "It looks like your town is stuck with me whether they like it or not. It sounds like I've bought a house. Who do I see about a mortgage?"

"How much do you need?"

"It all depends on who does the repairs, and I want to keep $50,000 invested in my son's education. I will need a max of $65,000."

"We will give you what you need at 4% fixed thirty years, no points, no early payoff penalty. We can help with the repairs. 'Mike Murphy and Son' will furnish the labor and buy the material needed at cost. You will only have to pay for building material."

"You aren't doing this out of a sense of obligation because I'm black." Vickidemanded.

"No," Mike snapped back. "We are doing it because you are one of God's creatures, and we love you whether you love us or not, and like it or not, you are a part of the family. My folks wanted a large family, but things didn't work for them. Murphy business policy is the same as family ties. The members of family and business work together, help one another when needed, and loyalty is for all members. Now, how about a hug for your brother!"

Vicki obliged and came apart. Through tears and sobs, she explained how all or her life she wanted to belong to a loving family, but it wasn't there. It seemed like all the men were abusers, sexually and emotionally. I am at last feeling like I was of some worth, because of the kindness and friendship you have given me. The police chief heard my whole story; accepted me for what I am, not what I was, and you are concerned about what I will become. I will be the best pilot I can be, and a damn good sister. I'm so tired. I need to take a shower and sleep."

CHAPTER 24

Kim," Mike called. "I want you to take Vicki to the ranch. She has clothes in her truck. She should not be driving without rest. Tell her- she is going home!"

Susan met Vicki at the door and greeted her with an honest hug.

"Hi, Vicki," Susan said. "Mike called and told me you were coming. The bedroom right across the hall is your room. You will be sharing it with my ten-year-old daughter, Mary, if you don't mind. The bathroom has plenty of clean towels and washcloths and a variety of soaps."

"Mike said I was part of the family. I must be her sister or her aunt," Vicki teased.

"You would be her aunt, since you are my sister," Susan answered. "When you finish with your shower, I'll be in the kitchen. Come in, and we'll have 'girl talk' before dinner. I don't know what we're having, but you can help fix it, okay?"

"Okay."

Vicki came into the kitchen with her hair in a towel, smelling of Estee Lauder, wearing a yellow sweatsuit and pink, fuzzy bear claw slippers.

"I feel so much better," she said. "A hot shower does take the stress away."

"How about burgers on the grill?" Susan suggested. "They're quick and easy, and we can sit on the patio while they're cooking."

"I know this will sound strange to you. I'm thirty-years-old and have never eaten a burger cooked on a grill at home. I've eaten a lot of fast food, but never cooked at home, and, of course, we never had a patio. It took two days of hard driving to get here, and it's a whole new world. I thought places like this were only in fiction books, but it is real. I can't wait to get my Mom and Jeffry, that's my son, here with me. I think I still remember something about cooking. I'll make potato salad."

Susan rang the bell on the patio calling Marie, Carl, and Robbie to dinner. Mike introduced Vicki to the children.

"Are you going to share my room, Aunt Vicki?" Marie asked.

'Aunt' Vicki, completely surprised Vicki!

"If that's okay with you, Marie. I don't think I snore, but when I'm asleep, I can't help it if I do."

"It's okay if you do," Marie said. "Mom snores, and so does Dad, but we're used to it. It doesn't bother us. If you hear a woman scream in the night, don't be afraid. It's only 'Old Noisy,' the cougar. We have an owl too, so there are sounds in the night. Daddy says that's God's voice telling us He is around watching over us.

Vicki laid in bed and thought how much her life had changed in the last three of four days. Noisy screamed and Hooter, hooted. The last Vicki remembered was the sound of the Columbia River splashing and gurgling on its way to the Pacific. *LA was never like this,* she thought to herself.

"You don't snore," Marie announced as Vicki came into the kitchen.

"That's good to know. I'll feel so good this morning. I haven't slept that well in years."

"The Schumann's will be by to pick you up in about an hour," Susan said. "Mike has already left. He is concerned about Angel Four. He won't tell me why. He told me he is worried that something is going on that puts Angel Flight in a bad light, but he doesn' know what to do about it."

Mike was on the phone when the crew of Angel Six arrived.

"She just walked in Howard. It's for you, Vicki," he said, handing the phone to Vicki.

"Miss Parks?" the voice on the other end asked.

"This is Howard Morrison. The owners agreed to $100,000. I'll have the papers drawn up and get ready to close. It will take two or three weeks before it's final because we have to use FEDEX to get important legal documents from place to place. Signatures must be original and witnessed. You can pick up the keys and order the moving van. Congratulations! You are a property owner, and unfortunately, a taxpayer."

"I just bought a home." Vicki squealed. "I'm going to call Mom and tell her to pack up and get ready to leave. She doesn't have a lease, and all she has to do do is tell the landlord when she is moving. A small truck is all she needs. Just big enough to hold relics, etc., Jeffrey's bike and his treasures. The furniture and appliances aren't worth the cost of the move. I will need $50,000 to close the deal,plus the repairbills and material costs. I'm already up in the air. Let's put an airplane under me. Let's go!"

CHAPTER 25

Angel Six was coming around for a series of T and Gs when Mike called on the radio.

"Go to our mystery channel, John."

"Roger. We're gone," John responded.

"Angel Four is at Beaver Air and is asking for you. She may be here with us. How about it, Angel Four. Did you make the trip?" Mike asked.

"Ten-Four, Hawk. It's lonely over here, and I need someone strong and handsome to hold me," Ronni said seductively.

"Hang tight, sweetheart, the Marines are coming. Angel Six out." John said. "Vicki, head west, and follow the river."

"What was that all about, John?" Vickiasked. "Susan said Mike had been worried about Angel Four this morning, but she didn't know why and he won't tell her."

"I honestly don't know, Vicki. She called me Hawk. That's the Police Chief's name. It must have something to do with some criminal activity. There's Troutdale. Put us down and taxi to Beaver Air. You can see Angel Four parked in front. Get close, but don't put us in a place where we have to have help getting out. I don't know what to expect. Follow my lead. I love you, Kim, and I'm not having an affair."

"I know that, John," Kim said. "Be careful. Vicki and I will both give you backup, all the way, in every way."

Ronni came running up to John and threw her arms around him and kissed him seductively on the mouth and whispered, "*Take me into Angel Four and close the door.*" She told him about the big crate that was always on board. "Sometimes it's heavy, and sometimes it's light. They load it with a forklift. When it's light, two guys just pull it out and walk away with it. It's full now. I need to know what's in it. I have my suspicions. Marco and Gerry went to a movie. They asked me to go, but I told them I had an old flame in the area, and he was going to get lucky; mess up the sheets on the gurney, John, we have about two hours."

"We've got to make this look real. Someone could be watching. We'll spend about thirty minutes messing up, and go to the terminal to clean up." John said. "I'll go see Jensen and get coveralls and tools, and go work on your airplane. Do you have a camera? I'll take a picture of it, and it's contents, that will give us a clue. Mess up your hair and clothes like you just had sex."

Hand in hand, they walked into the terminal and gave each other a passionate parting kiss. John left the men's room and went in search of Jensen.

"I need a pair of coveralls and tools to make it appear I'm working on Angel Four," he stated. "Don't ask questions because I wouldn't know the answers. All I can tell you is that activity around Angel Flight looks strange and suspicious."

"Frank!" Jensen called a mechanic who looked about John's age. "Fix up Mr. Schumann with coveralls and any tools he may need. Give him anything he asks for and don't question anything, do you understand."

"Yes, sir. Good morning, Colonel," Frank said. "It's been a long time, and I never had the opportunity to tell you what a great CO you were. Your men came first. I'm Frank Payne. There was a fire in Texas City that caused injury to me, and my kids and wife, and the Red Cross could not help me. You flew me home, personally in an old F-7 Tiger Cat. I didn't have a chance to thank you, and I have never forgotten it. My oldest son is named 'John Schumann Payne.' How can I help you?"

"I need to get into the cargo hold of Angel Four. I don't have a clue as to how to get in there, and we've only got about thirty minutes," John said.

"Piece of cake, Colonel, piece of cake." Just follow me," Frank said.

"Frank, I'm not in the service anymore. You just call me John."

"I'm sorry, sir, but I must disobey that order. Of all the CO's I had in the service, you are the one I most respect. The bastard that followed you, Luther E. Sommerville, undid all the good you had done. He said, I'm not here to make friends, and he didn't. Colonel, sir, follow me."

Frank had the cargo hatch open in a matter of seconds. John got in and noticed the writing and printing on the crate. *I don't know what it says, but it's Vietnamese, and Kim will be able to read it,* he said to himself.

"Frank! I need a very slender, solid pry bar. I need to get inside the crate without any visible evidence. Oh, shit! There are self-sticking seals all around, now what?" John said.

"Stand by, Colonel. I'll get a heat gun and some Elmer's glue and be right back." Frank said.

Handing the heat gun to John, Frank said, "Do one seal at a time and only get them loose enough to open the crate. To close it, apply a little Elmer's, spread it completely, and reattach the seals. They will never know."

Following Frank"s instructions, John loosened the seals and opened the crate.

"Holy shit," John exclaimed. "It's full of brand new sheets of $100 bills."

He carefully lifted the top sheet of bills and closed the crate and resealed it. Looking closely at his handiwork, he was satisfied that the crate showed no evidence of foul play.

Back in the service area, John asked, "Frank, Who told you how to do that trick?"

"In Korea, sir. We used that method to midnight requisition steaks and beer from the Officer's mess."

"Frank, I appreciate your comments on my command. I am truly flattered that you thought enough of me to name your son after me. Thanks for your help this morning. I don't know what I would have done without it. We come here on occasion, and I would like to meet your family and treat you all to dinner at any place you choose."

Ronni was watching John and Frank with intense interest. An audible sigh of relief escaped as she watched them close the hatch, and just in time. Marco and Gerry were coming through the door.

John went to Vicki and told her to meet Kim in the restroom. You wait for us in the coffee shop. Vicki went on her errand while John filled Kim in on what he had discovered.

"Give her this envelope," John ordered. "Tell her not to open it until she is sure she is in a secure place and e-mail us the pictures that are inside. Nothing happened in her airplane, and I'll prove it to you tonight."

"I know nothing happened, but I'll welcome your proof, Honey," Kim responded. Kim went to the ladies' room, and when she was sure she and Ronni were alone, she delivered the envelope and John's message.

"Be careful, Ronni," Kim cautioned. "We are ready to back you up anytime, anywhere."

Kim joined Vicki and John in the coffee shop. Ronni beckoned to John to join her and her crew.

Looking adoringly at John, she said, "Marco and Gerry, this is the old flame I was telling you about, John Schumann. We fanned the flame into a five-alarm fire this morning. Don't be surprised if you see him. I was to be his co-pilot, but yours was unavailable. That's why they assigned me to you. We want to get together as soon as possible, and I mean get together." She said seductively. "John, I see your crew is ready to leave, and we must be going too." Kissing John passionately on the mouth, she said," that will have to hold us until later." And she followed her crew out the door.

"There is something serious going on with her," John reported. "She introduced me as her old flame, and said I would be around, and they shouldn't be surprised. Let's get home and talk to Mike. Vicki! You drive."

John told Mike what happened at Troutdale about the crate of money, obviously counterfeit and the Vietnamese labels.

"I took pictures with her camera. She will e-mail prints to us, and Kim will translate them," he added.

"We better see Hawk, Mike said. "He should be in the loop."

Hawk was in his usual spot at Mary's café.

"What's new in aviation?" he asked.

"That's why we're here," Mike replied. "We need to talk, but not here."

"My office in fifteen minutes," Hawk answered.

In Hawk's office, Mike and John related the morning events. Hawk raised his eyebrows, frowned a little, and said, "Miss Johnson, call Sgt. Watkins and have him report to me ASAP. We need a war plan, and I think Bill should be in on it."

Sgt. Watkins was there in ten minutes.

"Mike! Tell the Sgt. what you told me."

"I promised Ronni I wouldn't tell anyone this, but I think for her safety, you should all know. She is an undercover agent working with the FBI. She told me the case she was working on would be coming to a head soon. The item she was looking for, we have found. We need to find who is producing, distributing, and what methods they are using. Any ideas, gentlemen?"

"I checked the log on Angel Four when she called in this morning," Mike said. "Most of their flights are deadhead. How much the rest of the crew know about this, I don't know, but we have to assume they are aware of what is going on, so we have to defuse it at warp speed. The four of us have got to keep her secret and be ready to act when she calls."

"Chief, I need a vacation." Sgt. Watkins said. "I've got time coming and feel the need for some big city, like Atlantic City, excitement. I don't want the children with me. It wouldn't be any fun for them, and as soon as I can make arrangements for them, I'll leave.

"If you don't mind coming home to spoiled children, you can bring them out to the ranch." Mike offered. "I've got an experienced grandmother, an elderly, but not old, Indian couple to see that they get spoiled, but not undisciplined."

"Sounds like a plan to me, Mike." Sgt. Watkins stated. "Thanks, I'll bring them out in the morning."

Mike said, "I'll have the bank issue you a card with a $10,000 line of credit. It will appear you are spending your money. Don't get careless."

"I've worked carnivals, and know Three Card Monte, learned to deal seconds and thirds and how to spot crooked games. I may be a hick cop from a hick town, but I get awful lucky when it comes to gambling," Sgt. Watkins explained.

"We have to let Ronni know about the information we have collected," Hawk said.

"I'll try the mystery channel," John said.

"I'll invite her for supper," Bill volunteered.

When Mike and John got back to Mike's office, Heather announced, "We got a strange e-mail. It looks like a big box with Oriental writing on it. I printed it out and put it in your 'IN' file."

"Thank you, Heather. Keep mum about this, please," Mike said.

Kim looked at the pictures and gasped,

"The boxes are from Northern Vietnam addressed to Terrance Widra Enterprises, Atlantic City USA. Printed Matter. It has an Official State Seal, which makes it almost immune from inspection. The US Government does not want to muddy the waters and is keeping a hands-off policy."

"Ronni was right on when she said it would reach into high places," Mike mused.

"We know what it is, where it's going, and who printed and shipped it," John commented. "All we need to do is figure out how to bust it and make it appear it was Ronni's plan. As Angel Flight, we can go anywhere anytime except overseas. If we could get the two sides fighting each other, all we would have to do is take out the winner."

"If Widra Enterprises got a shipment of blank paper, they would be pissed off and call the shipper and complain," Mike said. "The shipper thinks Widra is ripping him off because he knew he shipped the product. Widra will call him a liar because he knows he got blank paper. That should lead to a showdown hopefully, in Jersey." Mike paged Red.

"And what can I be doin' for ya, Michael, me boy?" he said as he came into the office. "It must be important because I never get invited to your Lordship's office," he continued with a smile.

"Do we still have that smoke pot we used when we got Susan's children out of Cuba?" Mike asked.

"Indeed we do, me boy, indeed we do, and it still works," Red answered. "I cleaned it and tested it last week."

"The next time Ronni is here, install it on an engine with the switch on her side, out of sight," Mike ordered. "Tell her where it is and what to expect when she activates it, and how to unload it. This plan is top secret."

"What's your plan, Mike?" John asked.

"We are going to make a duplicate crate and fill it with blank paper," Mike answered. "We're going to stash it in Cheyenne. When everything is in place, the first time Ronni is close enough to Cheyenne, she will activate the smoker and make an emergency landing at the Bodie ranch. Eli will be here to "Fix" the problem. Ray will use his forklift to switch crates, and Ronni and Virginia will keep Marco and Gerry busy. They will make the switch and remove the smoke pot. The whole operation shouldn't take more than a couple of hours. We sit back and wait for the shit to hit the fan!"

"I think it will work," John said. "How will Ronni know about the plan?"

"Heather!" Mike called. "Check the log on Angel Four and bring me the report, please."

Heather brought the log on Angel Four up on the computer. She studied it for some time and printed out a copy for Mike.

"It looks to me like they have an awful lot of deadhead miles, and I think it's time for a regular maintenance check." She reported. "They just delivered a patient to San Francisco, and are deadheading back to Atlantic City."

"Perfect," Mike smiled. "Get them on the radio and order them to come directly here for scheduled maintenance, and tell them it is a direct order. Failure to comply will result in pulling them out of service at their next refueling stop. Get Red in here please, things are about to happen."

"Something very important must be going on to be invited, twice in one day, to your Lordship's office," Red said.

"It is, Red," Mike said solemnly, "Angel Four will be here for scheduled maintenance. Install the smoker while you do the maintenance work. Be very busy and tell the crew it will be sometime tomorrow before it's ready. All I can say to you is, there is something big in the wind, and Angel Flight is right in the midst of it. Try to do the smoke pot secretly."

"I'll come in after midnight and do it." Red smiled.

Ronni set Angel Four gently on the tarmac, two and a half hours later, and taxied to Angel Flight Maintenance. The crew reported to the office and asked, "Why were they ordered in on such short notice?"

"I'm sorry, Ronni," Heather answered. "It's my fault. I completely forgot to go through the logs last week. You were due last Wednesday. I hope this doesn't cause your company any problems."

"We've got bonded cargo on board, and here we are stuck out in this hick town with no security," Marco bellowed.

"Back off, Marco," Ronni warned. "It was an oversight on her part, and she apologized. There is a damn good police force in this hick town who will provide us with security. I need to talk to the Chief and see what has happened to my assaultcase. While I am there, I'll arrange for security. Can I use the pickup?"

"I need to see Hawk myself," Mike said. "We'll get you checked in at the Marriott. Ronni will be in later. She and my wife are good friends. They will have dinner together and talk, 'girl talk.' Enjoy your stay. I'll see you tomorrow."

Chapter 26

Hawk was in his office and was pleased and surprised to see Ronni. "What's new in Jersey?" he asked

"That's why we're here, and we have information you don't have and a plan neither of you know. Let's get in your patrol car, where we will have absolute privacy. We need a security detail on Angel Four. It's only for show, and I'll explain in the car."

"I can't spare a patrolman: and turning to Ronni, continued; Sgt. Watkins decided to take a vacation to Atlantic City. Chief Hawk saw disappointment on Ronni's face immediately and added, "he will be there for a while."

Ronni blushed and smiled.

"I'll get in touch with the council, and they will stand watch."

"What is the council?"

"My Indian brothers," Mike answered. "They move as silently as clouds and are almost invisible. You could be on Main Street, and the council would be watching you. You would not see a one. The FBI could learn a lot about surveillance from them. They are too set in their paleface thinking to admit they could change."

Mike and Ronni brought the Chief up to date, explaining the plan in the privacy of the patrol car.

"We are going to get detailed pictures of the crate tonight and build an exact duplicate, and we will let Ronni know when it is ready and in place. John, or me, or someone will ask you if you remember Clint Walker, the actor in TV series, Cheyenne. He had a cabin on the river, near here and it burned down last night! Fax us your flight plans, and do not do anything to make them suspicious. When you have the first opportunity, go to your emergency landing routine and wait to see what happens. We will do all we can to help you bring this case to a close. Stay alert. I told your crew that you were close to Susan and was going to have supper with her, so help make me an honest man."

"It has been an eventful day, Mike," Ronni sighed as they arrived at the Marriott. "I'm going to shower, clean my gun, and watch TV. I'll see you in the morning."

Marco and Gerry went into the bar at the Marriott to have a few drinks. Theydrank until the hotel did not allow another. They decided they would see what this hick town did after a day's work. They took a cab to Fernando's Supper Club and were in subdued behavior, but watching people when a particularly attractive blonde caught Marco's eye.

"She reminds me of Ronni," Marco said. "I would sure like to lay down with her for an hour or two."

Gerry said, "You couldn't handle it. That's booze talking. Let's have another drink, and I'll buy it."

Fernando's closed at one a.m., and Marco and Gerry were drunk.

"I'm thinking about that good-looking, Ronni. Her room is next to ours. She might have left her patio door unlocked. It won't be any problem to sneak in on her."

"You're on your own, Marco," Gerry said. "That IS the booze talking. You're smarter than that, and I want no part of it."

"Okay, but that blonde we saw tonight has got me horny, and Ronni is going to take care of it."

"It'll be rape, Marco," Gerry cautioned.

Ronni had showered and cleaned her gun and put it under her pillow. It was a warm night, and she left the sliding door open, and went to sleep like usual, in the nude. The full moon shown brightly over her naked body.

Marco didn't hesitate, despite Gerry's protest. He went to their patio and was outside Ronni's room when he noticed, "My God, she's naked." He tiptoed into her room and was dropping his pants when Ronni woke up.

"Hi, Marco," she said. "Don't sneak around. Take your clothes off, shoes and all; nobody goes to bed with me with shoes on. I can see you are ready for action. Come over here."

"I don't dare," Marco whined.

Ronni rolled over, reached under her pillow and pulled out her gun, and put a shell in the chamber.

"Get on the bed, face down, you greasy bastard," Ronni ordered. "I'll bet my thirty-two looks bigger than my matching thirty-sixes, doesn't it? Ronni took the laces from Marco's shoes, running the laces between his legs and tied one hand in front and the other behind his back. On your feet, and walk out the door. Not the patio door, you dummy, the hallway door."

Marco pounded on Gerry's door, but the over-indulgence turned out the lights for Gerry. He snored away in a drunken stupor. Marco slumped to the floor and passed out.

Ronni gathered Marco's clothes and put them in a trash bag, and leaning over the balcony rail, made a perfect shot into the dumpster four floors below. She smiled and slept peacefully through the night.

Ronni called the next morning. "Chief, I have to see you. How about you join me for breakfast?"

"I've had my breakfast, but I'll drink some coffee while we talk."

"Marco came into my room about one-thirty this morning," Ronni said. "He didn't come to talk. Sex was on his mind and was ready to rape me. He never got a chance. I don't want to press charges because, at this point, we don't need any new players. I can handle the situation. I humiliated him enough, and he was drunk. I'm sure it was the booze that caused it to happen.

"We got a call about two a.m. saying some naked drunk was running around the hotel, so we busted him. You do know how to hogtie a person, Ronni."

"Remember? I told you I had three older brothers and we were born and raised on a farm. That is just one of the many tricks I know."

"I will need you to file a report on the attempted assault and rape for the record," Hawk stated. "Then I'll deliver you to Mike. I can rest a little easier now that I've seen more of your handy work."

Ronni closed the door to Mike's office.

"Marco tried to rape me last night, but didn't even come close." She told Mike the whole story.

"Gerry was not involved in any way. I think the story should stop here and now. We don't need to bring somebody new into the picture; I am not filing charges. Only you, the Chief, Marco, and I know the true story, and I'm sure Marco has been humiliated enough that he's not going to talk. He froze the instant he saw my thirty-two pointing his way. Has Gerry showed up yet?"

"No, and from the sound of things, he nor Marco will be in any condition to fly today," Mike said.

"I'm fine to fly," said Ronni. "I've had my rest, and Red said it would be this afternoon before he's finished with Angel Four. Gerry should be sober enough, by that time, and if not, I can put on autopilot and relax. I don't think we should delay things unnecessarily. We are too close to the finish line."

"Okay, Ronni. You're good to go when Red signs off, but be careful," Mike cautioned.

"Excuse me, your Lordship," Red teased. Everything is done, including pictures. I'll show you how it works, and where the switch is if you'll come this way, Missy."

"Vonnie is singing and whistling this morning; I should work late more often," as Red went out the door, talking over his shoulder.

"Ronni returned to Mike's office, and The Marriott courtesy car was just leaving. Marco was in his stocking feet and some ill-fitting clothes. Gerry was correctly dressed, but was suffering from a world-class hangover.

"You two look like death warmed over," Mike said. "Ronni has taken the responsibility of your flight. I wanted to fire you both when the hotel called and said you came in after one a.m., stumbling drunk, but Ronni told me you have been so over-extended you didn't have enough time off at home, and that's why you lost control last night. I will have a 'come to Jesus talk' with your dispatcher to tell him to allow you more free time at home. I am not going to ask questions."

"Marco, I'll have one of the servicemen take you downtown, and you can get some decent clothes, then, if you are ready to go, Red has signed off on your bird. You can finish your mission."

"Sir," Marco whimpered, "I got mugged last night. I don't have a dime, a credit card, a checkbook, or even a billfold."

"Heather! Cut Marco a check for a grand. We will deduct it from his pay at a hundred dollars a month, no interest."

Marco returned with new shoes, slacks, and a shirt.

"You look a lot better, Marco, and when the booze wears off, you'll feel better," Mike said.

"Ronni! Your crew, such as it is, is ready when you are. You are in command, for the moment. You two, indicating Marco and Gerry, will act accordingly. Now get out of here.

Chapter 27

Ronni said, "Gerry, you go file the flight plan. I'll be waiting n the cockpit. Marco, while Gerry is out of earshot, listen: You and I know what happened last night. Here is your wallet. I put your keys and stuff in my flight bag. You will not have another warning. The next time I'll blow your brains out. Do I make myself clear?"

"Clear," Marco said guiltily, " I got a lesson that I'll never forget, and thank you for keeping this quiet. I am always a friend. It will take time and circumstances to prove it to you, but I am as serious as I have ever been. You stuck your neck out for me. I will return the favor whenever I can."

Gerry climbed aboard and secured the door.

Ronni spoke to Gerry while waiting for the engines to warm up.

"I don't know how much you know about last night, or very early this morning, but it's forgotten and forgiven. We are a crew, and we have to trust each other. I have been too aloof, and for that, I'm sorry. We will do everything except sleep together. We are a new crew starting an hour ago! We each have a job to do, and we'll do it, and help each other when they need it. Okay, with you, Marco?"

"Better than okay," Marco said,

"You mean like The Three Musketeers, all for one and one for all?" Gerry said

"Close enough, pal," Marco laughed. "Oh!It hurts to laugh. I know I brought it on myself."

"Gerry, you're the Medic. Don't you have something for his hangover?" Ronni said.

"Just some extra-strength pain killers, and some coffee."

"Give him a couple of pain killers, and a little coffeemight make him feel better."

Marco woke up three hours later.

"I'm hungry,"

Ronni said, "Good timing, Marco. Des Moines is just ahead. Gerry, get on the horn and get us clearance to land; non-emergency status. We would like to refuel and get something to eat. We are in fourth place behind that United."

Ronni made a show-off landing and said to the tower. "Not bad for a broad is it? I'd do it again to show you it wasn't an accident, if I had time. We will be at Hawkeye Park."

Ronni continues, " Okay, guys, let's do our pit stops and get a bite. To eat."

"We will probably get some heat from the boss for being late," Marco said.

"I'll cover it," Ronni volunteered. "Just agree with whatever I say, understood?"

"Understood," Marco and Gerry said together.

"Will the commander of that Angel Flight at Hawkeye Air Park please pick up the red courtesy phone?"

"Without hesitating, Marco said, "Ronni, you take it. You are more capable. I run second seat."

"I'll be the commander, but you will be the pilot of record, and there is no debate. Excuse me and get my coffee renewed. "Angel Four command pilot, Veronica Lane. How can I help you?"

"This is Dr. Barger at Broadlands Hospital. We have a NASCAR driver that was in a bad wreck at the Fairgrounds. His injuries are not life-threatening but very painful. He is sedated and needs to get to Atlantic City. Can you help?"

"The gods are smiling on him today," Ronni said. "Encourage him to buy a lottery ticket. It just happens we not only have room for him, but are being dispatched to Atlantic City. We will get him on board pronto and take off."

"His wife wants to know if you take checks or credit cards for your service?" the Dr. asked.

"We don't take cash, check, credit cards, or any other form of monetary exchange. The service is free, for Bill Gates or paupers, the service is the same. We would expect Gates to write a nice tax deductable check out of gratitude, but he would never get a bill from us. Where is the patient?"

"In the recovery room, but we can have him ready to transport in fifteen minutes."

"Ten minutes after he arrives, we'll be wheels up and heading for Atlantic City."

"Finish our lunch, guys, we've got a patient to transport. I'll file another flight plan and get a weather report. Marco, you make the walk-around and start the APU. Gerry, get ready to take on a patient."

The ambulance arrived, and everything was ready. The patient was now on the gurney. Gerry helped the patient's wife with her luggage and seat belt and secured the door. Ronni started the engines, and when everything was running as it should, she said, Marco, let's 'aviate.' I don't believe we ever worked together this well. I think we are a real team at last."

"This is ground control, Angel Four, and you have priority clearance for departure. Use runway 65S."

"Roger, ground control, runway 65S, thank you. Angel Four out."

Gerry entered the cockpit to report, "The patient's wife would like to speak to the commander."

"That's you, Ronni," Marco said.

"I agree with Marco," Gerry said. "You are the one that pulled us together, and your smooooth touchdowns are incredible. Mike always explains the electrifying feeling of a perfect 'Angel Flight' landing to new pilots, and yours are perfect! Gino was not a team player, and nothing went right. Marco might be the pilot on record, but you are the commander."

"Okay, I'll be the commander," Ronni said, "and my first command is, we forget what happened in The Dalles. I'll go back and talk to Mrs..... What is her name, Gerry?"

"Marge Chambers. Her husband is Dale, one of the better known NASCAR drivers, and has a huge following of fans, including me."

"Hello," Mrs. Chambers. "I'm Veronica Lane, the commander of Angel Flight Four. You wanted to speak to me?"

"Yes, I do. I understand there is no charge for this service. Is this true?"

"Yes, it's true. It started several years ago when a very wealthy man's orphaned granddaughter needed life-saving surgery. They were in Portland, Oregon, and the hospital was in Galveston. The pilot of the man's corporate jet was drunk and couldn't fly. A former Navy pilot heard the tirade and stepped up to the plate and saved the day, and the little girl. That's her portrait on our logo. The grandfather and Navy pilot bonded. The pilot said all his training had been to kill and destroy, but what he wanted to do was save lives. Angel Flight was born with the premise, there would never be a charge, no matter what the financial status of the patient. Those who have the resources are encouraged to give a tax-deductible check to Angel Flight, but they never receive a bill. Let their conscience be their guide. We are dependent on the generosity of corporations and people of means."

"Mrs. Lane. NASCAR has a huge fan base, and I am sure most of them are not aware of your service. I will personally work to correct that situation. Dale is very popular and has a lot of press coverage. The nation will hear of your service. Dale and I will encourage the NASCAR sponsors to pony-up some money for your company. To whom do they make the checks payable?"

"Make the check payable to 'Angel Flight.' Mail it to State Bank of Oregon, The Dalles, Oregon 97058. Thank you, Mrs. Chambers, and please call me, Ronni. I'm no longer married. If you need anything, just ask Gerry. He is a registered nurse and very competent. We should be in Atlantic City in about two hours. The temperature is 60 degrees Fahrenheit and raining. I foresee no problems."

"Dr. Barger called the hospital in Atlantic City. They will be waiting for us," Marge advised.

"Atlantic City, right on schedule," Marco announced. "Would you please take control, Ronni. I need to work on my landings. I'll do the checklist."

"Okay, Marco. Tomorrow we will use that obviously abandoned strip Northwest of the city for some T and GS."

Chapter 28

Once on the ground, Ronni told Marco to taxi to the terminal where they saw the flashing red lights of the ambulance, then taxi to Garden State Sky Harbor.

A black stretch limo was waiting, and the crew was escorted to it by a determined-looking large, curly-haired blonde man.

The 'boss' sat in the back while his body-guards took positions on either side of him.

"Where the hell have you been. You were supposed to have been here yesterday," he screamed.

"Our orders were, do you hear; our company ordered us to go to The Dalles for scheduled maintenance." Ronni snapped back. "It was an oversight on their part. We were due last week. These two, (indicating Marco and Gerry) spent the night guarding your precious cargo, that's why they look beat-up. We shouldn't be here yet. Marco has too many hours on duty, but I convinced the company that I could handle it. Marco and Gerry took the responsibility to stand guard while I got some rest. It was the last night's sleep I've had in a long time. You do have a contract with Angel Flight to transport patients, and we transported a patient from Des Moines to here. Get off our backs, and I don't care if you are done listening or not; I'm done talking. We are off-duty. Tell your goons to let us out before I get pissed off."

"Supposing I decide not to let you out," Blonde said.

"That would be one of your biggest mistakes." Ronni said. "and I have Misters Smith and Wesson to back me up, not that I would need them. I think you are all mouth and no guts. If you want to try me outside, let's do it. Marco, take charge of Misters Smith and Wesson for me and, Gerry, you and Marco stay out of it. Come on, Blonde, try me."

Ronni exited the limo with Blonde right behind her.

"Okay, bitch. I'm going to whip you and then take you down right here on the tarmac and in the rain."

"I deserve it when you prove you can," Ronni said, "delivering a solid right fist to the mouth, followed by a hard left to the belly area. Blonde bent over and puked up his dinner, and Ronni straightened him up with a vicious uppercut and a kick in the nuts. "My three older brothers taught me how to take care of myself." She looked straight at the boss, and said, "you don't have any protection at all, if this is one of your best,you don't pay enough to hire me. Come on, guys, I'm wet and hungry. Let's hotel and have dinner. I'll buy it."

Ronni noticed a fork-lift unloading Angel Four and depositing the crate into the van with a sign on the door, Terrance Widra Enterprises. She was on the way to the terminal to catch a ride to the hotel.

"There goes the limo. TWE on the plates," Gerry said. "I wonder what that stands for?"

"I'm moving to the Heath Plaza," Ronni said. "If you gentlemen would wait for me in the dining room while I get out of my wet clothes, I'll buy dinner and drinks,"

"Dinner, yes, drink, no," Marco said.

"That goes for me too," Gerry agreed. "You are one tough lady, Ronni. It sounds weird 'tough lady,' but you are both tough and a lady."

"Thank you, and I'll be right back."

"Did you see how fast she threw that right hand? Ali, in his prime, wasn't any quicker." Marco commented.

"She doesn't weigh more than a hundred and a quarter, but she put it all in those punches. Blonde got a lesson he will long remember."

"Here she comes now," Gerry said. "She is a damn, good looking woman. No! she's a beautiful lady."

They both stood up as she approached their table. Gerry held her chair until she was seated.

"Thank you, Gerry, you're such a gentleman, you too, Marco."

"You bring out the best in us, Ronni," Gerry said.

"I did that without thinking. It was the natural thing to do."

Over dinner, Marco said, "You told us you don't mess with a married man, but your old flame is the pilot who gave us our orientation and that little dark-haired lady is his wife. What's going on."

"It was a ruse that could interest me. There he is now. Bill, BillWatkins," she said, standing up, hoping he could see who was calling. "Come and join us for dinner. I'm buying, and there is no debate.Marco and Gerry, this is Bill Watkins, a friend, the one I just mentioned, Bill, this is my crew."

Marco and Gerry finished dinner, and not wanting to be in the way, excused themselves to spend some time with their families.

"I've got so much to tell you, Bill," Ronni said. "We, Hawk, Mike, John, and I have found out Angel Four is transporting counterfeit money from the west coast to many places in the US. It is printed in North Vietnam and shipped to Terrance Widra Enterprises here in Atlantic City. We have also worked out a plan to break the case."

"I want to hear more, but not here," Bill said.

"If not here, where? Your place or mine, big boy," Ronni said seductively.

"I've moved over here. We have connecting rooms. It makes no difference, where.I'll get a shower and shave. I've got a big-screen TV, and there's a Steven Segal movie on tonight. I like his movies. I don't know what discipline of martial arts he practices, but he makes it look effortless," Bill said.

"I'll freshen up and put some sitting-around clothes onand join you on your couch."

Ronni went over the plan that they had approved. Bill made a few suggestions. She nestled up close to Bill. He put his arm around her protectively, and didn't notice she was sound asleep until she snored. The movie was one he had seen before. He shut the TV off, and carefully stretched her out on the couch, and covered her with a blanket, turned down the lights, and went to bed.

When Ronni woke up, the sun was up, and Bill was in her room watching, 'Fox and Friends,'

"Good morning, sleepyhead," he smiled."How did you sleep?"

"I don't know. On my side, I think, but I'm not sure. I was unconscious most of the night. How did the movie end? The last I remember, Segal had a cue ball in a sock or something, and took someone's teeth out. I've got to remember that move. What do you have planned for the day?"

"I thought I might play the hick cop and get real lucky at the Casino, and then go see Jim Walker and tell him what you told me. I want him to be ready to move in when the time comes. Let's have some breakfast and have some fun. I'll go to the casino, and when you see me wipe my brow, come on to me. I'll say, ' it looks like this is my real lucky day. I'm no gentleman, but I do like blondes, especially real blondes.' You say whatever comes to mind."

"It sounds dangerous and fun. Let's do it."

Chapter 29

"One more thing, Ronni. It's only dangerous if you don't know what you are doing. If I ask, How much cash you got, baby? Open your purse, look inside, and say a little over five grand."

Bill went to Heath's Taj Mahal Casino, and wandered around, staring wide-eyed, like some country bumpkin. "This place would sure hold a lot of shelled corn," he said aloud to nobody in particular.

A casino hustler asked, "Where do you live?"

"Oketa, Kansas, just south of Barneston, Nebraska. Population 116 when everybody's home. I sold my farm, and ain't going back, andthe population will be 115. It stays about the same because when some girl gets pregnant, some guy leaves town. Is there anything besides these nickel dime slot machines? I've got a bunch of cash to spend, and I don't want to stay here forever trying to get rich."

"We do have a blackjack table with a ten thousand dollar limit, and a poker room with the same, ten thousand buy-in."

"Here is my line of credit. How do I get the cash?"

"Follow me, sir."

At the cashier's cage, the hustler said, "This man has a line of credit of ten grand. Give him that amount, and as a courtesy, we will extend it to twenty thousand. Enjoy yourself, sir. The blackjack table is through that door and to the right."

"Thank you, young feller. I will have fun."

Bill found the blackjack table, and found a seat open as a disgusted player left. He bet cautiously, paying close attention to the dealer. One or two players, in particular, were constant winners; the rest, including himself, were losing. The light went on in his brain. The dealer is dealing seconds, and using a marked deck. When he figured out the code, he asked what the limit was.

"Whatever you can afford, and backup with a line of credit." The dealer answered.

"I'm in a hurry, sonny. I've got about eight thousand, or grand, as you folks call it. I'm betting all of it. "Damn," he snorted. "Busted again. The girl in the cage in front says, I can have a courtesy line of ten thousand more, is that true?"

"Just a minute, sir, I'll check."

"She said to cover anything you bet."

"I'm not about to bet the farm, cause I don't own it no more. There was some developer from Kansas City, Missouri, offered me fifteen hunnert dollars for my six hunnert forty acres of blood, sweat, and tears. I owned it free and clear, and by the time I sold my equipment, I cleared way over a million dollars, so here I am."

The hookers tipped off by the dealer started moving in.

Bill wiped his brow, and Ronni came up and said seductively,

"Do you feel lucky today, honey?"

"Whooee, do I feel lucky. Darlin,' I ain't no gentleman, but I do like blondes, especially natural ones."

"Then you are going to love me, honey."

"I'm betting twenty thousand on this hand. Is that okay with you?"

"Yes sir, I was told to cover whatever your wager is."

"Deal the cards, sonny. My luck has just changed for the better."

The players before Bill all went bust. Bill put his massive hand over the dealer's, and said sternly, "Call your pit boss over here NOW."

A slender man in a tuxedo followed by two armed bodyguards appeared.

"I am Charles Bird. What seems to be the trouble?"

"Charlie, your dealer is dealing seconds, and not very well. I might add, in addition to using readers."

"I don't believe you, Charlie said.

Bill said to Ronni, "Darlin', call the police and ask for my cousin, Jim Walker. Tell him Bill Watkins is staying at Heath's Taj Majal with a problem that has to be solved fast."

He looked at the nearest bodyguard, without taking his hand off the dealer's, said to Ronni, "Darlin, I hate to drag you into this, but I promise to make it up to you in spades later today, and probably all night and well into tomorrow. Take that piece I noticed in your purse, and if anyone threatens me, put one between Charlie's baby blue eyes. I hate to be called a liar."

"Oh, Honey, this is so exciting. I can hardly wait to see what comes next."

A uniformed officer appeared and asked if there was a problem.

Bill said, "Officer sit next to Charlie, there. Darlin,' this officer gets the second round. We will wait for my cousin."

Lt. Jim Walker entered the scene and asked, "What do you have here that is critical to solve now?"

"That uniformed, useless excuse for a man with the phony Lt. Walker is a bonus. The dealer is dealing seconds, and using readers. I told Charlie about it, and he called me a liar."

"Bill, I hope you can back up what you say about this dealer and this club. Don Heath has a lot of clout. He won't tolerate any crookedness. These guys are toast, if what you say is true, and, of course, when you provide the proof."

"Yeah, big shot! Put your money where your mouth is," the dealer sneered. "I'll bet you fifty grand, and you can't prove a thing."

"How about it, Charlie, are you ready to cover the bet?" Lt. Walker asked."

"You bet your badge, I am." Charlie snapped back."

Lt. Walker ordered one of his men to escort Charlie to the cashier's cage, and bring back fifty thousand in cash. "I don't want that phony counterfeit, only real money."

Charlie threw a stack of money on the blackjack table and said, "Don't get used to it because you ain't going to win the bet."

"What's going on here?" a voice sounded from the rear.

"Mr. Heath, this hick farmer accused us of running a crooked game, and I just bet fifty thousand dollars he can't prove it," Charlie said.

"I'd like a piece of the action if you're that positive. Would you accept a check?" Heath asked.

"No, sir, I only know you by reputation. You wouldn't accept a check from most of your patrons unless they showed you proof of financial responsibility. Why should I trust you? Show the cash or get out of my way if you want in, my hand is tired, and I'mbeginnin' to run out'ta patience."

"You show a lot of smarts for a hick. Here's the cash. Now win your bet."

Taking the cards from the dealer, he handed them to Mr. Heath. Just to show there is to trickery, study the cards, shuffle them, and let Charlie cut them."

While that was taking place, he asked Ronni. "Darlin' would you get me a towel? I need to dry my hands."

"Here's a napkin, Honey. Will that do?"

"That will be fine. Put your gun away. It might go off and hit one of Charlie's bodyguards and blow his brains out."

"Okay, ladies and gentlemen," Bill announced. "Watch and see how they cheated you. I said he was dealing with seconds and using readers. I'm going to deal thirds and call every card as I deal it. Please note the top two cards are the ace and king of spades. Mr. Heath, when I have proved to you that I've won my bet, tell me to stop, and I'll show you a winning hand."

Mr. Heath told Bill to stop when he had dealt 15 cards.

Don Heath said, "I can't bet you shuffled these cards well."

Bill said, "Here it is. Did I call every card like I said I could."

"Yes, you did. Now show me a winning hand. "I said, "the winning hand."

Slowly so everybody could see, Bill pealed the top five cards from the deck. The first two were the ace, king of spades followed by the ten, jack, and queen; all spades, a Royal Flush. "Not bad for a hick farmer," Bill said. "Charlie, I'm going to leave most of my winnings here. I want a receipt for the deposit, and when I retrieve my winnings, I want a cashier's check. I'll expect to receive all you cheated me out of as well. Your bookkeeper can figure out how much you owe me, and don't forget you are dealing with a hick farmer. Come on, darlin', let's have some more fun. Cousin Jim, if you are going to be in your office this evening, I'd like to come by and talk about the good old days."

"You know my latch string is always out for you, Billy boy. Bring your blonde friend with you. My office needs prettying up."

Donald Heath caught up with Bill and Ronni as they were leaving the Casino.

"I don't know whether to be mad or glad about what just happened," he said. Nobody has ever talked to me the way you did. The part that hurts is, it's the truth. I expect instant respect because I am the Donald, and most times, I get it. With you, I have to earn it."

"Let me tell you, Bill interrupted; "before you go any further, you can't buy my respect, even with your millions."

"I wouldn't even try, sir. You earned my respect by your actions, and I'm hoping to win yours the same way. I am going to locate the patrons we have mistreated, and try, in some way, to make it up to them. I have fired the entire staff at the casino and closed until the reorganization policies will establish security; and providing customer information concerning the casino industry via printed brochures, handouts, posted bulletins, etc. It will be costly, but the news of the events of last night, and the publicity of our clean-up campaign should attract new people. Bill, Would you consider becoming the 'head pit boss?' Name your price."

"Mr. Heath, I am flattered with your offer, but where I live, we never lock doors. We leave the keys in the ignition, and when somebody needs it, they use it and fill the tank before they return it. Our local grocer forgot to lock up over the Fourth of July holiday, one year. On Tuesday, he found over $200 in cash and some checks, plus a signed note saying she couldn't make change and would come in Tuesday to square up – and she did. This town is where we will live, raise our children, and try to be worthy citizens. We are not wealthy, but we are one of the richest communities in the world. Fate may bring you to The Dalles, Oregon, if so, ask for Bill Watkins, that's me. I'll show you heaven on earth. I just spotted a three-card Monte come to town. I think I'll educate them!"

"Do you mind if I watch and learn?"

"No, watch the shill; He will turn the corner of the payoff card up far enough that you can see it from across the street, but the dealer doesn't notice it. The shill wins, of course, and the payoff is two to one."

They watched as the game went on. There are three or four shill winning, but no one else. The reason nobody wins is because the dealer has the payoff card palmed. It isn't in play, and knowing that, you announce the payoff card won't be there – and it isn't. Thus you think it must be the remaining card and reach for your money, but watch your back! They hate to lose. Come on, darlin', I feel lucky again."

"Look here sugar, a game of chance with pretty good odds, Bill said. "Can anybody play?"

"We've got the time if you got a dime," was the answer.

'Hon, how much cash you got?"

"A little over five thousand."

"Oh, that's way too much for them to cover. I was thinking more like ten or twenty dollars, so, when we win, we can play the slots."

"We can cover five grand okay," the Monte dealer said.

"Fine, Hon, give me the money."

Ronni pulled five, crisp, thousand dollar bills from her purse and handed them to Bill.

"Here's mine, let me see yours."

"I don't carry that much cash with me," the dealer said.

"Then how were you going to pay me when I win?"

"Don't go away; the cash will be here in a while." He made a phone call and said, "It's on the way."

A Harley pulled up a short time later, and a bigdirtbag handed an envelope to the dealer, who counted out twenty thousand dollars.

The dealer spread the cards, and as Bill predicted, each had a corner bent up.

"Oh dear, Honey, it looks more difficult now," Ronni said. "Let me help you, sugar. Would it be cheating if I talked to my Grandma, up in Heaven for advice?"

"Lady, you can talk to anybody, any place. Just pick a card."

Ronni looked heavenward and said, "Are you sure, granny, thank you." She stepped up to the dealer's table and turned the cards over. "Granny said, It ain't this one, and it ain't this one; it must be that one." The dealer grabbed her wrist before she could turn the third card over. "Here's your twenty grand, now beat it. Bill dragged the dealer by the shirt collar, telling him, "If you ever touch my wife again, I'll pull your tongue out and stuff it down your throat."

The dirtbag was about to step in when Ronni put a round in each tire, and one in his toe, The shills had run off wanting no part of the problem.

The police arrived and asked, "What happened to Mr. Heath?

"That man with the torn shirt assaulted, Mrs. Watkins. The dirtbag and the sap he has behind his back headed towards Mr. Watkins; then, Mrs. Watkins fired two wild shots, hitting the tires on the bike. The gun discharged accidentally, hitting him in his toe. You make out the report, and Ronni and I will sign it."

"Mr. and Mrs. Watkins, I would very much like to visit with you further. You are not what you look to be."

"We're staying at the Plaza. Let's have lunch there about one p.m. tomorrow."

"I'm looking forward to it. You two are a real pair. Until lunch tomorrow, Good-day."

"What now, Bill?" Ronni asked. "I've had about as many thrills and chills as I can take for today. Can we take a break and just sit and talk?"

"Good plan, let's get some coffee, and sit on the boardwalk and watch the ocean."

CHAPTER 30

They found a donut shop on the boardwalk and got coffee and donuts to go.

"There's an inviting-looking bench over there, Honey," Bill said.

The breeze of the Atlantic was cool. Ronni snuggled up to Bill for warmth. He put his arm over her shoulders and pulled her close. They sat in silence, sipping the coffee and munching on the donuts.

Ronni broke the silence, "Do you realize you referred to me as your wife. Mr. Heath assumed we were married, and you have called me hon or honey. I'm sure the darlin' was for show, but how about the rest?"

Bill sat in silence, squeezed her shoulder affectionately, cleared his throat, and said, "You've been on my mind since the first night, when we had supper together, and that unbelievable love-making session in the hotel! I've been trying to put my feelings for you into words. I don't have an eloquent vocabulary, or a talent for romantic prose. I guess what I'm trying to say is, I'm sure I'm in love with you. I feel like we have always been together. I will never forget my late wife, but I know I'm with Veronica Lane. These words are honest, and directed to you, sincerely. I want to spend the rest of my life with you, but we have to build a relationship on solid ground. I am not going to spring a new mom on my children. I want them to know you and accept you, and eventually, love you, not only for who you are, but also because you make me very happy. They remember the happiness we all had together.

Willy asked me not too long ago, why I didn't smile or whistle anymore. I tried to explain that even though they were both with me at home,that I was lonely for their mother. I want you to fill that void in my heart."

"Yes, I accept your proposal." I agree we should build on solid ground. My marriage failed for that reason. My brothers put a damper on my social life. I didn't know how love was supposed to feel. I believe it's about how I feel when I am with you, rather than about you. I feel secure and cozy when you are near, like when you are snuggled in a warm blanket, drinking hot chocolate in front of the fireplace, at ease, and in comfort. Times occur of anger, illness, discontentment, and all, but love keeps the judgment and misunderstandings at a minimum. That's the way I define 'love.' I'm ready to marry you right now, but we've just started to build a relationship to learn the whims and bad habits of each other. I want to be a 'stay at home' wife and have your supper cooking when you get home, beer in the fridge, and coffee ready to pour. We will always plan for time with the children between supper and bedtime. Our time together will be after they have gone to bed. It will take six months or moreto build this foundation for a lasting marriage. I'm going to resign and go to work for the chief. What are you going to do with your winnings?"

"I want to give the city back it's ten grand, invest the rest for the children's college. We will spend our money wisely, but have a new beginning, a new house, and neighborhood. We will, of course, value Willy and Cindy's suggestions as well as objections. I can wait as long as it takes, but I will be happy when the wedding day comes,"Rose had a difficult delivery, and after Cindy was born, I made the hard choice of having a vasectomy, Now that we've discussed enough for today, let's go see my cousin, Jim."

Chapter 31

Lt. Walker was busy booking a prostitute.

"Hi, you lucky lady. Make sure he gets his money's worth," she said to Ronni.

"Oh, he will get his money's worth. We are going to be married, and I'll get half. Not bad for a one night stand. It beats the hell out of a $250 night trick", Ronni said.

Lt. Walker indicated to go to his office and take the seats across from him.

"What's new?" Billy boy, Jim laughed.

Bill and Ronni gave Jim all the information, including TWE. They laid out their plan for the capture of the printers of the counterfeit money.

"I think it will work, Jim stated. They are going to want their money, and Widra is going to want his counterfeit. Get the two sides fighting each other, and you can whip the winner. Damn good plan. When are you going to spring the trap?"

"We'll put the details together, bait the trap, and when the rats take the bait, we'll spring it. The code is 'remember the TV show, Cheyenne. That will tell you the counterfeit cargo is in the air, headed this way. The ball will be in our court. Ronni is the aircraft commander."

"I need to interrupt you here, Bill." Jim should know. "I'm undercover FBI," Ronni flashed her badge. "I give you jurisdiction in this case. You will have all the information the department has and full cooperation. Anybody gives you trouble, call me."

"You two are one hell of a crime-fighting team. In less than a day, you expose a crooked casino, and take down a three-card Monte gamewe've been trying to shut down for weeks. That fake cop you caught for me is singing like a canary. The mob pays these guys to do whatever it takes to keep one of their own from going to jail or testifying, including murder. We have him in protective custody. If I could put you two on the force, I could retire half the force and still get more done than we donow! You are welcome here anytime,Cuz and Mrs. Cuz."

"Where did you come up with the $5000 you gave me?"

Bill asked Ronni.

"I've been carrying that around for weeks.It's counterfeit, and if you lost it to them and they tried to spend it, they would be detected and arrested. Harry Truman's picture is on the bills. I don't know who's picture is on the real money. Let's call it a day, go to our hotel, clean up and have a quiet supper."

"I heartily endorse that plan, Honey."

John ordered a huge glass of cold milk to wash his chopped sirloin down, and Ronni ordered iced tea with her pork chops. A large man at the next table mocked John about ordering milk.

"Why not have a real man's drink, like three or four beers?"

His hooker girlfriend giggled, "Yeah, a real man's drink."

John walked over to the couple's table and said, "How much do you weigh, sir? I weigh 285."

"310. Why?"

"Would you like to arm wrestle to see which is a real man's drink, beer, or milk?"

"I outweigh you by 25 pounds, and I ain't never lost an arm-wrestling match. Do you still want to try me?"

"Yeah," the hooker echoed, "Do you still want to try him?"

"I don't do this for fun. Would you like to bet a little money on the outcome?"

"Don't mind if I do. How about a grand?" John said.

"Honey, how much cash do we have?"

"Not counting our original investment, twenty grand."

"I'll cover all bets up to twenty grand," Bill announced.

"And I will cover any amount over that." Mr Heath said.

"Miss!" Bill said to a waitress. "Would you bring two votive candles, a half-gallon of milk, and the same amount of light beer."

Bill measured where the back of the hand would be for the loser, and placed a lighted votive candle in each place. He then set the milk in front of his challenger, and the beer in front of himself. "I'm Bill Watkins from The Dalles, Oregon," he said, extending his hand. "This match will prove a champion in arm-wrestling."

"I'm Walt Livingston from Tacoma, Washington." the challenger said, accepting Bill's hand. "You are right; this is a no grudge match. I suppose if I lose, I drink the milk, and if I win, you drink the beer.

"That's the way it plays, Walt. Are you ready?"

"Yeah, Let's get it on."

Mr. Heath made sure the combatants were comfortable, putting their elbows on the table and locking their hands together.

"I'll count down from three to one and say go, then you start. Good luck, gentlemen. Three, two, one, go!"

The air was full of tension as the two combatants strained. Bill stared straight ahead, expressionless. Walt was straining, and the sweat was starting down his face. The hooker wiped the sweat from his face. You could see the muscles in both men straining to gain the victory. Walt was slowly losing ground when Bill said, "I'm not going to burn your hand, Walt you're too good a man. You should drink more milk and less beer, and stopping short of the flame, asked, "concede?"

"Yes, I do. You are one hell of a man, Bill. I salute you." He picked up the milk, chugged kit down, and wiping his chin said, "Hey! That's a damn good drink."

Bill took Walt aside. You have more strength than I, and you outweigh me. The reason you lost is because you were trying to figure out a way to beat me. I just stared straight ahead and concentrated on not getting burned. Here is your grand. Take it before I have to kick the crap out of you, too."

Walt grinned and said, "I ain't ever been beaten twice in one night, but chances are it probably would have happened tonight." The two giants exchanged friendly hugs, and each went on their way.

Chapter 32

Mr. Heath handed Ronni a stack of money. "I don't know how much is there, but Themob owns the casino across the street, and they lost $50,000. If I just followed you around and bet on you, I would make another fortune. I'll see you for lunch."

They were halfway across the lobby, when a wormy-looking hood approached them.

"Mr. Cascio from across the street, wants to see you.It's late, and we're tired," Bill said.

The worm opened his coat, exposing a Military 45.

"He insists."

"Bill Honey, you've worked hard all day let me handle this."

She waited for her chance and tossed her purse to Bill. The worm watched the purse land in Bill's hand, and turned when he caught a substantial right on the chin, and a left on the mouth.

"The man insisted we see him. Let's go. Put your purse in the hotel safe, and we'll see what Mr. Cascio wants. We are on a roll."

Tossing the unconscious worm over his shoulder and taking Ronni by the hand, they crossed the street and burst into Mr. Cascio's office.

"This garbage belongs to you. Throw it away. By the way, I didn't do this, my 125-pound wife did. I just carry the trash out. What the hell do you want? We're here on your insistence. Honey! Take one of your thirty-eights out and show it to the ugly goon by the door."

Ronni unbuttoned her blouse. The goon was salivating until she pulled out her chrome-plated thirty-eight caliber Beretta.

"Is this the one you meant, Bill, Honey?"

"That's the one. I never get tired, looking at it.".

Bill turned to Mr. Cascio, and said, "I asked you what you wanted, and I expect an answer, or I'll tear this place apart piece by piece, and throw you and that goon, into the ocean! I'll do the same to the one behind the screen, and that wormy piece of crap you sent to bring us here. Mr. Heath, across the street or my cousin, Lt. James Walker of the Atlantic City Police Department, will tell you I WILL carry out my threats!"

"I can see I have made an error in judgment, Mr. …what is your name, sir?"

"Watkins, Bill Watkins. I am sorry I lost my temper, but it has been a long day. I'm going to ask you for a favor."

"Certainly, sir, anything I can do, I'll do willingly."

"I'm going to be away on business, frequently leaving my wife alone. I'm going to ask you to protect her while I'm gone. I will hold you personally responsible if she gets a run in her hose, a cold, or even a hangnail. Do you understand, and am I clear on this point?"

"Yes, sir, clear," Cascio replied nervously.

"Come on, Honey, let's go, but button your blouse before 'goony's' eyes fall out."

Ronni collected her purse, and they finally made it to their rooms.

"Your place or mine, Honey?" Ronni asked.

"Let's call it our place, and just use one room," Bill answered.

The next morning they moved Ronni into Bill's room, and reregistered as, Veronica Lane and William Watkins. They had breakfast, and went shopping for nightwear and a swimsuit. The rest of the morning, they enjoyed each other's company, and strolled the boardwalk. Mr. Heath met them for lunch as planned.

"You two are the talk of the town. I heard you went across the street and braced Cascio in his office, with his bodyguards present. Is that true?"

"It's true." I put him personally in charge of Ronni's safety. I told him I needed to go on a business trip and made him understand, clearly, that I would repeat the actions of yesterday if any harm came to her."

"Tell me who you are and what you do."

"I'm just a hick cop from a small town in Oregon. One of your local bad boys let his mouth run, and it was his gun that killed an NYC undercover cop. The investigation examined a spent round, and the serial number and linked the crime to Gino Consiglio. I delivered him to Lt. Walker."

"Did you arrest Gino Consiglio without a fight?"

"Oh, he protested when I took his gun away. His finger got broke in the scuffle. I squeezed a bit too hard. Later I saw this lady I knew from home, and here I am."

"How about you, Ronni? What brings you to Atlantic City? I fly a MediVac Jet for Angel Flight."

"I've heard good things about them. Is it true you don't charge for your service?"

"That's correct. Never a charge. We depend on the generosity of people who would like to donate money to us, rather than the IRS. There are generous and numerous contributors out there! Patient's families and friends, businesses, doctors, and others. We are fortunate to have a Casino that donated a plane to us."

"I would consider it an honor if you and Mr. Watkins would keep The Plaza as your home. Your rooms would be private with maid service and meals included. I'll show you what we have after lunch, and you can take your pick. I'll get keys for both of you and have your belongings moved in this afternoon. What do you say?"

"We say, thanks. Our plans are not final yet, and we don't know for certain how long we will be here, but we do appreciate and gratefully accept your offer. It will be nice to have an address," Ronni stated

They picked a fifth-floor apartment featuring a balcony where they could sit and have a clear view of the Atlantic.

"Let's get a pizza and eat on the balcony tonight," Bill suggested. "It will be a pre-honeymoon, honeymoon."

Ronni and Bill enjoyed the first evening of their newhome resting on the deck, snuggling in the romantic atmosphere, under a full moonshine.

CHAPTER 33

A moving van marked, 'Garcia and James, Movers', The Dalles, Oregon,' was unloading at Vicki's house. Her mother and Jeffery were helping the best they could. Vicki was out on dispatch and wasn't expected back for several days. Hawk came by to see how things were going. Jose and Jesse smiled and shook his hand.

"Thanks for letting us escape, Sen`orChief," Jesse said. "We got a job with a moving company and liked it and started a business for ourselves. It was hard going at first because we didn't have a truck, but we kept trying and got a good one. We are not wealthy, but are happy and healthy.We are going to get a better house. One of my long-ago friends told me we were lucky, and I told him I learned the harder you work, the luckier you get. Just a minute, Jose, let me help you. Thank you again, Sen`or Chief."

"Hello," a voice sounded from the back door. "I'm Elaine Moss, your next-door neighbor. I can see you are very busy and I won't stay. I've got coffee, lemonade, soda and some sandwiches for your lunch. We have supper at six, nothing special, just common food. You all have a place set at the table; come over any time."

"I'm Doris Parks, Mrs. Moss, and this is my Grandson, Jeffrey. His Mother works for Angel Flight and is gone a lot. We aren't used to this kind of hospitality. I'm sorry if we seem standoffish. Thank you for the invitation. I'll make some barbequed short ribs for us to share, after I finish cleaning the stove. I do believe I have died and gone to Heaven! Is everybody this friendly, or are you the exception?"

"There are a few that will insult you, through ignorance or fear whenever they can, but by and large, we accept people for who they are. I'm looking forward to our friendship. I'll see you and Jeffery for supper."

"Sen'orChief, we saw a black dude in an older Cadillac while loading the truck in LA. We didn't think anything of it until we noticed he was following us." Jesse said. "He just turned the corner and went East."

"Thanks for the tip, Jesse. I'm sure I know who he is. I'll take care of it." Hawk got on his radio.

"To all cars. Locate older Cadillac with California plates and let me know where it is."

"Chief, he just went into Mary's. Do you want me to bust him?" Sgt. Gibson asked.

"Negative, we have no reason to arrest him. I'll handle it."

Hawk went into Mary's and went directly to the stranger's table.

"You must be William, 'Blacky,' Harmon," Hawk said.

"And what if I am?" the stranger said. "I ain't done nothin' wrong."

"I know that," Hawk said. "I didn't come in here to arrest you or give you a hard time. I came to talk straight talk. Vickie Parks has a great job and a future here. I know she stole money from you that you were dealing drugs and served time for it. You are; at this time in your life, even with society. Vicki used your drug money to get out of the Ghetto. Your ill-gotten money did some good. You are welcome to stay here as long as you obey the law. Nobody from this office is going to bother or harass you, but if you break the law, I will personally see to it that you get full Shoshone justice. There are plenty of opportunities here for you to make a fresh start. It's up to you. They call me Hawk, I'm the Chief of Police, and my door is always open. Think over what I said. Now I'm going over to my usual spot and have some coffee, feel free to join me, if you like."

Halfway through his second cup, Blackie joined him.

"I've never had a cop talk to me like that. It is usually, 'Hey, get your black ass over here,' or something like that. I felt I was never going to get a chance to make an honest, decent living. I've got a college education, but because I wore an afro and was more belligerent than I should have been and because I had a chip on my shoulder, I never got a good job. I realized long ago I had made my bed and had to lie in it. I'm going to stand up and turn around. I want you to take my forty-five, check it out, and throw it away. I want you to direct me to a place that needs a hard-working man, willing to start at the bottom and work his way up. I would appreciate it and tell Vicki she has nothing to fear from me.

"Higgins Construction can never get enough men. It's all hard work with great pay plus benefits. They are one of the best employers in the state. What was your major?"

"Engineering with a minor in Architecture."

"There is a hospital under construction here. You passed it on the way into town. I'll give you my card, and you ask for Pat Harrigan. Take a lunch and make sure you've got proper work clothes with you. Pat will start you on the job, as soon as your tax form is complete. Higgins will advance half a week's pay if you need startup cash. The payback is deducted from your checks a little at a time. You will have a probation time of six months to prove yourself, and then benefits kick in."

"Thanks Chief. Please take my gun. It is suddenly too heavy to carry. Good-night."

Chapter 34

Dorris and Jeffery knocked on Elaine's back door at five forty-fivep.m.

"Come in, Doris," Elaine called. "I'll be out in a minute." She came into the kitchen, pushing a wheelchair. The occupant was a man holding an oxygen tank. "This is my husband, Ronald. Ron, this is our new neighbor, Doris Parks, and her Grandson, Jeffery."

Ron extended his hand and smiled. "Pleased to meet you both," he said weakly. "Excuse me if I don't get up. The spirit is more than willing, but the flesh is weak."

"Supper is ready," Elaine announced, helping Ron to the table.

When everyone was seated, Jeffery took Elaine's hand and his Grandmother's hand and bowed his head.

"Our Heavenly Father, we thank you for this food, Bless it to nourish our bodies that we may serve you. Thank you for our new friends and a chance to have a better life. Watch over Mommy and bring her home safely to us. Help Mr. Moss to feel better and help us to understand and accept thy will be done. Amen."

Elaine and Ron had tears in their eyes.

"What a beautiful prayer, Jeffery," Ron said. "Where did you learn it."

"I just prayed what I felt. I only know the 23rd Psalm and The Lord's Prayer. When I talk to God, I just tell him what I feel."

"Out of the mouths of babes," Elaine said.

After supper, Doris and Elaine did the dishes while Ron showed Jeffery his stamp and coin collection.

"Elaine, I've spent thirty years working in rest homes and caring for people. I would like to lighten your load and tend to Mr. Moss. You could do some of those things you and I both know you want to do. Like get your hair done, not that it needs it, but you need time for yourself.We have a beat-up lawnmower Jeffery likes topush, and he will do your lawn when he does ours. In LA, we didn't have much, but what we had he made look like a park, and we had the only fresh off the vine tomatoes in the area. His greatest pleasure besides eating them was to share. I don't know where he comes by his attitude, but he is a joy to both his mother and I. Vicki swears by the fact that when he was three days old, she promised him and herself she was going to turn her life around, and he strengthened her enough to do it. She was a whore at fourteen and an unwed mother at sixteen. Now, she flies a jet airplane. She says you can do anything you want to do if you want to do it bad enough and are willing to pay the price."

"We have a brand new self-propelled mower in the garage. It's Jeffery's. He can start a small lawn mowing service and earn some extra money.

"If he accepts, and I'm sure he will, he will give ten percent to church or charity, save ten percent for himself, and split the rest with you."

Vicki returned home four days later. The windows glistened, the house was immaculate, Jeffery had the yard beautifully manicured as well as the garage. Jeffery had made a place for his bike and lawnmower plus a space for Vicki's pickup. He had cut and trimmed the Moss's lawn and made a coral for their garbage can that was more convenient for Mrs. Moss. Vicki stared with pride and amazement at the change that loving care can make. When she last saw it, it was a house, and now it was her home. Doris and Jeffery greeted her with hugs and kisses. Doris told her about their neighbors and Jeffery's new lawnmower. When Doris told her about Jeffery's prayer at supper, Vicki picked him up and hugged him tightly.

"I am so proud of you. Your strength helped me to get where we are now. You are too young to understand, but someday you will. Thank you, son."

Payday was the next day. Vicki, Doris, and Jeffery dressed to go to the bank, get some shopping done and have dinner at Mary's Restaurant and Supper Club. Vicki was pulling into her parking place and noticed a man in a Stetson Hat and expensive hand-tooled boots getting out of a shiny, red country Cadillac with training wheels, visiting with another man. The red pickup had blazoned on the sides, ZEEK RANCH. They were patiently waiting in line to make deposits, etc. when the dude rancher said to Vicki and her party, "Get out of my way, I'm in a hurry."

"Sir, I will get out of your way in a moment," Vicki said quietly."

"Get out now," he screamed, "and get that old tin can you call a pickup out of my way, too. We don't need your kind here."

The bank lobby was hushed.

Vicki said, "Sir, I must respond to your crude remarks. Number one; that paid for old tin can you called my truck. Number two; it will out-run,and out-pullyour shiny, red unpaid for country Cadillac. Number three; I travel a lot and keep a log on the people I meet, nice, not so nice, and others. I tallied up this morning, and I want to thank you. I'm five assholes short for the week, and you filled my quota, plus two for next week. Would you like to challenge number two?"

The people in the lobby roared in appreciation. Mr. Zeek was furious. He had never been confronted in that way, and humiliated in front of his neighbors. Mike, hearing all the commotion entered the scene.

"Mr. Zeek, do you want to challenge that lady's pickup?" he asked.

"I would take that bet in a heartbeat, plus, and my truck for $50."

Mrs. Ward. " What is the balance in Miss Parks checking account?"

"This deposit makes it $125,154.14."

Mike said, "The tarmac is 7000 feet long. Are you sure you want to race?"

"I'll forget the pulling end of it, but you damned right, I'm ready to race. How about you, you black bitch!"

"I want the title on your red toy, free and clear. Any time you're ready."

"I will be the judge and hold the stakes," Mike announced. "Mrs. Ward, clear Mr. Zeeks account except for $50 plus the debt on his truck. Cut him a cashier's check for the balance. Mr. Zeek, we need a lot of people like Victoria Parks here. But one like you is one too many. Here is your check. Take your loud mouth and rotten business elsewhere. Now, go out there and try to beat that old tin can."

Vicki and Zeek went to the end of the runway. The tower confirmed there is no traffic.

Mike took a green towel to use as a starting flag. "Just like NASCAR," he said. "I'll hold it up, and you rev up. I'll drop the flag, and you go. Red Kely is at the end to declare the winner. Mr. Zeek, you will be guilty of grand theft auto, if you lose and don't surrender your truck. The penalty means two years minimum as a 'guest' of the state."

"Shut up. Let's get this charade over. I've got company coming."

Mike dropped the flag, and Zeek pulled ahead. Vicki caught up with him and stayed even to the halfway mark, blew him a kiss, and ran away from him like he was on blocks.

The crowd went crazy.

Jeffery was jumping up and down, screaming with pride, "that's my Mom. That's my Mom."

Mike approached Zeek and held his hand out for the keys.

"How about the out pull, part," Zeek demanded.

"You said to forget that part. Your big mouth wrote an insufficient funds check; now, give me the keys and title."

"And supposing I don't?"

"You will go to jail, directly to jail," Hawk said, "anddon't think you won't!" he chuckled.

Vicki peeled the Zeek Ranch decals from his truck. "Stick one of these on your back, and maybe someone will be impressed enough to give you a ride. The body on that tin can is original, floppy fenders, worn-out seats, and all. It's a different story under the hood. I'm not a mechanic, and I don't know the upgrades on the engine, but I've been clocked at a raceway in Riverside California at 145 mph and let up because I was running out of track.I entered a tractor-pull competition at a fair and learned later, I had pulled twenty-five yards farther than the winner. Farmer's have a saying, 'you can never judge the depth of the well by the size of the handle on the pump.' This day has been great! Thank you, Mr. Zeek. Mike, while you are transferring the title on my new truck, I'll take 'Lilly Belle,' the pet name for my truck."

"I'll follow you home and bring you back, Vicki. I have some news for you."

On the way back to get her new truck, Hawk told her about Blacky's supposed turnaround.

"He said to tell you that you had nothing to fear from him, and I believe he means it," Hawk said. "Did I hear you, right? You clocked at 145mph?"

"Yes, chief, and I still had more left," Vicki said. "The keys are in the ashtray if you ever feel the need for speed."

"You've only been here a short time, but you've made a big positive impact on our town. We would like more folks like you." Hawk said.

CHAPTER 35

How much do I owe for the repairs, Mike?" Vicki asked.

Mike answered, "Materials came to $4795.67, labor zero. Like I said, you are family. Your mom and son are great people. You can bring them out to the ranch anytime. Are you going to keep that big pickup?"

"I don't want a big pickup; I'd like to have a mini-van."

"Dad's company could use a big pickup like that one. You go to Kozak Motors and ask for Jason. Tell him what you want, and it will be an outright cash deal with no trade-in. I'll find out what the pickup is worth, and one of us will owe the other one some money."

"Okay, that sounds fair to me. Mom and Jeffery are waiting, so I'll be on my way."

"This is a big truck, Vicki." Doris said. "Do you need another truck?"

"No. One of our errands today is to shop for a mini-van. Mike wants me to buy what I want, and he will buy the truck for his Dad's company. What do you want or need, Jeffery?"

"Mr. Moss showed me his stamp and coin collections. He said the longer you have them, the more they are worth. I would like to start a hobby like that. Mr. Moss said he would help me get started and give me some of his coins and stamps, but I want to buy them."

"How about you, Mom. What do you need or want?"

"How can I want anything? I've got a home in a peaceful town, a neighbor who accepts me for who I am, a daughter to be proud of, and a grandson who shows wisdom and caring beyond his years, and my health. I'm forgiven and going to Heaven. What more could anyone ask?" We do need milk, a popcorn popper, and popcorn. I want to put my feet up, eat popcorn, and watch a movie on TV."

"Okay," Vicki said. "A big screen TV, cable but no games, Jeff. You are not going to be a couch potato. I will get you a computer, and you can teach Mom and me how to use it."

"I don't want nothin' to do with no computer. My brain is as full as it can get," Doris commented

The following days Vicki spent practicing her landings. Jeffery went with her and was mesmerized by it all.

"Do you think I could learn to do this, Momma?" he asked.

"You can do anything you want to do..."

".. when you are willing to pay the price and want it bad enough," Jeffery finished.

"That's right, son, and don't forget it."

CHAPTER 36

Vicki drove Jeffery and her mother in her mini-van to the ranch. All came out to oooh, and aaah and kick tires and all those things you do to a new car.

When the commotion subsided, she said, "Mom and Jeffery, you aren't going to believe this, but in time you will know it is true. I will tell you who these people are: The taller of those two ladies is my sister, Susan; next to her is my sister, Kim; the Indian couple are my grandparents, Faun and Bear Claw; the lady next to her is my mother, Celestina; over by the grill is Jeffery's brother, Carl and his sister, Marie. You've met my brothers, John and Mike."

Dorris was overwhelmed and speechless.

Jeffery'sinterest was watching the horses.

"Are those your horses, Carl?"

"Yes, Grandpa Bear gave them to me and taught me how to talk to them."

"Do they buck and bite and kick?"

Carl explained," They used to buck, but when I learned to talk to them, they stopped bucking. The horses don't bite and seldom kick, unless they become abused. They will buck if you use a whip or sharp spurs. Some cowboy at the Pendleton Round-Up climbed on Scout without asking me. He thought he was the most important man in town and didn't have to have anyone's permission to do anything. Scout tossed his head and turned to see who was in the saddle, then trotted to the center of the arena. The cowboy stood in the stirrups and waved his hat to the crowd. He sat down and put his two-inch Mexican style spurs to Scout's flanks, and Scout just tossed him into the messy wet pile of mud and poop and trotted to me. The cowboy came running over at me, and Scout turned his rump to the cowboy and was between the cowboy and me. He raised his hand with the whip in it, and Dad said, before you use that whip, make sure you have insurance. I don't think Scout would intentionally kill you, but you can bet your ass and all your prize money that you could end up in the intensive care ward at the hospital!"

"You give me a chance, and I'll teach that damn horse a lesson or two."

Mike said, "You have to be smarter than the horse, if you are going to teach him anything. Get out of here before my son kicks the crap out of you and don't think, for an instant, he can't do it."

Carl asked Jeffery, "Do you want to ride Scout? Scout won't buck, I promise."

Jeffery paused, deep in thought.

"I've never been close enough to touch a horse. I'm not afraid. I just don't know what it will be like."

"I'll help you on and lead you around until you feel comfortable. Next, I'll mount Beauty and teach you to ride. You will be sore in the morning, but the more you ride, the easier it is, and you don't get sore anymore."

Vicki called to Jeffery, "Come, Jeff, we have to be going. You can come back again and learn more about horses."

CHAPTER 37

Ten days later, the crate for the counterfeit money was ready.

"It looks exactly like the one in the picture." Hawk commented, "right down to the splits in the boards on the sides."

"We'll load it into the dog, and Red can fly it over to Bodie's tomorrow, Mike said. "I'll let Ronni know, and she can be ready. I hope her crew doesn't give her any trouble."

"I'll send Bill Watkins back," Hawk said. "He can ride shotgun, and I think there are some serious emotions there. We may be having another wedding. He cleaned up in the casino, won a bunch arm wrestling, and beat three-card Monte out of twenty grand. Jim Walker wants to hire the two them, Bill and Ronni, for his police force, and Donald Heath wants him for the head pit boss. He spotted a crooked blackjack dealer, who denied he was crooked, and the casino put up a total of $100,000 that Bill couldn't prove they were crooked. He dealt thirds, fourths, and fifths, calling every card and turned over the top five cards showing a royal flush in spades. Remember, he told us he knew a little something about crooked games?"

Vicki, her Mom, and Jeffery were watching their big screen TV and enjoying popcorn and a tranquil and peaceful Friday evening, and the doorbell chimed. Vicki opened the door.

It was Blacky with a dozen yellow roses. "Before you throw me out, please listen to what I have to say," he pleaded. "I watched your house for weeks, waiting to get my money back. I saw the moving van loading, and I decided to follow it. I came here to get my money. I think one of the movers spotted me and called the cops. I was eating when the police chief walked up to my table and called me by name. He talked to me like I had rights. He explained that I was even with society and had no reason to be looking over my shoulder, and the chief told me how you had used the money and that some good came out of my ill-gotten cash and I should forget about it. I told him I had to find a good job, and he sent me to a construction company that was always looking for hard-working help. I talked to Pat Harrigan, the superintendent, and I went to work that day. I got the first honest paycheck I've ever had today, and it feels good. I've got a small apartment, and at the end of the day, I clean up, eat supper and watch TV, just like real folks! The flowers are a thank you for stealing my money. I probably would be dead by now if you hadn't.

Please come in and have popcorn with us. I'll make coffee, and you can help us finish off Mom's apple pie," Vicki said.

"I'd like that. I haven't had a homemade pie of any kind in my life."

"Mom, Jeffery, this is Bill Harmon. His name was once 'Blacky.' Everything we have, we owe to him. He has come here from LA and hasn't had a home-cooked meal in years and years. Could you stop by here for supper tomorrow about five-thirty? What are you planning for supper tomorrow, Mother?"

"Barbecued short ribs, baked beans, and coleslaw, sweet tea and cake of some kind."

"How about it, Bill?"

"A man would be a damn, excuse me. A man would be a fool to turn down an invitation like that. Yes, ma'am, I'll be here. Could I bring anything?"

"Just a hearty appetite and the attitude you have now."

"I think 'Big Bad Bill' is 'Sweet William,' now." Doris sang."

Angel Six dispatched early the next morning.

"Sorry I have to leave. Go ahead with your supper plans, Mom, Vicki said. Bill needs someone to kind of spoil him, and Jeffery can use a man around the house to help him. I don't know how long I'll be gone.

Sometimes we're out and right back, and other times we are out for several days. If you have to get in touch with me, call Mike or dispatch. The numbers are on the pad under the phone. I love you guys, bye."

Angel Six dispatched to Klamath Falls. Rod Olavsson, a log hauler, had depended on his 'jake brake' for too long without checking on his air brakes. They were out of adjustment when he needed them. The Peter Built trailer and load of logs rolled down the mountain. By the grace of God, he survived. He has multiple fractures, a concussion, and severe internal injuries. He will go to a specialist in St. Louis, Mo.

Vicki, set Angel Six lightly on the tarmac. "Don't' you just love it when things go right?" she giggled.

"You've got the groove, Vicki. You've got the groove," John commented.

The patient was sedated and secured in place. Mrs. Olavsson, tightly clutching her infant daughter, looked wan and exhausted. She hadn't had any restful sleep since Rod went over the mountainside.

"Mrs. Olavsson," Kim said. "Let me hold your baby while you lean back and try to sleep. Your husband's vitals are okay, and he is resting. The doctors assured us that although his injuries are serious, they are not life-threatening. We are three to four hours out of Saint Louis, and you can use those hours to rest. There is nothing for us to do except wait."

"Thank you, and please call me Donna, said Mrs. Olavsson. "The baby's name is Judy. She has brought so much pleasure to our lives, and she is such a happy baby. She has just been fed and changed and should be alright."

Kim put the baby on the seat, and before Kim had Donna covered with a blanket, Donna was sleeping.

Vicki held Judy,and the soft sweet glow of the forgotten joys of motherhood, brought tears to her eyes.

"I wish I had been sober when Jeffrey was a baby." She said. "It was a constant fight to stay sober. I didn't take the time to enjoy him. I'm not going to waste another opportunity."

"Lindberg Field at one o'clock," John announced. "Vicki, set us on the tarmac. I'll do the checklist. Just relax. Like I said at Klamath falls, you've got the groove and that electric shock of perfection.

"Kim woke Donna and helped fasten her seat belt.

"Thank you for the use of your baby," Vicki said over the intercom. "It reminded me of how much I missed while my son was a baby. Please don't miss any opportunity to hug and kiss and tell her how much you love her. Don't forget to attend the pageants, plays, no matter how juvenile and make sure you and her dad, aunts, uncles, grandparents, the whole family is there to see her, not the performance, but to see her."

"Beautiful touchdown, Vicki," John commented. "I might just as well sit in the passenger cabin. You are a great airplane driver."

The crew went with the Olavsson's to the hospital. Vicki rode in the ambulance with Donna and Rod.

"I wanted an opportunity to hold your baby," Vicki said. "She is beautiful."

Rod was on his way to surgery. Donna and Judy had a room close to the recovery room where they could rest while waiting for Rod. John gave her the standard check from Angel Flight to cover any unexpected costs.

"You can call the 800 number you see on the check if you need additional funds, and they will wire you that amount," he added.

John called dispatch in the cab on the way back to Lindberg Field.

"Angel Four is on the way with a burn patient. They would like you to wait for them, and since you are on stand-by, you might as well hotel it tonight." They said.

Tell them we'll be the Express, near Lindberg Field." John answered.

CHAPTER 38

It was mid-afternoon when the two flight crews rendezvoused for refreshments. In the course of conversation, John mentioned he and Kim had bought a home site near Mike and Susan.

"We came across a burned-out cabin while we were looking the site over. It was obviously, abandoned for some time. We checked the records at the courthouse and found that the previous owner, John Cauldwell, liked the TV show called 'Cheyenne.' The star of the show, Clint Walker, was wanting a place to get away from the Hollywood crowd and found this place. Mr. Cauldwell agreed to let him build his cabin there, and the two became fast friends and fishing buddies."

"Interesting," Ronni said. "I don't believe I ever saw the show, but my folks talked about it. It was well before my time, but I suppose somewhere in cableTV land, there is a station showing reruns. Some shows, like M.A.S.H., never die. Let's gussie up this evening and have a nice quiet dinner and maybe dance a while." We are three couples, and it would work out fine. John, you and Kim are already a couple.

Gerry cut in. "Everybody, if it's alright, I'd like to have Vicki as my date."

"That leaves you and me," Ronni said. "We'll meet in our suite at seven-thirty. Vicki and I have plenty of room."

The men wore their custom-tailored suits, white shirts and cufflinks, tie tacks and lapel pins with the Angel Logo.

Ronni was a striking blonde, in a bronze, faille, Capri pants suit. The jacket was long-sleeved, mid-length. A becoming antique gold satin vee-neck blouse underneath. Her lithesome, long-legs enhanced the Capri style. Her shoes were antique gold pumps with four-inch heels.

Vicki was also a tall, dark-haired beauty. Her garnet red, sheath-style, full-length dress, slit to mid-thigh, accented her slender and beautifully developed figure. Four-inch heels on her black pumps enhanced her already beautiful long legs. Simple gold disc earrings complimented her lovely facial features.

Kim was the petit one. Beautiful, tiny, and exuding charm and personality. She chose luxurious, green sateen with sparse, but noticeable black embroidered edges on the mandarin-style neckline and cap-sleeves. She covered her shoulders with a soft wide, almost sheer, stole. Black purse and pumps with three-inch heels finished her ensemble.

Each of the girls wore a cameo necklace with the Angel Flight Logo carved on it, suspended on a golden chain.

Vicki called down to the front desk and asked.

"Where would you take a date, one you thought a lot of, to make it a special evening?

"There is only one place for that kind of date. "The Inferno." Marvelous cuisine, live music for dancing, and it has been in the same family for five generations."

"They must be doing everything right to stay in business that long. Would you call and make reservations for a party of six for seven-thirty this evening?"

"What name shall I use?"

"Parks, Victoria Parks."

"Consider it done. I'll have our courtesy van take you there, and when you are ready to return, give us a call, and we will come to get you."

The night manager gasped at the sight of the six coming out of the elevator!

"We see our share of attractive people, but I have never seen a party of six looking so beautiful. You three ladies aura is the look most women want to achieve."

A man carrying a briefcase in one hand and a suitcase in the other was so entranced, he walked up to the decorative fountain and fish pond, stumbled and fell in. The only injury was his pride, and the papers in the briefcase. His suitcase fell away from the water.

They were met at the door by a distinguished-looking gentleman with a fresh carnation on his lapel.

"You must be the Parks party, and I'm Mr. C. The first letter of a long, Italian, hard to pronounce, name. Mr. Reinheart from the Express called and told me you were on your way and suggested I greet you personally. I'm glad I did. Your table is ready. Just follow me."

Vicki, being the hostess, took his arm as he escorted them to a table near the dance floor.

He said, "I notice you ladies have identical cameos, and you gentlemen have the same cufflinks. What is the symbol?"

Ronni answered, "It's the logo of our company, Angel Flight."

"You are the people that take emergency patients and especially injured children to the nearest and best hospital for their treatment, and you do not bill or charge for your service."

"That's correct, sir. We feel the parents, or wives, or husbands, whoever is the significant person in the life of the patient, has enough worry already. They don't need the concern of how to pay us. The smiles of relief, the hugs, the thank you cards, especially from children, are rewards enough for us. The practical side is that we are dependent on the generosity of those of means. The best check we got was from the classmates of an eight-year-old girl. The class members went to their parents, grandparents, aunts, uncles, friends, and neighbors and told them how Angel Flight helped their friend, and they wanted to help us. They sold ice water in the park, they gave up their allowance, and even had their teachers' help. That was a true love gift. I think the check was $97.37."

Mr. C. excused himself, saying, "I must get back to business. Thank you for your patronage, and have a pleasant evening. Trina, my granddaughter, will be your server."

Dinner was over, Mr. C. sent a split of Sangria to their table; just enough for a small glass each. The band started playing a fast-paced tune.

"Would you like to try this one with me?" Gerry asked Vicki.

"You know, we blacks all have natural rhythm," Vicki laughed.

It was a quick-step type number, and Gerry and Vicki danced like they had been partners for years. They had the floor to themselves, while their fellow crew members watched in amused fascination. When the music stopped, a hearty round of applause from an appreciative audience burst forth. Vicki and Gerry held hands and bowed in acknowledgment.

Mr. C. came rushing to their table.

"My wife has just had a massive heart attack and has to go to Boston! Can you help?"

CHAPTER 39

"Angel Six is ready to transport. We're at Lindberg Field. We can be wheels up in less than an hour. We won't have time to change. We will grab our clothes and meet you there." John said.

Mr. C.'s limo was waiting at the door as the Angel Flight crews ran outside.

Kim said, "I'm not comfortable in this situation. I don't think I have the experience or training to handle this."

"I am a registered nurse, and familiar with this kind of emergency, Kim. You move to Angel Four, and I'll go to Six. We can switch back later, Gerry said. "Is that all right with you, John, Ronni?"

"Getting her to Boston is the most important thing right now. Who does it, and how, doesn't matter," Ronni stated.

"Amen to that," John agreed.

The service personnel at Lindberg had been alerted. The APU was up and running; the lights were on.

It was a strange sight; Three formally dressed couples, women in high heels, men in custom-tailored suits helping the medics load Mrs. C. onto a gurney Mr. C. boarded and was holding his wife's hand and crying. Kim kissed John and joined Ronni and Marco.

"This aircraft has been thoroughly serviced, and is ready for immediate departure," the service manager said to John.

"Thank you, sir. Gerry secures the door and makes Mr. C. comfortable. Vicki, if you are through the checklist, let's 'aviate.'"

Gerry was continually tending to Mrs. C. while her husband watched and asked, "Why are you doing this? Why does this need to be done? Is she going to be alright?"

Gerry patiently answered each question, explaining what they were doing, etc. "Is she going to be alright? Nobody on the planet can give you a definite answer, only God makes that decision, and we have to accept, Thy will be done. We, humans, are doing all we know how to do, and she is resting comfortably."

Gerry went into the cockpit and said to John, "I think you had best push to the max."

"We are at max now, Gerry. The only thing faster than us are a few military planes. We have informed Logan we are on the way, and the Med-Fly is standing by. It's two hours from St. Louie to Boston. All we can do is keep going."

"Gerry," Vicki said. "You are a marvelous dancer I haven't had that much fun in years, and never with a honky. I am impressed with your nursing skill and how you explained the facts to Mr. C. You also got a little preaching done. Good job."

"Fasten seatbelts, Logan International in five minutes," Vicki announced. We have priority clearance and go straight in, no waiting."

"Angel Six. Ground control. Pull off the tarmac as soon as you can. Med-Fly will come to you."

"Roger, ground control," Vicki answered.

The Med-Fly crew had Mrs. C. and her husband on the way to the hospital in a matter of minutes. Vicki taxied to 'Bean Town Sky Port' for servicing.

John noticed they were stared at as they were deplaning. He then realized how they appeared, especially, Vicki in her four-inch heels.

"Shall we change or go to the hospital dressed like this?" he asked.

"I'd like to change into something more comfortable," Vicki said.

Mrs. C. was on the way to surgery when they met with her husband.

"I'm surprised to see you here. I thought you would be gone, once you had delivered the patient."

"No, Mr. C," Vicki responded. "We don't leave until we are satisfied the parents, husbands, or whomever are in control of the emergency, as well as their emotions, are under control. We could go into the Chapel. There is nothing more we can do except wait. It will be a respite to reflect on all our blessings. Ronni, you and Gerry go to the hotel. And get some rest. I'll stay with Mr. C. until we know the prognosis. I can handle the situation."

Vicki and Mr. C. sat in silence, holding hands, each deep in their thoughts. The sun was coming up when Mr. C. heard a page for him. A tired doctor and nurse were waiting to see them.

"It was touch and go. Nurse Mann's quick action when we lost her once, brought her back. Mrs. Mann is my right hand. I believe if I were to drop dead in the middle of an operation, she could step in and complete it without a hitch. I expect a full recovery. We did some bypass and other surgeries. She will be sore for some time and will want to go home soon. Please don't rush it. I'll monitor her regularly, and when it's time to release her, I'll give you some literature to follow about making life easier for you both. She is resting and will be sleeping for several hours. I suggest you do the same thing."

The hotel courtesy car came for them.

"Angel Flight is a very appropriate name for your company," Mr. C. told Vicki, and you are a special lady. You are not only beautiful on the outside; you also have an inner beauty of which you aren't aware. I saw and felt it while we waited. I felt the caring in the way you held my hands. I have never felt that from anyone, not even my family."

Gerry was about to have breakfast as Vicki, and Mr. C. came in.

"How did things go? Is she alright? What's the prognosis?" he asked.

"Everything is good, young man," Mr. C. said. "We shall forever be indebted to you."

"The smiles of relief and tears of joy are more than enough payment for doing our job knowing our talents and resources are from God. Will you two join me for breakfast?"

"I'm too tired to eat right now, but thanks for the thought." Mr. C. answered.

"I'm hungry," Vicki said. "I'll join you and then shower and crash. Yesterday was a long stressful day."

"I'd better call my wife and tell her where I am, and that I am now on Angel Six." He dialed his home phone. A man answered." Is Connie there?" Gerry asked.

The voice on the other end said, "It's for you, sweetheart. Gerry heard his wife say, "Get off me, if you're finished, give me the phone, Hello." Gerry turned ashen and hung up the phone.

"Gerry. What's wrong?"Vicki demanded.

"I just talked to my cheating wife," he answered, choking back tears. "A man answered and said it's for you, sweetheart." She said, "get off me if you're finished and give me the phone."

Gerry came apart. "What did I do that caused her to do this? What am I going to do? Where am I going to live?"

"Calm down, Gerry. One step at a time. Let's get out of here and go someplace to talk. My room is perfect. Don't get any ideas about sex because it won't happen, and I'll explain why later."

In the privacy of Vicki's room, she held him tight and let him cry. Nobody's going to know about this. There will be talk and whispering, but you and I know the truth. Our friends don't need an explanation, and the rest won't believe the truth. I am your friend. You can live with me. I'll even share my bed with you but not my body. Remember this above all else. It is not your fault. Things like this happen. Don't do anything stupid. You will make a decision when you have a chance to think clearly. Divorce may be the answer, but make that decision after you have calmed down. Don't think about getting even or revenge. What goes around comes around. You have two cheaters and what makes you think they won't cheat on each other. I'll take my shower, and you get your things and move in. You should not be alone. I'll let John know what has happened, and he will be supportive. When someone slams a door in your face, God opens a window, now get."

Chapter 40

Angel Four continued it's dispatch to San Francisco, where they picked up a patient for Atlantic City. He was in his mid-thirties, swathed in bandages. According to the chart, second and third-degree burns over a large portion of the body. He was with a tough-looking man who spoke little, but watched every move. Kim came forward and reported something is suspicious. "Nothing shows me he has burns or anything else wrong with him, and that gorilla with him undresses me with his eyes."

Ronni whispered, "Kim, Marco, listen to me carefully, I think we are carrying illegal cargo, and they are the watchdogs. Don't do anything to jeopardize yourselves. We'll stick together, and we can beat them, but we must cover each other's back."

They had just cleared Cheyenne's air space when Ronni turned on the smoke.

A scream from Mr. Tough guy alerted Marco. "We're on fire!" the toughie cried. "We're all gonna die!"

"There's a likely looking place at ten o'clock. I'm going through the checklist, get us on the ground, quick, Marco."

"Take over, Ronni," Marco cried. "I'll finish the checklist. You're better at emergencies."

"Okay. Call central dispatch and explain we have an emergency, but we are under control and preparing to land at a strip East of Cheyenne."

Ronni spoke on the PA," As soon as we stop rolling, get out. All of you. I'll stay with the aircraft and get it away from the buildings. Good luck."

Kim popped the door open, as soon as they stopped rolling, the first one out was their patient, and right on his heels was the tough guy. Marco jumped down and caught Kim in his arms. " You are one cute little one, Kim."

"Thank you. My husband says the same thing, often."

Ronni called Mike on their secret channel and said, "The bait is in place waiting for the rats."

Eli was rushing towards the plane, sirens blowing, red lights flashing. An Oscar-winning performance.

He towed Angel Six, after the 'fire' was extinguished, to the service center where Ray was ready to do his part. Eli parked in such a way that no one could see the transfer of cargo. Eli had the smoker removed and put it in the firetruck, out of eyesight. The operation happened in less than an hour. Mr. Tough guy demanded to see his box. Marco opened the cargo door for him to investigate.

"It looks okay to me, let's go." He said.

"It seems the high altitude and clean air has done wonders for your burns, sir," Kim commented.

"You get paid whether or not we use your services, just sit down and shut up." Mr. Tough guy said.

Ronni came back and confronted Mr. Tough guy. "Sir, can you fly?" she asked.

"If I could, we wouldn't hire some damn broad to take us around."

"I didn't mean fly an airplane. I meant fly like a bird,"

"No, I can't. A dumb question from a dumb broad."

Ronni fumbling around in her bra said, "Ah, here it is and produced her 38 Beretta. Unless you adjust your attitude in one second, you are going to get a chance to learn. You are a nonpaying passenger on this airplane. I am the commander, and I will be treated with respect as will all of the crew members. Don't tell us to sit down and shut up, but I suggest you take your advice. Have I made myself clear? Kim, take Mister Beretta and, if you feel the urge put the barrel between his legs and blow his brains out. It's only fair to warn you, looking at the wide-eyed 'patient,' that also goes for you. Kim has not been with her husband for a very long time. She has a hair-trigger temper, and PMS can strike at any time. Good Luck"

"You are one cool chick, Ronni. I know just how they feel," Marco commented.

Kim stuck her head in and handed Ronni two forty-fives. The gentlemen said they weren't going to need them and would feel safer if you kept them up here. PMS, hair-trigger temper, where do you get such ideas," she laughed.

The last leg of the flight was uneventful.

Chapter 41

At Atlantic City, Marco taxied directly to Garden State Sky Harbor. The same limo TWE was waiting for them and the same goons.

Blonde said, "Mr. Widra would like to speak to you."

Marco said, "You tell Mr. Widra it's just as far for him to walk as it is for me, and I have been working all day. Tell him to get off his butt if he wants to talk to me. I ain'tmovin'. How about it, Blonde? Do you want to try it again?"

"No, I'm going to do cutie pie over there."

"Ronni, stay out of this. PMS and my hair-trigger temper just kicked in. Come on, try your best if you want to sing soprano for a while."

Blonde lunged at Kim, and she side-stepped and slapped him as he went by. He lunged again with the same results.

"Ronni, are you going to talk to the big shot," Kim asked,

"I guess not. I'll only go to old Widra when Blonde moves."

"Hey, Blonde, did you get tired or just lose interest?"

"No, cutie pie, I'm changing my strategy. Slow and steady wins the race." He approached cautiously. Kim took a couple of steps back, and then a feign to the left and her size five hard-toed right shoe in the crotch and a left to the point of the chin, a right-hand chop to the Adam's Apple and Blonde was out.

Ronni shouted to Mr. Widra. "He's lost two out of two to dumb broads. When will he ever learn?"

Mr. Tough guy said, "And I was afraid of the gun. The blonde cleaned his clock with her fists, and cutie pie used her feet and hands. They earned my respect."

Widra was fuming. "Take that impotent piece of crap to his place. Stay with him until he wakes up and tell him I want to see him when he is clean and sober. We are going to have a come to Jesus meeting. Let's get out of here."

Marco went home. Ronni and Kim checked into the Heath Plaza.

 Good evening, Mrs. Lane, Mr. Watkins arrived earlier, and I believe he is having coffee with his cousin.

Kim went to her room, and Ronni joined a surprised Bill and his cousin, Lt. Walker.

"We just delivered the bait," Ronni reported. "Everything went as planned, but Kim and I had to beat the two goons to collapse."

"What is Kim doing here, and what happened to Gerry?" Bill wanted to know.

"It's a long story, and I'm tired. I want a shower and a nap. Excuse me, Lt. I'll be in touch."

Terrance Widra sat in his plush office.

"This is the easiest money I have ever made. I order, Angel Flight ships, I collect and pay for the product, and our hands never touch the stuff. Life is good." He said.

The phone rang, and one of his hired hands picked it up.

"Yeah," he answered. "You better speak to the boss."

"What do you mean, it's blank paper?" Terrance screamed.

"I paid good money for that product, and I 'll get my money. Them damn chinamen are gonna learn you don't screw Terrance Widra! Send them two watchmen in here NOW!"

Mr. Tough guy and the burn victim went to Widra's office.

"I've got some questions for you two, and I want straight answers. "Were you there when they off-loaded the crate? Were you there when hey loaded it into the truck to take it to the airport? Did you watch them load it on the plane? Was it ever out of your sight?" Widra demanded.

"Boss, we watched that crate every minute. The only time it was outtaour sight is when it was in the cargo section of the plane." Mr.

Tough guy answered. "I double-checked itbefore we took off after the fire, and it was just like it was when I sealed it in Frisco. That box ain't been outta our sight since we signed for it. It had to be shipped full of blank paper. Otherwise, I don't know how it was in there!"

"I'll call them chinamen and ask them to explain why they shipped me blanks. There's another load due in LA in a week. We'll wait and see what's in that box."

Widra called his Vietnamese supplier, who denied shipping the blank paper. The shouting match ended after the Vietnamese said they would be over and personally inspect the crate of blank paper.

"Your last order is on the way as we speak. It is being shippedthrough the port of Los Angeles and should arrive next week. We will see you as soon as travel arrangements can be made. Good-bye."

"Business as usual, with a slight delay. We are short on inventory. I will double my next order when the orientals get here," Widra stated. "Make damn sure we have an airplane available. I want to keep the crew we've got. That blonde has gotme thinking. I'd like to have two gorgeous broads, instead of you ugly goons, who could whip ass. I would get a lot of respect and be invited to places and see the mob salivate, like you do, when you see them."

"Boss! You should see where that blonde keeps her rod. I'll give you a clue," Tough guy said. "She's got three thirty-eights under the hood, and one of them is a Beretta. I'm going to a Casino and find a hooker. Are you done with me for now."

"Go on and get out of here," Widra said. "I want to know where you're staying if we happen to need you. I'm going home, maybe I'll get lucky."

Blonde was in a foul mood. He had been totally humiliated in front of Mr. Widra and his fellow mobster, by two women. He sat on the balcony of his fifth-floor apartment. He was on this third Scotch and water, no ice and musing to himself what he was going to do to those bitches. *I'll do the blond on the bed and drag her ass out here, tie her wrists to the rail, then untie her and toss her over the side. Yeah, that's just what I'll do. I'll think of something for cutie pie too.*

CHAPTER 42

Bill let himself into the apartment he shared withRonni. She had taken her shower and put on a T-shirt, but the shirt did very little to hide her natural assets. Bill looked at the sleeping beauty and said to himself. "*Therewillbe plenty of time for us later.He* picked up the paper, poured a large glass of sweet tea, and went to sit on the balcony. The warm sun and relaxed atmosphere worked their charm, and his head dropped, and the paper fell, as he drifted off to sleep.

The sun was setting, and the darkness was racing the sun in their eternal contest that always ended the same way; Ronni kissing Bill awake and sitting on his lap.

"Why didn't you wake me up when you came in?" She asked.

"I wanted to, boy, oh boy, did I want to. That T-shirt covers you up, but I know what lies beneath and decided we would have time for us later with no guilt feelings. I don't feel guilty, but how am I going to explain it to my kids? Put your clothes on, and let's have supper."

Over supper, Ronni told Bill about Mr. C., and explained why Kim was on Angel Four.

Bill said, "We will rendezvous someplace and get the crew status straightened out before the computer crashes and burns. Hawk saidI should ride shotgun until this thing is over. He is like a father the way he worries over hispeople. I will stay out of your way. It's your case, I'm just covering your back. See that guy pretending he is reading the paper. He has not taken his eyes off you since we came in. I'm going to talk to him."

The man put his paper down as Bill approached.

"Excuse me, sir. I couldn't help but notice you payingparticular attention to my lady. Can you explain?"

"My boss, Mr. Cascio, said I should watch, so she don't get no hangnail or run in her stocking. And if anything happened to her some big dude; hey, that's you ain't it? Would take it personally and tear Cascio's wheelhouse down."

"You can relax now. I'm here, and I'll take over. I would like to speak with Mr. Cascio if he is in later this evening."

Bill returned to Ronni, laughing.

"What's that all about?"

"That is one of your bodyguards, compliments of Mr. Cascio. I think I should thank him when I see him later this evening."

Bill and Ronni walked over to Cascio's club and asked to speak to Mr. Cascio. "Tell him Bill Watkins is here."

A nervous, Mr. Cascio opened the door.

"Yes, Mr. Watkins. Come in, please."

"I want to thank you for watching over Ronni while I was gone. What is the name of the bodyguard that watched Ronni?"

"That was Frankie Medly. He's amiable,not the sharpest tool in the toolbox, but very dependable."

"I know we parted on, notthe best of terms, but that was in the past, and I have cooled down. We can probably never be friends, but I will tell you something that I heard from a reliable source. You can use the information as you like. If you want to expand your operation, be ready to move quickly. A bigtime mob is going down, leaving an opening for someone. You are the only person I have shared this with, and the word stops here."

They were leaving the club, and Ronni said, "Isn't that Frankie at the bar?"

"Yes, it is, and I am going to buy him a drink. Hey, Frankie, you did a good job of protecting my ladies, and I'm going to buy you a drink. Bartender, whatever he wants. Here's a twenty. Buy one for yourself. Thanks again, Frankie."

Chapter 43

"Kim. Would you like to do or see anything in particular?"

"I would like to see a casino and watch gamblers."

There's several in town. All the casinos are similar except the décor. Did you have one in mind?"

"No. Just close enough to walk to. They went to the 'Star Dust', a short walk further.

Kim was amazed at the amount of money that changed hands after each game. "Is there a simple game I can play?" she asked.

"Blackjack and craps are the simplest rules and the easiest to learn. Skill comes with practice."

"You show her, Blackjack, Honey."

"Okay. We'll watch a while, and I'll explain what is going on. You'll have an idea as to what's going on when you are ready to play.I'll let you play your hand unless I see you about to make a big mistake. Then I'll stop you."

A seat opened, and Kim was ready to play. She had bought $2,000 worth of chips. Bill watched intently as a new dealer and a new deck were introduced. The dealer made a big show of breaking the seal on the cards, and shuffling and fanning them to impress the crowd.

"Bet the minimum until I tell you otherwise."

"Ronni." Get the manager quietly."

Ronni came back with a gentleman in his late fifties, steel gray hair and neatly trimmed mustache.

"I'm Harry Gillmann. I own this club. This lady said you wanted to see me."

"Sir, my name is Bill Watkins. I'm going to assume you try to run an honest game?"

"Absolutely. The odds are always in favor of the house, we don't want to cheat the betting public. Somebody hits for ten grand and is happy as a clam and brags about his skill as a player. He never mentions the twenty grand or more he lost. Yes, sir, I try to run an honest game. What are you implying?"

"Don Heath fired your new dealer last night. I caught him dealing seconds and thirds and using a marked deck. Don was sure I was wrong; he bet fifty grand to prove it. Today I am that much closer to a paid education for my children, and he is that much shorter in his checking account. Let me prove it to you. The Red Head has fourteen, a ten of hearts and four of spades, and the top card in the dealer's hand is the seven of clubs. The dealer has king, jack of diamonds. He will stay unless he can bring up an ace, but either way, he wins because the Red Head is his partner."

Harry watched the game unfold just as Bill called it.

"Security! Escort this slimeball and his whore girlfriend to my office. If he should trip and fall and get a bloody nose make sure it doesn't get on my carpet. Clean out his pockets and the whore's purse. Let her keep her condoms. Give them ten dollars each and show them the door."

"You big bastard." The dealer shouted at Bill as he was being escorted unceremoniously away. I'll deal with you later."

From the back of the crowd, a voice said, "You would have to deal with Frank Medly first, and I know you, and you ain't got the balls it takes to do the job. Take your bimbo, and go to Vegas."

"Hello, Bill, ladies. It's a pleasure watching you work. I've got a bad pump. The doc says I should avoid excitement, but watching you is like laying in the sun getting some rays."

Kim played for almost an hour, and was quick to catch on. She won $500 and decided it was time to call it a day.

"Life is never dull around you two," Kim said.

"Let's get to our apartment before you get into more trouble," Ronni suggested.

"I'm going to shower and shave before I come to bed."

"I just might join you."

"You do at your own risk. You don't have Frankie watching out for you."

"That's what I'm, counting on. While you shave, I'll get the shower ready, you know, not too hot, just sensuously warm."

"I've never shaved so fast in my life. I hope I didn't miss any.When we aren't together, I miss you so much. It's not the sex. It's the excitement you bring. The things we've done together like three-card Monte, and the way you groped in your bra for your Baretta; the hooker act. That's the excitement you bring."

"All I do is follow your lead. Are you going to wash my back or stand and talk all night?"

They washed their backs and held each other tightly, kissed passionately, and tenderly and continued their shower. They dressed in their sleepwear and had a glass of wine on the balcony.

"I wanted you to make love with me, the minute I saw you with Lt. Walker, and was disappointed you didn't wake me. We should save water and shower together more often."

"As I told you earlier, I really wanted to wake you, but I wanted you to know I'm in love with you and not just horny. Let's hit the beach tomorrow and work on our tans. I can hardly wait to see you in your new swimsuit. I'm tired, let's go to bed now."

The beach was crowded as usual on the weekend, but they found a place and spread their towels and rubbed sunscreen on each other. Then laid back to soak up the sun.

Bill said, "We're scheduled for dispatch Wednesday. Deadhead to LA. I think this is where the shit is going to hit the fan. We better alert Jim."

Ronni's cellphone chimed.

"Hello. Yes, this is Angel Four commander. We can be wheels up in one hour or less. We will pick them up in Philly. Good-bye."

"What's that all about."

Chapter 44

"Some vital brass has to be in Seattle, yesterday. They got a hold of Widra and paid him a bunch of money for us to fly them there. This cuts our vacation short, but we had yesterday, and that will last us for a while. Besides, we are going to be together.

Marco and Ronni looked impressive in their uniforms. Bill and Kim were just passengers and wore casual clothing. Bill wore jeans, a western cut shirt, and custom made cowboy boots. Kim chose a white pleated skirt and a short-sleeved blouse. Her long raven black hair fell loosely from a red bow. The three paying passengers were executives of a prominent company, based in Seattle, with US Government contracts. Bill took an instant dislike to them.

The youngest said as he threw his briefcase on the gurney. "Look here. I've got a place to take my nap."

Kim said, "Sir, this is a MediVac Aircraft, and that gurney is for patients not for naps or to be used as a desk."

"Look, honey, We paid good money for this ride, and I expect to get my money's worth."

Ronni was taxiing to the runway, and suddenly turned off the taxi strip.

"I'll just be a minute tower.

She left her seat and faced the young man.

"Sir, you paid for a plane ride, and you are going to get just exactly that, a plane ride. We don't serve coffee, tea, sodas, or booze. We do have a restroom you may use. This silent gentleman here is my flight attendant. After you use the toilet, he will check it out, and if it looks like hogs were in it, he will invite you to clean it. He can be very forceful. Do you have any questions?"

"Yes, I do. Do you have any idea who you are talking to?"

"Yes, some ignorant asshole who cannot put a simple sentence together. Correctly you would have said, 'Do you have any idea to whom you are speaking?' and I would have said, no, and I don't care. You are on my airplane. You will act like a gentleman. It's up to you."

The eldest of the trio said, "Commander, can you taxi back to the gate, please? This piece of impotent snot has just been fired. I apologize for him. He is my nephew, the son of my only sister, and I hired him out of love for her. He has been a thorn in my butt from the first day. He has never worked in his life, and it is way past time he starts. My sis will be hurt, but she will get over it."

Marco stopped at the gate, and Bill opened the door.

The former employee was about to say something when Bill, in his intimidating manner, said, "I suggest you keep your mouth shut, before my little sister's PMS kicks in."

His uncle said, "Don't look for a check in the mail. You haven't earned your first one yet. Boy, do I feel good. It will be too late to get anything done today. We'll stop in Omaha, and I'll treat us all to their famous steaks."

"Can't refuse an offer like that," Ronni commented. "Marco! Let's 'aviate.' What is your name, sir?"

"Dale Marten, and my right-hand man, Fred Knouse."

"Mr. Marten, we will be in Omaha in time for lunch, and with the time changes, we'll be in Seattle before sixp.m. Just sit back and enjoy the ride. We have coffee, soda, milk, and ice tea. Kim can possibly find a Danish or a donut if you would ask. I'm sorry I came down on your nephew. I was out of line."

"You did what somebody should have done long ago. If you worked for me, I would give you a bonus, a raise, and two-weeks in Hawaii.

Thank you. Now, if you will excuse me, Fred and I have some figures to go over."

The Omaha steaks were as delicious as expected.

"I've got to find time to come here and spend an evening, and a leisurely dinner. Food this good should be savored and not rushed through." Dale commented.

When Angel Four flies over The Dalles, Ronni said, "Leave a light on, we'll be back shortly."

"There's no one on the gurney, Marco. You can set us down."

"Okay, Commander. Are we going to make The Dalles tonight?"

Marco made the perfect landing.

"You can do that again in The Dalles, and we'll know the first time wasn't an accident." Ronni laughed.

When Dale and Fred were clear, Kim secured the door, and Angel Four was 'wheels up' fifteen minutes later, and Marco proved the first wasn't an accident thirty minutes later in The Dalles. John was waiting for Kim, and as far as they were concerned, they were the only people in,andafter a long, homecoming kiss, they walked to their car hand in hand.

Ronni said to Bill, indicating the Schumanns, "There's a couple in love."

" Marco, all of my possessions are in Bill's garage. I'm going to get them and check-in at the Marriott later. I'll see you in the morning for breakfast."

A patrol car took Bill and Ronni to Bill's house to get his car and to the ranch for his children. He gave Ronni a quick look at his house.

"I'm sure it was a lovely home," Ronni said.

"It sure was, but after Rose died, it was just a house. Do you want to meet the children?"

"Do you think the children would think I'm intruding?"

"They know you exist. I mention you a lot. No, I don't think they would object."

"Follow me to the Marriott. I'll check-in. We can get the children and maybe get ice cream before you drop me back at the hotel."

Ronni stayed in the background, watching Bill's children running to greet him. Bill crouched down to hug and kiss his children. Willie was embarrassed at being kissed, but his little girl couldn't get enough affection. It was obvious she and her daddy were very close. Willie walked up to Ronni and held out his hand.

"Are you Veronica?" he asked. "My Dad talks about you all the time. It's nice to meet you."

Bill brought Lucinda over to meet Ronni.

"I know who she is,Daddy. You told us what she looked like. Are you going to marry Daddy, Veronica? You make my Daddy very happy."

"Yeah, are you going to marry Dad?"Willie asked.

"We have mentioned it, but you really ought to get to know me better. I might be the Wicked Witch of the West or like Cinderella's stepmother. Stepmother's have a bad reputation. When two people get married, it should be forever. It takes a lot of time to really know another person. I've only known your father for a short time, but I will tellyou this. I have never loved anyone as much as I love your dad. I hope we can be a family someday. I can never be your mother, and you should always remember her. I would hope you would love me because I love your father, and I make him happy.

"Thank you for watching them for me, Susan and Mike. I'll be needing your services again, Wednesday. We are to pick up a load Thursday or Friday. The way it looks, that end of the operation will be closed down while we wait for the suppliers. What they can be charged with, we don't know, but they will be slowed down until they find another distributor. Come on, kids. We'll get some ice cream on the way home."

They stopped at a newly opened ice cream shop, where you sat at tables, and ate off glass dishes, and had real spoons, not plastic. They each had a sundae of some kind.

Willie said, "Dad, remember when Mom was alive, and we would go to that ice cream store downtown. It was fun like this is. Can we do this again sometime?"

Choking back tears, Bill said, "I forgot how much fun it was for you two. Yes, we will do this again, and as often as we can, but not so often that we forget to have fun."

"Veronica. Are you going home with us and sleep with my Dad?" Willie asked.

"No, Willy. Only married couples sleep together."

"But I know lots of people who live together and aren't married."

"That's up to them, Willy. Times have changed, but the rules haven't."

"Where are the rules written down, Dad?"

"In the book, your mother and I used to read together. It's the Bible, and I have neglected your Christian Education for too long. "Is Mommy in heaven?" Lucinda asked.

" Yes, she is definitely in heaven, and we will all be with her for eternity someday?"

"How do you know, dad? Some kids at school said you have to be perfect to get to heaven. Was Mom perfect?"

"Nobody is perfect, even your mother, but she was forgiven and surrendered herself to Jesus. Jesus promised that was all you had to do to get to heaven, and Jesus doesn't lie. Let's start our road to heaven now. Ronni, if you would like to make the trip with us, join hands."

The family at the next table joined hands with Bill and the circle. A pair of teenagers joined the group. When the circle was complete, Bill said, "I will pray for my family and myself. You must pray for yourselves. My prayer goes like this. 'Father God, Brother Jesus. I am a sinner. I ask your forgiveness and blessing on my children. I turn my life to your service, Amen.'"

"You mean that's all there is to it? The gentleman at the next table asked. Our priest never said it was this simple."

"Have you ever opened the Bible on your own? I've found a simple way to get started studying the Bible. There are thirty verses in Proverbs, and if you read one each day of the month, you would gain great knowledge and probably be interested in continuing to read the entire Bible. My name is Bill Watkins. I'm not a preacher, I'm a cop."

"Bill, you've opened my eyes and turned on a light! Wait until I tell Father Elio I'm going straight to heaven and pass purgatory."

"Well, it's been a good time, but I'm going to take you guys back to the hotel," Bill said wistfully.

"I'm going to read Proverbs 23 from the Gideon Bible," Ronni stated.

Lucinda spoke up, "Don't forget to kiss Daddy good-night and me and Willy, too."

"I don't think we are going to have a long courtship," Ronni said.

"The shorter, the better. Good-night."

CHAPTER 45

Ronni's phone rang at seven-thirty the next morning.

"Good morning, my sleeping beauty," Bill said. "It's a beautiful day, and I'm about to cook breakfast on the patio. If you're up to it, come on over. I'm fixing bacon, eggs, hash browns, toast, juice, and coffee. I thought I might take you and the kids for a ride to Timberline Lodge on Mount Hood, and then just tour. I want to show you the beauty and majesty of it. We'll drive to Portland, and cross over into Washington, and come back on that side of the river."

"I'll be there in fifteen minutes. You kids just as well get used to how I look first thing in the morning. I love you, see you in fifteen minutes, bye."

Vicki called Marco and invited him to spend the day with her family. He was surprised to discover Gerry living with Vicki, and they explained the reasoning behind it.

"We are good friends," Vicki explained. We share the bed, but there is nosex, and that is the truth. Sex is way down my list of priorities. I sold it, I traded it for drugs, I had it stolen from me. I'm not saying I'll neverhave sex again, but if and when I do, it will be a total commitment, not a one night stand. I don't know how love is supposed to feel, but I am sure I will recognize it. You can hangout with us, since you are going to be here a while. I'll introduce you to Blackie Harmon. He lives next door. He has a story about why he is here; ask him to tell you about it.

"There is nothing that smells as good as coffee brewing outdoors mingled with bacon frying. I'll eat way too much and have to do extra crunches in the morning, but it is worth it." Ronni said as she came onto the patio. "I love you, Honey, and you can cook too."

Willie was shooting hoops, and Lucinda was rocking her doll.

She came over to Ronni and put her arms up, and Ronni took her and sat her on her lap. Lucinda put her head on Ronni's shoulder and nestled down with a happy and satisfied smile.

Bill looked at his baby. "She has not had that comfort since Rose last held her, over a year ago. She has adopted you, that's for sure. Willie is trying to be macho, but he misses mothering. He asked me last night when we were getting married. Today was his idea. He doesn't want you to leave, so be prepared for tears when we have to go. I think as soon as this case is over and the dust settles, we should go ahead. The children are all for it, and so are you and I."

"How about the Fourth of July? There is only one thing that concerns me, and that is the ghost of Rose. I don't think I would ever be comfortable living in her home, with her children, and married to her husband. I think we should find our place. The children will grow up and leave home all too soon. Willie can choose his room and decorate as he wants to, within reason. Lucinda can do the same. She will outgrow dolls and find other interests, but it would be a room that is hers by choice."

"I've got the winnings from Atlantic City. Let's build just what we want, maybe out on Mike's place."

"I think that's a great idea, and I insist on kicking in as much as I can. I've got some savings and Cds. It's going to be for better or worse as long as we live. We are going to be one, and it is our home. I would like to be a stay-at-home wife, if possible, and have supper ready when you come home. You make a living, and I'll make the living worthwhile,

We'll work on floor plans, kitchen and bath fixtures, exterior, landscape, décor, and have Murphy and Son build it. Breakfast is ready. Willie, wash your hands and bring a washcloth for Lucinda.

CHAPTER 46

It was a perfect day for Bill's plan. The road to Timberline Lodge was mostly cleared of snow. The sun was out as were the skiers. The view out the huge windows was mainly two colors: the purest sky blue and the pure white of the snow. The skiers are the only things detracting from the spectacular vista.

"Will you teach me to ski?" Ronni asked. "I think it would be a perfect family activity, and as we will be fairly close, it would be affordable."

Rose and I wanted to ski, but never found the time. I guess the answer is, 'take the time.' I'm not letting anything stop me from being a dad. I've neglected the children for too long already. Let's finish our ride. There are some cascades, waterfalls as you call them, I want you to see."

It was late in the afternoon when they crossed the bridge into The Dalles. Lucinda had fallen asleep cradled in Ronni's arms. Willie was fighting sleep, but was losing the battle. Before he surrendered, he said, "This is the best day I've ever had, and after you are married to my dad, we can do it again."

"Absolutely, and do other things like picnics, and we'll cook on an open fire, and if you and your dad catch fish, we'll clean and cook 'em right on the river bank!. You have never tasted real fish unless they are cooked right after they're caught and over a campfire. When I was younger and living with my parents, we would go to the creek and catch catfish and bullheads and cook 'em fresh. Those times are in my fondest memories."

"It sounds to me like you are planning on building some fond memories here, honey," Bill said.

"That's the only kind to have."

The following days were spent building a family relationship. They talked of building a new house and wanted Willie and Lucinda to have some input. Willie wanted room for his computer, but Bill told him there would be a computer room with a door that would remain open.

"I trust you, son. I don't know your friends that well. I feel it's better if we can watch what's going on. There is a lot of bad things on the web, and I don't want you to get started watching it. I'm not so old that I can't remember how it is for a boy growing into manhood. I had the same urges you have, and as you get older, they are going to get more intense. That's when you are a man in charge of yourself or a boy with no control. The choice will be yours. Nobody can make it for you. Whatever happens, I will still love you, and if you tell me the truth, I'll stick by you, but if you lie to me and I find out, and I will, you will suffer the consequences by yourself."

"I hope you've had the birds and bees talk with him," Ronni commented.

"Not as thoroughly as I should have. I believe I'll do it right now. You and Lucinda go do your girl's thing while Willie and I go fishing. I have no idea how much he knows already, but it's time to find out. You know you're acting like a mother."

"I'm just doing what comes naturally. I was raised with three older brothers who protected me. How much they knew about the birds and bees, I don't know. I learned about It in college and had some hairy moments. Fortunately, my brothers taught me how to box and fight dirty, and my reputation spread. 'She's a fun date, but don't try to get in her panties. She says there's only room for one asshole.' When Lucinda needs the talk, I'll take care of it. Go fishing. I'll have supper ready at six."

"Now, you're acting like a wife, and I can get used to thatquick."

"Lucinda, while your dad and Willie are fishing, what do you want to do?"

"I want to play house and have a tea party."

"That sounds like fun. Let's go to the store and get what we need for a tea party. Would you care if I called you, Lucy? Lucinda is such a long name for such a sweet little girl. Lucinda comes from the Bible, and it's a beautiful name. It will always be your name, but I would like to call you Lucy. My name is Veronica, but most people call me Ronni. What would you like to call me?"

"I miss my Mommy so much, but when you are here, I don't miss her. I'll call you, Mommy, and you call me, Lucy."

Ronni was walking on air; It was a happy afternoon. Lucy was helping with supper. Together they decided, on roast beef, mashed potatoes and gravy, green beans, biscuits, apple pie, and ice cream.

Willie and his dad got home around five-thirty. "What smells so good?" Willie asked.

"Oh, just supper," Ronni answered.

"Daddy, I had one of the funnest days. We had a tea party and fixed supper together. I told Veronica that I really miss Mommy, but when I am with her, I don't miss Mommy so much. I call Veronica, Mommy, and she calls me, Lucy.

"Did you catch any fish, Willie?"

"No. Dad talked all the time. I don't think he intended to fish at all, just talked about things all boys should know. I knew a lot already, but some things were wrong, and Dad straightened me out on the BS the guys are telling. He said I should ask him questions, and he would give me straight answers. I guess it was a good day, after all. If Lucinda is going to call you mommy, what shall I call you?"

"How about Ronni?" Bill suggested. "It's a takeoff of Veronica."

"I like it," Ronni said. "Is that okay with you,Willie?"

"Yes. Can we eat now? The smell makes me hungry."

Supper was placed on the table, and as they sat, Lucy asked everyone to hold hands.

"Thank you, God, for this food and for Veronica, and Mommy, I miss you. I want to call Veronica mommy, because she makes me happy like you did. Amen."

It's hard to eat when you're choking on tears, isn't it Bill?"

"Yes, it is, and such a wonderful supper."

"We've got apple pie and ice cream for dessert. I helped mommy pick the apples from the tree in our back yard."

"I'd forgotten about that tree," Bill said. "You have a lot of depth, Veronica Lane, and I'll bet few people are aware of it."

"I seldom get a chance to show it, but it is so natural with your children, I don't know how to be a mother, and I just do what feels natural."

"You have a natural talent that you didn't know you had. Some women are terrible mothers that should never have had children. There are some women, like yourself, that have never had children who are wonderful mothers. Don't worry, the kids will teach you what you don't know. We are anxious for your first lesson, aren't we, kids? We will be leaving in the morning to finish a job we started. We will be back as soon as we can, and start getting ready for Ronni to move in."

"If you are going to get married, anyway, why can't she move in now?" Willy asked.

"Yeah, why can't she move in tonight?" Lucy echoed.

"We don't have enough time tonight, but when we get back, she will move in. We are going to be married on the Fourth of July." Bill said.

Wow! Can I have some firecrackers to celebrate with?" Willie asked.

"That we will decide later, son. They are dangerous, and there will be other people around. We have to have consideration for the safety of others. Go pack for the ranch. We want to get an early start in the morning."

"Speaking of packing. I better get to the hotel and get my stuff together and make sure Marco is ready. I'll see you in the morning, Honey. Good-night, Lucy and Willie.

"Mommy, will you say my prayers with me?"

"Of course, I will, Lucy. How about you, Willie?"

"I'm going to ask Dad to help me with mine, but you can kiss me good-night."

CHAPTER 47

Marco was watching a western on TV when Ronni called him.

"Wheels up about nine in the morning," she said. "Were you bored to death out here in the sticks?"

"No, I spent most of my time with Vicki and Gerry. He caught his wife cheating on him and went off the deep end. Vicki insisted he move in with her, so she can keep an eye on him. They share the bed, but no sex. Everything seems to be working out for them, It's a wonder Gerry doesn't gain a lot of weight. Vicki's mom, Dorris, is a good cook. I'll be ready in the morning."

"You file a flight plan and get a weather report for LA, and I'll do the preflight. Happy dreams, I'll see you in the morning."

She called Gerry and told him, wheels up at nine in the morning.

"I'll be there. Vicki will bring me over." He said.

Vicki had Gerry there on time, and it was not a natural parting for them. They had grown close in a very short time. Could true love be very far behind?"

Bill arrived with a smile from ear to ear.

"You look like you had a lucky night." Ronni teased.

"You have no idea how lucky I got. I'll tell you. Willie said his prayers and thanked God for having me as a father, and for you, he called you Ronnie, for making me happy again. He said I smile and whistle like I used to, and then he hugged me and said, I love you, Dad.

It was a voluntary thing, not a response. I haven't seen Lucy sohappy, since Rose died.She is excited to have you move in. Yes, I got lucky last night. There is no such thing as luck. We ask God's help, and if we get out of his way, He can and will help us; in His own way and in His own time. I don't recall what I prayed for except for help raising my children, and He sent an angel named Veronica. Let's get this mission over and get back home."

"Here comes Marco with the weather report, and flight plan, so fasten your seat belt and enjoy the ride."

There was no hurry, and they just loafed along, enjoying the leisurely pace and the scenery. Gerry seemed unusually quiet, and Ronni finally asked if he was okay.

"I guess, with all that has happened lately, I'm okay. Vicki, literally saved my life. This is the first time she hasn't been around for me to lean on, and I'm scared."

"You have three people in this airplane to lean on when you need support. I don't think you will need us, but we are here. I'm going to ask you a question, and I demand an honest answer. Please be truthful, and no matter what your answer, nothing is going to happen to you, but I've got to know. First off, I am an undercover FBI agent working on a huge counterfeiting operation. You know this aircraft hauls damn few patients, but we log a lot of miles. We have been transporting counterfeit money for Terrance WidraEnterprises. We are on our way to pick up a load now. I've set a trap, and it's about to snap shut on the mob. My question is this. How much do you know and how involved are you?"

Gerry was the first to answer.

"I don't know anything about the mob, or counterfeiting. I was beginning to get suspicious. I talk with other Angel crews, and they hardly ever haul cargo unless it's hospital supplies. I'm a damn good, well-trained nurse, and to see my skills wasted on cargo, pisses me off. I know about the mob and Widra. I want to get away from them, and I can't think of a nicer place than where we just spent our downtime, but I don't dare leave because they will hunt me down or hurt my wife and kids, but, like I told you, you stuck your neck out for me, and I owe you a big one. I will not do anything to help them or hurt you. That's a promise."

"Suppose I told you, Widra and his entire operation are going down. If you are on our side, I can promise you that if you have a record, it will be sealed or expunged. The chief of police inThe Dalles is noted for giving second chances. There are plenty of jobs, or you can stayon with Angel Flight. I'll give you a recommendation."

"Lady, you got a deputy."

"That makes two," Bill said. "I'm on assignment from the Chief she was just talking about, to help close this case."

"I'm not going to stand by and let you guys have all the fun and glory." Gerry chimed in. "I can use a club or something.

"This is Ronni's case," Bill said. "She is calling the shots. You will do what she says. There is going to be some shooting probably. Be ready. The Atlantic City Police Department is going to be there; don't shoot them. The common-sense rule: know your target, aim, and squeeze. Ronni will work out the details on how this is going down, and fill you in on what you are expected to do. Are there any questions? Stay out of the way if you do not want any part of this action. Your decline will be honored, and no one will think less of you. I'm talking to you, Gerry. Your experience with guns, shootings, and violenceis not at all in your field of occupation. The rest of us are trained, for better or worse. You will be better assistance to stand by and care for the wounded."

"John Wayne Airport just ahead. Fasten your seat belts." Ronni announced. "Okay, Marco. Show us how good you are and taxi over to Duke's Air Park."

Angel Four was serviced immediately, and towed to a parking place. Ronni called the warehouse where the merchandise would be and was told that there had been a delay. "You can expect the freight Friday morning."

"How about late Thursday?" Ronni asked. "We need the merchandise, badly. We are out of stock."

"Thursday evening; seven-thirty for you, sweet cheeks."

"Careful, honey. I forgot and brought my husband with me. Maybe next time."

"I'm looking forward to it. Thursday evening, seven-thirty, bye."

"Gentlemen," Ronni announced. "We will receive our merchandise at seven-thirty Thursday evening. We have free time until then. Marco, keep an eye on Gerry. There is not much to do for entertainment. Please stay out of trouble."

The crew checked-in at the Best Western Motel, and Marco and Gerry shared a two-bedroom suite. Bill registered as Bill and Ronni Watkins.

"Wemight as well get used to it. The mob will be with us soon."

They ordered a pizza and soda for supper and watched the Dodgers and Cardinals play on TV.

"I wonder how Mr. and Mrs. C. are doing?"

The game ended in the eleventh inning when the Cards pulled a suicide squeeze that worked. Final score Dodgers 3, Cards 4.

"I'm going to shower and go to bed. Want to join Me?" Ronni asked.

I'm going to watch the news first. Ronni soon came to bed, and they discussed how their privacy plans would be during the construction of their new house. A tender good-night kiss and a whispered, *I love you,* and they fell fast asleep in each other's arms and slept like only contented, lovers can sleep.

Chapter 48

"I want to have a big breakfast this morning," Bill said while he was shaving. " A western omelet, home fries, toast, and coffee and a huge glass of milk."

"I'll have the same," Ronni said, "but without the milk. Let's rest today, and as soon as we are loaded, we'll take off. St. Louis is three hours away, which will be about twelve-thirty a.m. their time, and Atlantic City is twoand a half hours further. We can get a good night's sleep and close this case down tomorrow afternoon. I'll call Marco and Gerry, and we can meet for lunch and go over final plans and strategy.

The merchandise was delivered at seven-thirty. Command pilot, Ronni, signed the receipt and accepted the bill of lading for it.

"You are all set sweet cheeks. Your cargo is secured and sealed." The warehouse driver said. "Don't forget toleave your husband home next time."

"Sure thing, honey. Thanks for your cooperation. We are completely out of supplies. We'll be leaving now. Okay, Marco, I've done the walk-around and preflight, see if you can remember the routine to get us off the ground."

Yes, Ma'am. Let's see what happens when I do this. Oh, that starts the port engine, then this must start the other one. It's all coming back to me now. Let's 'aviate.'"

Three hours later, Marco announced, "Lindberg Field on the horizon, fasten your seat belts. Ronni, if you don't mind, would you set us down."

"Yes, I need the practice. We will stay at Express Motel, and get started abutten in the morning, and review our plans for the bust, while we have breakfast together. Tower, can you patch me through to the Inferno, thank you. Hello, Inferno. Is Mr. C. there? Mr. C., I didn't recognize your voice. This is Command Pilot Veronica Lane, of Angel Flight. I want to know how Mrs. C. is doing. We are about to land at Lindberg Field. We will be staying at the Express. ... Just a minute, I'll ask. Can anybody eat a steak? Mr. C. wants us to come over to the Inferno for steaks."

"I can always eat a steak," Bill said.

"I know Marco and I can," Gerry answered

"Yes, Mr. C., there will be four of us. See you soon, bye."

Mr. C.'s limo was waiting for them at Sky Harbor.

"The boss is so excited to see you," the driver said. "All he has talked about is how you saved his wife's life. He asked all of his employees to kick in as much as they could to give to Angel Flight. I know be gives ten percent of net earnings every week, plus he has given them some stock. He says, Why not use my money to help others instead of hoarding it for myself?. I've been with him twenty years, and have never seen him so energetic. His doctor said his health is like a forty-year-old. Just a short time ago, he was worried about his blood pressure and cholesterol, but everything has improved. Business is way up. Mr. C. says, the more I give, the more I get. I should have done this years ago."

Their table was ready, set with Mr. C.'s personal fine china, linen tablecloth, and napkins. The centerpiece was a hand-carved small blonde angel on a sky-blue doily. Except for the chef and Mr. C., the club was empty.

"Thank you for the opportunity to personally thank you for saving my wife." Turning to Gerry, he said, "Thank you is not enough. The outcome would have been grave, were it not for your expertise and skill. My wife is at home, resting and getting better every day....How do you like your steaks? We 'flame broil,' which leaves no extra fat to taint the flavor."

"I like mine pink in the middle," Gerry said.

In unison, they all said, "Mine too."

"Will salad, baked potato, and breadsticks be okay for the sides, and what to drink?"

"The sides are fine, and bring us the dressings for the salad," Bill said,"andI would like an extra-large glass of cold milk and coffee."

"Coffee, all around," Marco ordered.

Mr. C. brought the salads and a basket of fresh, warm breadsticks. He brought Bill's milk and poured the coffee leaving a large thermos of coffee on the table. He and the chef brought the rest of the meal on two large silver trays.

"Before you start, would you all join hands with us?" Mr. C. asked. "Our Father in Heaven," he prayed, "I thank you for bringing these people into my life. Angel Flight and especially Gerry for saving my wife, and my chef, Mario Diblasi, for taking over in my absence to run the club as well as his duties in the kitchen. Most important of all, opening my eyes to the opportunities to help others. Bless this food, and these friends. In your blessed name. Amen."

"I didn't realize I was hungry until I sat down," Ronni said.

Mr. C. presented a serving of Spumoni ice cream for dessert, then joined them for a glass of Sangria. "To help you sleep," he said. "Please make it a point to call me when you are in the area. I don't want you to feel obligated to come to the club. I'm interested in you as friends. My wife and I have a few friends because of my business. It doesn't leave us much time for a social life. I'm going to change that. I'm going to name Mario the club manager, and take some time off. She loves baseball, and I have a season ticket with box seats on the third baseline. I see maybe three games a year, she seldom misses one. When you are in town and have the time, I would like to treat you to a game. That goes for all Angel Flight crews."

"I'll pass the word around," Ronni said. "We have to go, Mr. C., I speak for the entire crew when I thank you for your hospitality. I'm not a hand shaker, Mr. C., I'm a hugger. Let's have a hug."

"A hug is better than a handshake. Who is this large gentleman?"

"This gentle giant is Bill Watkins. He and I are going to be married on the Fourth of July."

"Pleased to meet you, sir," Mr. C. replied. "You two make a handsome couple. My best to you, good night."

Mr. C.'s limo took them to the Express.

Chapter 49

"I feel like royalty in blue jeans," Bill said.

"We really touched him," Gerry said, and all we did was do what we get paid for."

"I've got to shake the mob," Marco said. "I can't deal with it anymore. Can you help me get my family away?"

"Absolutely, Marco. Widra is going down tomorrow, and you won't have to worry about him for a while." Ronni answered. "You're going to have to leave with your clothes, and that's about all. Call your wife in the morning and discuss it with her. If she says go, have her pack only those items that are precious to her, and have she and your children check into a motel. This airplane will be out of service for a while. We will take you all to The Dalles, where you can start over. Hire a reliable moving company, load up the rest of your belongings and put them in storage as soon as possible. You can move your stuff to the Dalles when the heat is off."

"I'm no coward," Gerry said, but I just can't bring myself to hurt someone. All my training has been to ease pain, not cause it. I'll stay in the plane."

"That's fine, Gerry. You'll be out of harm's way, and we won't have to worry about you."

"But I'll worry about you guys."

"We'll be okay," Ronni assured him. "Wheels up at ten in the morning. Good night."

"Let's see just how much self-control we have and just shower and go to bed," Bill said.

"We had better take separate showers. I like mine lukewarm, and you like your's steaming hot. I'll see you between the sheets."

Showers were over. Ronny dried her hair and slipped between the sheets. Bill rolled on his side and kissed her tenderly on the lips.

"I love you, sweetheart."

"I love you too, Honey."

They nestled in each other's arms and slept soundly through the rest of the night. The alarm clanged at eight-thirty.

"Up and at'em," Bill said, smacking Ronni on the butt.

Marco landed Angel Four on the tarmac at five after ten.

"Sorry I'm late boss," he said. "My wife and I had a long talk this morning. She had never thought of moving, and I caught her completely off-guard. She said she was going to pack as much as she could and get to the city. She has Angel dispatch number, and when she is settled, she will call and let me know where she and the kids are. When I told her about The Dalles and how the people treat each other, she said, let's get there and start over. We got married and had nothing, not even a future, and we didn't do too bad. Now we have a family and a future to be happy in a city that seems like an ideal place to live. Let's kick some ass today and get this case solved, and I'll throw my gun away."

"I can't let you do that, Marco," Bill said.

"I'm an officer of the court and will have to have a spent round and the serial number of your gun. We enforce the law equally. You are not going to be arrested, and your record will be expunged or at least sealed. We need the information for the record. It may clear up some open cases."

"I think it will. After you get all the data you need, do what you want with it. I don't ever intend to use a gun again unless it would be one of those fancy hunting rifles to shoot a deer or something, but I'll never aim at a human again. I hope my change of heart won't get in my way today. I'll gladly take a bullet for any of you, especially you, boss."

"I'm touched by your loyalty, and I pray it doesn't come to that. This is a solemn pledge. If the worst happens to you, your family will be well-taken care of, including college. Your wife will have everything she needs as well as our friendship. Marco, you are a true friend, and I love you."

"You've got my eyes leaking, boss. You'd better land this bird because I can't see too clearly right now. I have a good friend, Gerry, but he never said he loved me."

"I thought it was a little sissy to tell another guy you loved him," Gerry answered.

"I tell my boss, the Chief of Police, I love him, and nobody has ever called me sissy," Bill commented. "One of Jesus' commandments tells us to love one another, and no one called Him sissy."

Bill continued, "Jim Walker has been alerted, but we may be a little early. We'll play it close to the vest and by ear." I will have Widra sign a receipt acknowledging he has received the goods. The manifest lists what he has signed for. We will walk to the terminal, and when they are all inside his warehouse, and can't see us, we slip in and hide. We wait until he opens the crate, and has the goods in his hand, then we bust him. Take a deep breath, and say a little prayer. Here we go!"

"Good afternoon, Mr. Widra, Ronni said. "I need you to sign this receipt for your goods. You get the original, and I keep the copy. Where is Blonde? I was looking forward to humiliating him again."

"He's around someplace. Watch your back. He does not take rejection at all. He will not be satisfied until he gets even, and he is brutal. I'm only telling you this because I admire your guts. Nobody ever talked back to me and got away with it. Blonde tried to teach you a lesson, but lost, and that cute little bitch that put him down really pissed him off. I laughed so hard I almost peed my pants. I would like to hire you, two women, as bodyguards. You won't eat as much, and you are a hell of a lot prettier than the goons I got now. Watch your back."

As planned, Ronni, Bill and Marco headed for the terminal, while Gerry stayed with the plane. As soon as the warehouse door closed behind the forklift carrying the crate of counterfeit money, the trio ran across the parking lot to a side door. It was locked.

Marco said, "this is from my misspent past," and he produced a set of picks, and in a minute or less, they were inside. They moved silently toward the sound of voices.

"Here it is, by damn," Widra said. "Good quality, them Chinamen do good work."

Ronni stepped into the light, flashing her badge and gun, and said, "Freeze, I'm Special Agent Veronica Lane FBI. You are all under arrest."

One of Widra's men turned out the lights and started shooting wildly in Ronni's direction. Bill returned fire, and someone turned on the lights; a shot rang out from the shadows in the back of the warehouse, and someone fell from the catwalk to the warehouse floor.

He was hurt and said, "She doesn't get a run in her stockings, a hangnail or nothin'. That's what the boss told me."

Jim Walker and his men arrived to mop up.

"Where's Ronni?" he asked.

Frankie came from the shadows with his hands up, and his gun was hanging from a thumb.

"He's on our side, Jim."

"Take my heater, please. I am retiring. I put that guy down, pointing to the one on the floor. I saw that blonde goon of Widra's turn Ronni's lights out busting her with his gun. He tossed her over his shoulder like a sack of flour and ran out the back door."

Bill faced Widra and demanded, "Where did he take her?"

"I don't know, and I don't care."

"Don't look, Jim," Bill said, grabbing Widra by the throat and starting to squeeze.

"Hey, cop, this is police brutality," Widra screamed.

"I can't see any police-involved, so it can't be police brutality. I think you had better answer Bill's question before he saves us the cost of feeding you while you wait for a trial for the next twenty years. Oh, hell, don't answer his question, squeeze, Bill. See if he pisses his pants, dies, or talks first."

Bill lifted Widra off the floor and started to squeeze. Widra nodded his head in surrender.

"Talk fast. Every minute counts."

Widra named an apartment complex where Blonde lived.

"I know where that is," Frankie spoke.

"Bill, you drive, my car's out front," Jim ordered.

"Can I turn the siren on and the flashing lights?" Frankie begged.

"Turn the siren off when we get close. I don't want Blonde to know we are on the way. When we get there, stay in the car. I don't want any witnesses."

Blonde had stripped the clothes from Ronni's unconscious body, and using old neckties had tied her to the four corners of the bed. He had worked her over with his fists in a drunken rage. Her lips were puffed, one eye was beginning to swell, her nose was bleeding, and she had a split lip. Blonde poured himself another glass of courage and took his clothes off. Looking at her nude body, he was getting out of control.

Bill, not taking time for the elevator, ran up the steps to the fifth floor. He located Blonde's room, and tried the door. In his haste, Blonde had not shut the door entirely, and it swung open. Spotting and reaching Blonde's gun, he silently removed the clip, and ejected the shell from the chamber.

Blonde was between Ronni's legs. She spotted Bill and forced a smile.

"Are you smiling in anticipation?" Blonde asked.

Through swollen lips, she said. "I can hardly wait."

"That's as close to heaven's gate as you will ever get," Bill said. 'Here is your gun. You won't have to look for it. I don't know what you are so proud of. You do a pretty good job beating up unconscious women, but you can't do it when they are conscious. I'll give you the facts. I weigh 235 lbs, height 6ft 4in. You get the first shot."

Blonde raised his gun and pulled the trigger. "You don't think I'm dumb enough to give you a loaded gun, do you? That was your first shot. I'm going to beat you silly for hurting my wife. You better be prepared to defend yourself."

Blonde threw a left, Bill ducked and countered with a vicious backhand across the mouth, knocking his opponent down.

"Get up and try again."

Blonde kept trying. Bill kept slapping.

I'm not going to put your lights out. I want you to feel everything I do." Bill stated.

After twenty minutes of cruel punishment, Blonde's face was a mass of blood. Most of his teeth were on the floor. His nose was smashed and broken.

"I think I'm over my mad, now. It's time to get rid of the trash." He drug Blonde to the balcony, and tossed him over the side to a dumpster five floors below. Untying Ronni, he bathed her swollen face with cold water until she was able to navigate, although unsteadily, on her own. He helped her dress and held her tight.

"Sweetheart, let's go home," She whispered.

Frankie was waiting for them and apologized for letting her get a hangnail. "Where is that blond bastard, Bill.'"

"Yes, where is he," Ronni asked. "When I knew I was safe, I relaxed and went to sleep. I remember you telling him that was as close to heaven's gate as he would ever get."

"He thought he was Superman and fell to his death."

Back at Widra Enterprises, Jim Walker was just wrapping up. He looked at Ronni and asked, "Where is Blonde?"

Bill said, "He thought he was Superman and fell to his death."

Frankie turned ashen and collapsed.

"Gerry!" Marco screamed.

Gerry came running from the plane and began CPR. Lt. Walker called for an emergency unit. By the time they arrived, Frankie was breathing again.

Chapter 50

"He needs to get to Boston General yesterday." The Medic said.

"Get him loaded, and we are out of here in ten minutes," Marco stated.

Bill helped Ronni into the copilot's seat and read the dials and gauges for her. Marco finished the preflight, and Gerry secured the door, and the engines were up and running.

The emergency unit asked the tower for immediate clearance for Angel Four. Good luck and God speed."

Ronni went back to sit with Frankie and hold his hand. She looked at Gerry with questioning eyes. He made the sign of the cross as to say, it's in His hands now. Ronni went back to her seat and asked Marco if her speech was clear.

"For us that know you, yes, but a stranger might have a hard time understanding you."

"Bill, I need to talk to the people in Boston. First off. We can't have any delays. We must go straight in. The Medfly from Boston General has to come to us, and their surgical team has to be ready. Tell them a VIP named Frank Medly needs immediate attention."

"Walker must have a lot of clout," Bill stated. "Everything is ready. Medfly will be waiting for us on the tarmac. The surgical team is ready. They all want Frankie's autograph when he recovers. They didn't say when, which is a good sign."

"Logan has us on the scope," Marco announced. "Are you able to make the checklist?"

"Bill can help me like he did before."

Marco rolled to a stop beside the Medfly. Ronni gave Frankie a kiss for luck, and within five minutes, the transfer was complete, and Frankie was on the way to the hospital.

Marco taxied to Air Park. "We will be here for a day or two, maybe more." He said to the service manager. "I want this aircraft ready thirty minutes ago, in case we have an emergency. That large man gets really upset when we have to wait because some airhead didn't do their job. Do you understand?"

"Yes, sir. We have been instructed to give all Angel Flight aircraft priority. No exceptions. As you can see, the fuel tanks are being filled as we speak, and the gurney, and other equipment is being sterilized."

"I'm sorry I came across hard, but I've been in a gunfight, my copilot got the crap beat out of her, and a friend of ours is on the way to Boston General.It has been a hell ofa day."

"No apology is necessary, sir."

The quartet from Angel Four took a cab to Boston General to be with Frankie. One look at Ronni, and the intern ordered a nurse to get her a hospital gown and check her vitals.

"We just came to see how our friend is doing." Ronni protested.

"All I can tell you is he is in the hands of our best team, and the prognosis is positive. It will be several hours before he is conscious. In the meantime, I'm keeping you at least overnight, maybe longer. You have had a brutal beating, and may require some dental work. I hope whoever did this is caught and made to pay."

"He was caught, but in resisting arrest, and being drunk with power, he thought he was Superman. Five floors down, the dumpster stopped his fall."

"Could I get a shower?" Ronni asked. "I need to wash the pain away, and found in the past that a steaming hot shower does wonders for that."

"The nurse will help you." The intern answered. "We don't want you fainting with no one around."

"I'll wait for her to get settled in," Bill said. "Why don't you two check-in for us. I'll be along later."

Marco and Gerry said their good-bye's and carefully hugged her.

"We love you, Ronni," Marco said.

The nurse had a new gown ready, and wheeled Ronni to her room. Bill had filled out the necessary papers to get her checked in and was waiting for her.

"It was a good shower." She said.

"I'll wait for your shot to take hold, and you go to sleep before I leave. I'll be back to have breakfast with you and bring you some decent clothes."

He held her hand, and tenderly stroked her arm until her eyes closed. He kissed her and said, "I love you." He thought he saw a trace of a smile on her face as he left.

He told Marco and Gerry that he would be leaving early to have breakfast with Ronni.

"I think they will keep her until tomorrow. Plan your day around that. I think the Sox are playing the Yankee's tonight if you're interested."

Bill packed Ronni's clothes, and as an after-thought, put her hairbrush and makeup in the bag. He stopped at an open twenty-four hour Seven Department store, and bought light blue silk pajamas for her hospital stay.

Ronni was awake, alert, and waiting for Bill and breakfast when he arrived.

"Good morning, sweetheart," she said. "How is my knight in denim jeans this morning?"

"Now that I see you're beautiful and beat-up face, I'm fine. "I've already got used to sleeping double. I had a lot of empty with me. I didn't sleep all that well. How about you?"

"That shot put out the lights, and I slept until the vampire came and drew blood and took my vitals. He said Frankie was alert, and is wondering why they are asking him for his autograph. I ordered pancakes, link sausage, two eggs, basted well, but nothard, large milk, and coffee. What's in the bag?"

"Decent clothes, your toiletries, and PJs."

"Let me comb my hair and brush my teeth while we're waiting for our food. Wow! Silk pajamas, she said from the bathroom, beautiful. They will be handy. In case of fire, I can slip intothese. I'll keep them beside the bed."

Frankie was sipping on his ice water when they walked into his room.

"Hey, you two. What are you doing here? I must have died and gone to heaven yesterday. I saw a battered up blonde angel, and she kissed me. What the hellhappened?"

"Your pump went bad, Frankie, and you fainted. Gerry gave you CPR untilthe emergency unit showed up. They finished the job Gerry started and said youneeded to be here,so we loaded you up, and here you are."Bill told him. "We told air traffic control we had a significant person on board, and could not afford any delays. Everything went as smooth as Ronni's silk pajamas."

"Who is the important person you had on board?"

"You, Frankie, you," Ronni answered. "You are an important person."

"That's why everybody wants my autograph? What will I do?"

"Scribble your name, smile, and say thank you," Bill answered. "Everybody deserves their fifteen minutes of glory. Enjoy it. Now that you have decided to retire, what are yougoing todo?"

"Ever since I met you guys, I've been wondering if there are more like you where you live."

"Almost everyone is like we are, just plain people wholove our neighbors as Jesus ordered us to do. We have an asshole or two, but we leave them alone, and they either have an attitude adjustment or move. Our police chief is a full-blooded Shoshone Indian who gives everybody a second chance. There are all kinds of jobs to be had, and we never lock our doors."

"I'm all alone, and it would be easy to pick up and go. I've got quite a bankroll; money wouldn't be a problem, but I would have to do something, or I'd go nuts."

"How about a security guard?." Ronni suggested. "You are a natural for that. I would love to have you out here, Frank. You are a special friend."

"I'm gonna give it a shot. If I don't, I'll always wonder what it would have been like. How do I get to this paradise you talk about?"

"Book your flight to Portland, Oregon, and give us the flight number and we'll be waiting for you," Ronni answered. "Marco and Gerry will be in to see you later. You rest. We have to go. I think we are going home tomorrow, but we will see you before we leave."

She bent down and kissed Frankie.

"You look like that angel that kissed me yesterday, but she didn't have silk PJs on, and wasn't nearly as pretty as you."

The doctor caught up with Ronni as she was leavingFrankie's room.

"I want to take some X-rays and run some other tests," he said. "If everything is okay, you can go home tomorrow, but I want to keep you overnight. I make rounds early. You should be discharged by eight-thirty."

"Nice pajamas. All the patients want some just like yours."

Marco and Gerry were looking for Ronni to see how she was feeling.

"Except for this mouse and some loose teeth and bruises, I'm doing okay. We will be going home tomorrow. I figure wheels up about ten."

"I got in touch with my wife," Marco said. "She is staying with an old friend in the city. She can be there before noon. We will have her paged and direct her to our assigned gate."

Chapter 51

The next morning the doctor released Ronni.

"You have a mild concussion," the doctor said. "The rest of the tests came back negative. I recommend rest for a week or more. You are tougher than you look."

"You don't know the half of it, doc," Bill commented. "Get dressed. We are going home."

Marco and Gerry were already on board. The APU was up and running. Marco had filed a flight plan and called Angel dispatch and reported them 'Out of Service.' Ronnimade the walk-around and took her seat.

"Let's go get the Mrs., you drive," Ronni ordered. "There is probably a lot of traffic above the city. We will use our status as an air ambulance to cut some slack.

Angel Four, you are cleared to land. Follow British Airways 747 and go to United Gate 17. We have directed Mrs. D'Angelo to that gate."

"We won't be long," Ronni answered. "We're just going to pick her and the children up and take them to their father. He's okay now, but he was in a gunfight with some counterfeiters yesterday."

"The way you throw bullshit around you ought to be a politician," Bill laughed. Marco taxied to his assigned gate.

"I'll be glad when we are out of here," he said. "The mob has long arms and eyes everywhere."

"You go get your wife, Marco," Bill said. "I'll watch your back. Ronni! Give me your badge. It may come in handy."

Marco spotted his wife and family, and was hugging and kissing each of them, when he noticed two tough-looking men watching him very intently.

"Get on the plane." He ordered. "Ronni and Gerry will help you get settled. I'll be along in a minute."

Bill watched Marco's family get on the plane and turned his attention to Marco. The thugs were forcing Marco to go with them.

Bill walked and pushed the thugs aside and grabbed Marco by the arm.

"You are Marco D'Angelo, aren't you." He demanded.

Marco's eyes widened, and he stammered, ah, yes.

Flashing Ronni's badge, he said, "I'm Wiliam Watkins FBI. I've been following you for weeks, but you were always a step ahead. I've got you now. You two stay right where you are. I'm going to lock this guy up and check my files. I might have pictures of you in there. Don't go away."

He drug the resisting Marco to the gate and turned to watch two thugs beat a hasty retreat.

"I believe you are clear of them for a while," Bill said.

"I didn't know what the hell was going on when you grabbed me. Those goons didn't know either. Let's 'aviate' boss."

"Go sit with your family after we're in the air. Put it on autopilot and enjoy the ride. Angel Six was dispatched to LAX to pick up a patient and his brother and transport them to Atlantic City. It was Angel Four's assignment, but dispatch reportedthey are out of service. There was some kind of serious altercation, and the command pilot got beaten up badly. They are on the way home as we speak."

John called Angel Four, "Are you okay, Ronni, and how is the rest of the crew?"

"I'm okay, bruised and sore. Marco, Bill, and Gerry escaped with no injuries. The bust went down almost exactly as planned. There will be someone from the other end heading for Atlantic City to straighten things out with Widra, but since he is in jail, they will have nothing to do except maybe find another distributor or go back to Vietnam. I wish there was some way to stop them, but there is nothing we can do. We know they made the product, but can't prove it. See you later, Angel Four, clear."

Chapter 52

LAX instructed John to taxi to Golden State Air Park.

"An ambulance is waiting with your patient, and you are cleared to go as soon as you are ready."

Kim welcomed them aboard, and as she was covering the patient, she noticed a scar on his neck. She stared at him, then went forward to talk to John. "Those are the ringleaders of the Viet Cong that destroyed my village." With tears streaming down her face, she continued. "The patient is the one who raped and killed my mother. Withher last ounce of strength, she clawed his neck. I saw the blood run before he kicked her to make sure she was dead. I'll remember that until my dying day, The other one just laughed as he shot women and children and old men. You were there and saw it too."

"I remember it well. I've never felt so helpless in my life. Ask them if they speak English. You have to fill out some forms for our government, and you want to be sure they understand."

"Yes," the patient answered. "I graduated from UCLA, so ask your questions."

"I'll be right back with the forms."

Kim heard them talking in Vietnamese about what they would like to do to her, laughing. Then she heard them say what theywere going to do with that round-eyed Widra for trying to rip them off.

"John, that's the people Ronni was talking about, and they dospeak English," Kim reported.

"I've got to find someplace toput down that's out of the way. Those bastards days on earth are coming to an end."

Vicki keyed the mike and asked Heather to get Jeffery on the phone.

'What are you doing? John asked.

"Swahili. I know just where to go. Just let it go at that. I'll put us on the ground in a place you asked for, and the rest is up to you."

"It's your airplane, Vicki. I have to work on a plan."

"John." Kim said, "I want the patient. I've got a lot of years of hate built up. I now have a chance to let it go."

"Okay, I won't step in unless it's absolutely necessary. Let's go ask the questions. I'll stick my forty-five in the mouth of the one with the scar. You tell them in Vietnamese what we witnessed them do, and how he came by that scar, and if he doesn't answer, this gun in your mouth is ready to fire. We are going to get off this airplane and settle the score. Be sure they know how we are paired up. Good luck, sweetheart."

"Fasten seat belts, please, fifteen-minutes to touchdown," Vicki announced. "John, it looks like there is an empty building down there. It could have been used for training or drug running or both. I'll taxi up to it."

"You stay with the airplane, Vicki. If we don't come out, get the hell out of here."

Vicki rolled to a stop. John and Kim went back to be with the confused passengers.

"I was told there was a large airfield in Atlantic City." The patient's brother said.

"Ask him his name, Kim."

The patient opened his mouth to answer, and John held his Colt 45 in the patient's mouth.

"Now, tell them what we discussed."

John moved the Colt 45 to point to the Vietnamese backs and said, "Get off this airplane and go into that shed."

The shed was a galvanized steel building that had seen better days. The one big door was missing, and there were no windows.

"We need more light, Kim, see if there's a lantern or something."

"I found one John, and it's got enough kerosene to last a while. I smell gasoline."

"It's coming from that barrel by the door. Set the lantern on the one next to it, and let's kick some ass."

Both of the Cong had some martial arts training, but neither had any boxing experience. Kim surprised her opponent with a kick in the face, knocking him back against the barrel of gasoline, almost tipping it over. He bounced back, feigned a move left, and got in a good kick of his own.

"Just luck, you slant-eyed bastard. That is the last opportunity you get."

She looked him square in the eye and said in Vietnamese, "this is for what you did to my mother and sister," and put her size five, shoe point in his crotch with all her hate and weight behind it. "That's just a start."

She proceeded to kick, slap, slash, and a vicious heel to the knee, and you could hear the bones snap over the screaming of the Cong. In the process, the gasoline barrel was tipped over and was spilling into the arena.

John's opponent tried a kick, but John caught his leg and delivered a straight right to the mouth, drawing blood. Each time the Cong tried a move, he met a left or a right or sometimes a combination.

The Cong found a piece of pipe and rushed at John, swinging wildly. John ducked and dodged and grabbed the pipe away from the Cong, who just stood staring hatred.

"Have you ever heard of Babe Ruth?" he asked.

"Yes, why?"

"They tell me that you could tell by the sound of the bat if it was a homer or not. John swung from the left side of the plate, "like this," in the manner of the Bambino. He swung again at the thigh of his opponent, breaking the bone. The Cong fell, screaming with pain next to his buddy into the ever-deepening pool of gasoline.

"How do you feel, Honey?" he asked Kim. "I feel like I can let go of the horrible past, and enjoy a bright future without thinking of these two. How about You?"

"I got even for all those MIAs they deny and the torture they went through. Let's leave this garbage for the rats or whatever. I don't want to touch them. Let's go home and retire and do some dancing."

"That sounds wonderful to me."

"Miss Vicki, take us home, please."

Vicki locked the left brake to turn the jet around, and as the plane spun around, the backwash blew the lantern off the barrel it was sitting on, spilling lighted kerosene into the pool of gasoline.

"What happened in there?" Vicki asked. "Did you kill them?"

"No. One has a broken knee. The other has a broken femur. It will be a long recoveringtime. Neither one will be dancing for a while."

When Vicki reversed direction to take off, they saw the shed totally involved in flame. As they flew over the shed, it exploded.

"They're burned toa crisp, by now," John said.

"I hope they suffered and had time to think about what they had done before they died," Kim added.

"If we don't refuel damn soon, I'll be a glider pilot," Vicki said.

"Go on into Philly, if we can't make it to Atlantic City," John ordered.

Chapter 53

We are going to Monopoly City, and check the Board Walk. We could get a load of JP4 and leave or take the rest of the day off and motel."

"I want a shower," Kim said.

"Garden State Air Park, here we come," Vicki giggled. -- - -"Full service, please," she asked the service manager. "We will be leaving in the morning, but I would like it ready in thirty minutes or less."

"Why the hurry, if you're not leaving 'til morning?"

"We are a Medivac Aircraft, and must be ready to leave on a moment's notice. A life may be in jeopardy, and every second counts. I don't need to explain anything to you. Just do what I ask, please."

"I don't take orders from a black, and especially a black bitch."

"Miss Vicki, ma'am, please," John said. "You did not s'plain to him like he could understand. Do you mind if I try?"

"Go ahead and do your best."

John reached behind his back and produced his 45, and he stuck it in the attendant's mouth.

"Listen, you impotent piece of slime. This lady asked you nicely that you do your job, and you call her a black bitch. We have been in the air all day. My wife and I just fought for our lives, and we are tired. You will apologize to Miss Victoria Parks. She has taken enough guff from red necks like you to last two lifetimes. I will call the police, and your boss after this aircraft is serviced."

The police arrived, and John handed his gun to the officer.

"I need to talk off the record to your police chief, or whoever is in charge of the counterfeit case, I've heard rumors about."

The officer saw Angel Six and said, "That would be Lt. Jim Walker. I'll get him for you."

A country Cadillac, with training wheels and a shell, screeched to a stop. A man in his mid-40's wearing muddy boots and bibbers got out.

"I'm Carl Hall. This is my business. What is the problem?

"Ask your service manager, Mr. Hall."

"Dad, that guy stuck a gun in my mouth, and ordered me to service their damn plane immediately."

"Is that right? You stuck a gun in my son's mouth?"

"Yes, I did, sir. Tell your dad why I did it."

"I don't know why."

"You have a chance, to tell the truth. I suggest you do just that," Carl said.

"Let's hear your side, sir."

Bill told the whole story. Carl listened and turned to his son.

"Is that the way it happened?"

"No. He's a damn liar, Dad."

Carl slapped his son across the mouth.

"He has nothing to gain by lying. Clear out your locker. Here is fifty bucks and a quarter; the quarter you can use to call a friend, if you have any. The fifty bucks you can do with what you want. Don't call home or come home until you've gotten your act together. I'm sorry this happened, sir. Is everything okay now?

"I would like your personnel to double-check the plane."

"Good idea. Bobby! Run a check on this airplane and check everything. Don't run a tab, they've already paid. I've got to get back to my farm. My kid thinks it's undignified to shovel dirt and manure, but that's what keeps me from going insane."

"You wanted to talk to me off the record?" Lt. Walker asked.

"Yes, sir. You can close the books on the counterfeit money. We picked up the manufacturers in LA. Bill went on to explain what he and Kim had gone through, and when the perpetrators of that massacre turned out to be the big cog in the counterfeit ring, Kim and I lost it. There is an abandoned airstrip northwest of the city. When we last saw them, they were alive. The building caught fire and exploded with them in it. They probably burned to a crisp.

"If what you say is true, and I have no reason to doubt you, I'd say justice is served. You people from Angel Flight are tough. I"ll mark the case closed."

They checked into the Heath Plaza. Mr. Burkehart saw the Angel Logo, he offered the Watkins suite.

"The Watkins are not here, and Miss Parks, there is a lovely large room just down the hall. It is on the house, of course. Mr. Heath says Angel Flight crews are our guests."

"Let'sfreshen up before dinner," Vicki suggested.

"How about we order a pizza and a six-pack and eat in our suite," John said. "We'll do clean-uplater and relax."

"That's a good plan. I'll wash my hands and be over."

"I can't remember when a pizza and beer tasted so good," Vicki commented. "I'm going to try my luck in one of the casinos. See you in the morning."

Chapter 54

"We had a nice evening," John said.

"Let's get dressed and meet Vicki for breakfast and go home," Kim said.

Vicki had finished eating and was waiting for the Schumanns.

"I won $500 playing blackjack last night." She said. "Did you have any luck?"

"Yes. Kim answered.

"How much did you win?

"We weren't gambling," John answered.

"We need a big breakfast this morning," he said to the server. "I' ll have a western omelet with extra onions, wheat toast, toasted not just dried out, orange juice, home fries, coffee, add a large glass of cold milk. I'd like my coffee now, please."

"That sounds good to me." Kim said, "but hold the extra onions and milk. I'd like my coffee now, also, please."

"Vicki," John said. "I'm going to retire when we get back to The Dalles.You might as well get used to running first seat now. You are in command from this moment on. You have earned it, and morethan able. You are as good or better than any pilot I've ever seen. You seem to have a natural instinct for flying."

Maybe it's because all us blacks have natural rhythm." She laughed. "Myfirst command is for you two to enjoy your retirement. The second order is to have a leisurely breakfast, then we'll 'aviate.' John, you file the flight plan and get a weather report. I'll make the walk-around. Kim, you're a passenger."

"I'll get coffee, sweets, and sodas, and we won't have tostop anywhere along the way," Kim answered. "I want to get home. I have a wedding to plan. We are going tohave a real wedding on the Fourth of July. I picked that date so John can remember it. His days of independence are over."

The six-plus hour flight to The Dalles was uneventful. Theytouched down shortly after noon PST.

Mike welcomed them home and thought a celebration of some kind was in order.

"Susan is always stuck with the party," Kim said. "I think we should have it at Mary's Supper Club, and Susan can relax and enjoy the party."

"Let's have Mary cater the whole thing and have it at the ranch. The kids can play, the women can gossip, and the men can stand around and BS," Mike said. "I'llset it up for Sunday afternoon. We'll eat about five. We will have a business meeting at two. There are some adjustments to be made, and everybody gets a chance to voice their opinion."

"Welcome home, everybody."

"Kim and John went to Hawk's office. They told him what had happened to the two Viet Cong.

"When we last saw them, they were alive and screaming in pain. We taxied to the other end of the runway, and when we turned around to takeoff, the building was in flames and exploded."

"I can't officially condone what you did."Hawk said. "they got what they deserved, and there were no witnesses."

Mary's workers had the tables and chairs all set up.

"The food will be here at four forty-five and be ready to serve atfive; the lead man for the set-up crew informed all. "There's coffee, ice tea, soda, milk, and water in the coolers and thermoses."

Mike called the meeting to order at twop.m.

"We have had a very successful year again. Thanks for your hard work and dedication. John Schumann and his wife, Kim, are retiring. This will mean Miss Parks will be the Command Pilot of Angel Six. She has asked Gerry Murdock to be her Medic.I would like you all to welcome Joseph Carter. He is full blood Apache. Joseph, please come up here and tell us a little bit about yourself."

"I adopted the Carter name from the family that raised me after my parents died of pneumonia. I am directly related to Cochise and Geronimo, and I did not go to college. I earned myliving unloading trucks. One day a paleface told me that I was in his territory and to get out or he was going to whip my redskin butt. He was a little taller than me and outweighed me by about 25 pounds. You do not threaten an Apache, especially this one. It was a relatively long fight, but I was in better condition than him. He got tired, and I put him to sleep.The fight drew a lot of attention, and a local fight promoter, Ray Clark, said he could get me some fights and make more money than I was making. I guess it was my heritage caused me to fight. I was a contender, and getting better matches and bigger purses. We were flying home from amatch when the pilot came back to congratulate me and thank me for winning. He had won a good-sized bet. He invited me to go intothe cockpit and observe. I asked himhow much he made as a pilot. I don't need to tell you what he said. I was and still amsingle, and my culture teaches to save, save, save. I kept my money. My next bout was with an older fighter trying to make a comeback. He dropped his guard in the fifth round, and I gave him a solid right to the jaw. He dropped like a rock, andhe never woke up. That was my last fight. I had heard about Cal Wero Tech, checked it out, and enrolled. I am a qualified multi-jet airplane pilot, driver, as you folks say. I have no commercial experience. I thank Mr. Murphy for giving me an opportunity, and Miss Parks for agreeing to put up with me. Thank you.

"He will fly as copilot on Angel Six. We have a complete casual crew who will relieve you once each month for a week of R & R. You will notice a ten percent increase in your checks beginning with this week's paycheck. This is possible only because of your PR.

"Now, I'm going to ask our good friend, who started this whole thing, and his granddaughter, who is the blonde Angel Logo, Mr. Walter Henderson and Missy, to say a few words."

"Thank you, Mike. Missy prefers to be called by her given name. She said Missy is a child's name, and she is old enough to be called

Michelle. It seems like only yesterday when Mike stepped upto the plate and hit one that is still going. It is through your PR, hard-work, dedication, and courtesy and caring for those we transport, that we have been successful. I should correct myself and say you have been successful. I have had such fun shaking money from multi-millionaires. Once they kick in a bundle, andget the joyful feeling that comes when you help someone, they get addicted to giving, and push their cronies to sweeten the pot. You will be the guest of most of the hotel and motel chains. Show your Angel Flight ID cards. Please do not abuse the privilege. Michele, would you like to say something?"

"Thank you, Mike, for being MY Angel!"

"I would like to say one more thing," Walt stated. "Mike, I forgive you for stealing the most beautiful and capable secretary anyone ever had. Margaret and I love you two as though you were our own."

"Before I close his meeting," Mike said. "Please, take a look at the 'Fleet of Angels' in front of your headquarters. It will make your heart swell with pride. Tomorrow at nine-thirty, a photographer will be here to take a picture of each crew standing in front of their aircraft, dressed in your uniforms. We will publish a calendar next year, and you will be in it with a short bio on each of you. A composite photo will be sent to you, and one will hang over my desk. If there are no questions, this meeting is adjourned."

It was like a family reunion, house warming, birthday party, Christmas, and Thanksgiving all rolled into one. Bear Hawk and Joseph talked about their heritage. Blacky was conversing with Senora Romaine in Spanish. Except for Susan, Blacky was the only person she could talk to in her native language. She spoke English, but it was hard for her, so she and Blacky shut the rest of the world out and talked. He told her about himself and his drug days. Her eyes welled with tears, as she told him about her son and what drugs had done to him

"He was my son, and I loved him, but if he or his friends had ever hurt Carlos or Maria or Susan, I would have killed them without any remorse. I would ask God for forgiveness and go on with my life."

Walt, Margaret, Winnie, and Murph were renewing an old fast friendship. Julia and Howard, Heather, and her husband mingled with the crowd.

Mike sought out Susan. "Just think a little over six years ago, Ihad only a mom and pop and Aggie. Look at the size of our family now. They are not an extended family, they are family."

Ronni and Bill were talking with John and Kim.

"Now that you have retired, what are your plans?" Bill asked.

"First off, we are going to have an official wedding," John answered. "We are legally married, but Kim wants a wedding on the Fourth of July. So be it!"

"Ronni and Kim looked at each other and at the same moment said, "A double wedding!"

The girls went off to tell Susan. She excused herself and ran to the PA.

Could I have everyone's attention, please, this is anexciting announcement. On the Fourth of July, there will be a double wedding here. John and Kim are already legally married, but Kim wants a real wedding. We are going to give her one. Bill Watkins and Veronica Lane are also getting married. You are all invited. On the day we celebrate the anniversary of our nation, Independence Day, we are going to witness two men giving up their's."

The next days were busy with wedding plans. Mike and John and Bill were wearingtheir dress uniforms. Winnie was helping Kim and Ronni decide on dresses, Neither of them even considered, white. They bothwanted full-length dresses, and perfect color was the sticking point. Winnie had always wanted a daughter and help her plan her wedding. "Now, I've got two,"she said.

The following days and weeks were spent finding the right material and patterns for the wedding dresses. Ronni chose soft, sage green, in soft silk, a trumpet style skirt designed to accentuate her lithesome full figure, and graceful movements. Bare shoulders with double spaghetti straps,form-fitted and flared from floor to knees, flowing gracefully in motion.

Kim picked adusty rose, also in soft silk for the warmer weather. An empire-style shows off a petit silhouette. The skirt is gathered to the bodice, floor-length falling generously and gracefully to the floor. The bodice has collected ruffles around the complete top, and spaghetti straps over the shoulders allow the ruffles to dropoff the shoulders, butbe held tolerable by the spaghetti straps.

"I've been wanting to make my daughter's wedding dress for years," Winnie insisted. 'and now that I have the chance, I am going to do it." There is no debate on the issue."

The men tried on their 'dress' uniforms and discovered they had to shed a few pounds before the uniforms would fit comfortably. They scheduled a six-thirty a.m. workout at the YMCA every Monday, Wednesday, and Friday.

Hawk, hearing about it, joined the group. "I think I'll insist that my entire department get in shape." He said. "I have officers that can hardly get out of their cruisers, and to run is impossible. I want them to get in shape for their own health and In the interest of public safety or be relieved of their duties. I can make a case for the decision by quoting the increasing costs to the taxpayer for health insurance and present it to the City Council. We can bring the wives on board by monitoring the diets. We can really shape up!I will ask the cafes to ask the officer if he or she really needs that donut or other high-calorie snack. The entire community can become involved, and we may get the civilians aware of their personal weight problems. We have too many big-assed people. Let's start a campaign to reduce, 'pun intended' the number.

"Angel Flight will foot the bill for the use of the "Y" for those who don't have the means," Mike spoke up. "I'm sure when the word gets around, others will join in. It is tax-deductible."

"We have a month to get ready for the big day," Susan announced at breakfast, andthere is no reason for any mistakes. We'll shoulder our tasks as follows: I will take care of the festivities and food;invitations will be Ronni, and Kim's job. Bear will officiate. Dorris, Faun, and Senora Romaine will take care of the decorations. Have I forgotten anything?"

"I can't think of anything," Mike responded. "You are the detail-oriented part of the family."

Mr. Bubb ordered a full side of Angus beef from the Bodie Ranch for a pit bar-b-que. Joseph and Blacky dug a pit for cooking the beef. They laid up dry hardwood for an enormous fire, and added large rocks to heat. The rocks would absorb the heat from the fire,and would be the source of heat for the actual cooking process. Everything was coming together as planned.

Frankie called,and Red took Ronni to meet him in Portland. On the way back to The Dalles, she asked him to walk her down the aisle.

"I would be most honored to," he sobbed. " Iain't never had nobody who gave a damn about FrankieMedly, until you guys showed up."

"We've arrangedfor you to stay at the ranch for as long as you like. Our boss, Mike Murphy, has built a few three-room lodges for our flight crews to get R & R. They have a bedroom, kitchen, living room, and bath with a whirlpool and shower. Everything is furnished except for groceries and personal items. If you need groceries, you call Bub's grocery store, and he will deliver it to you."

"I may not ever want to leave."

"That's fine, withus. After all, you are family."

Frankie was introduced to everyone. He was greeted with handshakes from the men and hugs and kisses from the women. "Frankie!" Mike said. "Welcome home."

"There are not enough words in my vocabulary to tell you just how I feel. I ain't had a home since I was five-years-old. I was moved from one place to another until I got sick of not having my own nail to hang my hat on. I went to Jersey and found a job washing dishes. It didn't pay much, but with that and learning how to pickpockets, I finally had my own nail. I graduated from the school of hard knocks and experience and worked for the mob as a messenger or whatever they needed. I packed iron and never pulled the trigger until that night you busted Widra. They were going to hurt Ronni, and I would have been responsible. I was told that if she even got a run in her stockings, a hangnail or anything else that 'Moose,' Bill Watkins, wouldtear down my wheelhouse. I shot that guy n self-defense. If I could find a job here,I want to stay, but Frankie always pays his own way. I don't accept handouts. I will try most anything legal that I can handle. It's so good to be finally at home." Then the dam burst and tears ran down everyone's face.

"We need ahead of security," Mike said. "When you have been released by your doctor, the job is yours if you are interested. We can discuss pay later."

"I'll take it, just pay me enough to get by," Frankie answered, extending his hand.

"You've just signed a contract," Mike said. "You will be paid above whatever the scale is for a person in your position, plus benefits. We've talked long enough. Frankie has had a long day, and I"nm hungry. Let's go to Mary's Restaurant and Supper Club. I'm buying."

The following days passed uneventfully. Frankie checked in with Hawk and registered the serial number and a spent cartridge of his gun as did everyone else. Many people, especially members of NRA, objected to it, but Hawk says," Get the rule on the ballot and let the voters decide. I will abide by the decision, but until then, you will register your sidearms."

CHAPTER 55

July Fourth, dawned bright and fresh, promising an ideal day for the weddings. Bear and the Tribal Council had secretly hired a company from Salem to set up a massive fireworks display, timed to go off as Bear unites the couples. The side of beef was ready to carve. Joseph had made some southwestern flavored sauce for basting the beef. Spicy,butnot toohot.

Susan cut some roses from Aggie's prize rose bush, and fashioned a simple corsage for the brides. "After all, were it not for her, none of this would have happened,she stated. "Agnes, we know you are in the arms of Jesus looking over us and are at last at peace. Thank you for the roses."

Blacky brought his keyboard, some of Hawk's officers brought theirinstruments and soon had a jam session going. The festivities started at noon with a prayer of thanks in Shoshone by Bear while signing it in native sign language. At the end of the prayer, Mary sang, 'Ave Maria' in a beautiful clear alto voice. Senora Romane had been giving her singing lessons unbeknown by anyone. Silence fell over the gathering as they contemplated in their own hearts and minds what they had just witnessed. In unison, they applauded and cheered.

The feasting was over,and time for the ceremony was at hand. Mount Hood was even more beautiful than usual due toa light snowfall last night. A beautiful backdrop.

Blacky and his group accompanied Senora Romaine as she sang in her native Spanishtongue, 'There's a Place For Us.'

They jammed softly and slowly while Frankie walked down the aisle with Ronni, and Mike senior walked with Kim. Both men kissed the brides and took their seats. Bear was officiating, and Vicki and Gerry standing in the rear, were quietly repeating the vows while holding hands. Just as the couples were exchanging kisses, the 'Blue Angels' did aflyover with their trademark fountain of colored smoke, and the fireworks display began!!

"I would say you two couples got a bang-up start on your marriage,"Hawk said. "When can I have my "Chief of Detectives on the job Mrs. Watkins?"

"This is Wednesday, We don't need a long honeymoon. Monday. Did you just say, 'Chief of Detectives'?"

"Yes, I did. I've been looking for someone to take that job off of me, and Bill is an outstanding Detective. I'm offering it to himbecause he is qualified and the best man for the job. A pay raise is included. I'll expect you Monday morning at seven-thirty a.m. rested and ready. Congratulations, and good night."

Lucy and Willie stayed at the ranch to give Bill and Ronni privacy. Kim and John went home. Vicki and Gerry had rented a lodge from Mike.

Kim cuddled next to John, and he realized she was nude. No bride ever had a more beautiful and exciting wedding. I have been anticipating this night since we first set the date. What follows is best left to the readers' imagination.

Gerry and Vicki were lying in bed in their quiet lodge. Gerry rolled over and kissed Vicki sensuously on the lips. Much to his surprise, she returned the kiss.

"I love you, Victoria Parks." He said. "I want to spend the rest of my life with you."

"I love you, Gerry, What the hell is your last name?" she laughed.

"Gilmore It's Gerald Paul Gilmore. It is funny that it never seemed to come up."

Gerald Paul Gilmore. I love you I wasn't sure what love is, but I'm sure I found what Bill and Ronni and Johnand Kim, and all the others we know have found.

The warm pine-scented July breeze wafted softly over the loving couple. The cougar screamed, the wolf howled, the owl hooted, and the Columbia River gurgled and splashed on its way to the Pacific, and under the moonlight, Mount Hood stood watch.

Chapter 56

The festivities and reverence of yesterday's celebration of adouble wedding ceremony will be a memory treasured by all the folks in this close-knit community. A good business yearfor Angel Flight Services tosustain operations on donations only as well as Murphy Electric Contractors business was in the black. These events were indeed, celebrated in good faith.The daily routine of work, daily chores, and duties necessary to make the town friendly and peaceful must resume.

Angel Flight Headquarters was getting an alert call. Heather heard, "This is Ogden Police calling. There has been a train derailment east of here and west of Cheyenne, and there are two victims. We are transporting them to Ogden airport. They will be admitted to Nebraska Med Center at Omaha for hospitalization. We need immediate Angel Flight services to pick up the awaiting victims at Hinckley Airport."

Heather responded, "Yes, I will call for dispatch immediately!Good-bye."She buzzed Mike's office phone and informed him of the situation.

Mike immediately called Vicki and gave her the dispatch orders and for her to get her crew into Angel Six as soon as possible for takeoff to Hinckley Airport.

This would be Joseph Carter's first assignment as an Angel Flight crew member!He was trained and eager to be active in a mercy flight.

Vicki said, "Joseph,you make the walk-around check, and I will file the flight plan and get the weather report.Angel Flight Six to Air Contol, we are ready for departure instructions."

Gerry was checking his supplies and making decisions that would beneeded for two victims.

The Gulf Stream rose upward into a clear blue sky and white clouds of heavenly array.

Vickie said, "Well, Mr. Joseph Carter, welcome aboard. I know you will have a proud and rewarding feeling when we have completed this journey."

"Thank you, Vicki. I am already feeling the anticipation of being a part of helping these people. Do you know any of the facts about the event?"

"No. Gerry, are you in control back there? I will check in now with Hinckley and ask if there is anything they can tell us.

Vicki keyed the radio to Hinckley channel.

"Hinckley Air Control Tower. Come in."

"This is "Angel Flight Six.Just took off from The Dalles, we are coming for the two victims of the railroad wreck between Ogden and Cheyenne. Can you give us any facts about it? Over."

"Hinckley Control Tower to Air Flight Six. The freight train was loaded with hundreds of containersenroute toPhiladelphia. It somehow ran off the rails androlled over. Lots of damage to the train but so far only two serious injuries.One life-threatening. Over."

"Thanks. Our ETA istwo hours from Dalles. We've been in the air for about 40 minutes.I will call for approach instructions later. Over and out."

The crew engaged inproductive and friendly shop talk and general conversation until it was time to call in for landing directions from Hinckley Control Tower.

Vicki keyed to Hinckley, "Control Tower, this is Angel Flight Six requesting landing instructions. Over."

"Hinckley Control Tower to Angel Flight Six. Cleared to land on runway 39. Ambulance is on the left, and your takeoff to Eppley Airfield atOmaha is scheduled on Emergency status to depart, immediatelyas soon as victims are secured onboard Angel Flight Six plane."

Gerry deplaned and went to the ambulance to evaluate the procedure to transfer the severely injured pair to Angel Flight Six gurneys. "These guys are in bad shape," he said to Vicki and Joseph. We will have to exercise extreme care, especially in take-off and landing for their physical comfort, or to avoid further injury to them." He talked to the medics, "What is the prognosis we can expect,and what medications are already administered?"

The Ogden Medical Team responded, "Both are heavily sedated and should stayunder during the transfer to the ambulance at Omaha. The older of the two is sustaining severe internal damage. His vitals are not stable. The younger is, of course, stronger, and his injuries are not life-threatening. God speed."

The three well-trained crew members were silent while doing their vigilance and care to their patients for most of the trip. Yes, silent to pray, in their own way, for the safety and recovery of the victims.

Vicki keyed to Eppley Air Control at Omaha.

"Eppley Contol Tower, come in."

"This is Angel Flight Six from Hinckley Utah with two male medical emergencies of the train derailment east of Ogden. Please have the Nebraska Health Med Center ambulance parked to beclose to the assigned runway and plane exit. These victims are suffering severe injuries and will need immediate attention. Over."

"Eppley Control Tower to Angel Flight Six. All alerts and preparation of the Nebraska HealthMedical team are in order on runway 62. Prepare for landing on runway 62 in 5 minutes. Over and out."

Vicki landed the plane perfectly,and the success code of electric thrill was felt by the crew at this crucial need for asmoooooth landing. The transfer of victims to the ambulance went without incidence.

Vicki, Joseph, and Gerry approached the hangar servicemen and asked them to refuel the plane to prepare it for the return flight to The Dalles in a day or two.

The crew returned to their seats in the cockpit, andfollowedthe hangar servicemen's direction to their designated parking area for refueling operation.

CHAPTER 57

They took a cab to Nebraska Medical Center hospital as was the policy of all medical flight service to follow up on the victims until they are secure in the care of loved ones or a protective source before the crew and Angel Flight end their services for that case.

Vicki said, "We will be here a couple of days until we are sure the victims are stable in a recovery prognosis. Driver, would you take us to a reputable motel, please?'

The driver said, "The DoubleTree is in a good location, if you might want to tour our city."

"That will be okay with us. We are a bit tired and need to rest. Thank you."

They walked to the check-in desk in their flight apparel and were greeted with mid-western hospitality plus!The news of their mercy flight had preceded them by a few minutes, and the welcome they received reflected the admiration for Angel Flight quite vocally by the onlookers in the lobby!

Joseph said, "This is an historic part of my folklore. Native American population here even now is quite substantial, I believe. We mayfindan interesting museum, activity, or landmark to explore while we are here. Does that sound ok with you guys?"

"Sure," Gerry said. "I have heard there are steak houses with superb tasting steaks, cooked to one's preference, and delicious. I'm sure we could plan one evening's meal for such a treat!"

"Great," said Vicki. "I'll see what I can come up with for one more adventure in this town that's almost smack in the middle of the nation." Let's not wear our uniforms tomorrow, we are tourists tomorrow.

They went to their rooms,Gerry and Vicki, where they left off after the celebration at Mike's Ranch, and Joseph, a competent and independent guy.They were all satisfied with a day's work well-done, they could relax and have a restful night's sleep.

They all awoke early and met in the refreshment room for a complete complimentary breakfast by DoubleTree food services.

Vicki said, " I have found The Bob Kerry Pedestrian Bridge to visit. The description points out that it crosses the Missouri River over to the State of Iowa. Does that sound okay for you guys?"

"Sure, Joseph and Gerry agreed. We need to call a taxi to take us there, right? We can have Double Tree call for us."

They began the walk and were wide-eyed to see the Missouri River was such an expanse of muddy water. They continued and stopped to read the many historical plaques along the way.

Joseph exclaimed, "Look here. There are some stories of my people's time in this very location. That makes me very proud. Every word is familiar to me as I remember,my grandparents told me when I was very young."

Gerry had gone a bit farther ahead of Vicki and Joseph and suddenly called back to them. "Hey! There is a boundary line painted right here underfoot, showing the Iowa and Nebraska territory. That is great! "

Vicki let it be known she was enjoying the view of the river banks and absorbing the written history of riverboats, the Morman Trail, the Union Pacific Railroad story, and President Lincoln's stay at the Dodge House in Council Bluffs, Iowa.

Time passed quickly, and Vicki said, " I really enjoyed this visit, tomorrow we'll find another place to go. We must go to the hospital now to check on the victims of the train wreck.

Gerry said, "I'll call a taxi to take us to Nebraska Med Center."

CHAPTER 58

The trio identified themselves and was escortedto Doctor Ward, who administered to the victims."I'm so sorry to tell you the older gentleman had severe injuries to internal organs,and it was not possible to save him. He passed away two hours ago. We are encouraged by the younger man who seems to beremaining stable. We cannot find any severe internal injuries.He has gone through all the extensive tests and examinationswe know of, andthat fact almost assures us that if he is stable throughthe night,he will survive."

"Vicki thanked the doctor and asked, " Have you any word from the Union Pacific people or the authorities in Ogden as to the names of these men, where they lived or why they were on the freight train?".

"Yes. These men are of Asian descent, and there is reason to believe they areessential employees of one of thecontainer company's. I don't think the family members have been located. That is sure to come soon, and the victim's travel itinerary will be found and reveal vital information. How long will you folks be staying?

Vicki explained, "It is Angel Flight policy that we stay with victims when we transport them to hospitals with severe injuries or illness until they are securely under a responsible caregiver or arrangement to provide care and future care."

Dr. Ward hesitated but asked, "I am curious to know what financial arrangement is required under these circumstances. It seems the UPRR would be responsible at this point."

Vicki described the charitable aspects of Angel Flight business policy and that the finances for company operations rely on philanthropy practices of corporations, individuals of high income, and donations from groups and individuals. It has been several years since the beginning, and the money is always there. It is a good cause, and people do have charity in their hearts. The monetary giving aspect is genuinely a rational formula. Thank you, Dr. Ward. We will return tomorrow."

Joseph said, "it's a shame the old man didn't make it. I wonder if they are father and son? I am thankful to be working with you guys. The day has been pleasant, and the pedestrian bridge was a magnificent sight. Maybe we should find a fast food place and have a bite to eat before we call it a day – there should be one close by. Let's start walking."

"I see a Burger King sign just ahead," Gerry said.

They got closer and saw a mixed group of folks, obviously of different nationalities and arguing loudly and broadcasting a growing anger from the tone and actions they were showing.

Vicki keenly observed and said, "They have a racial dispute that probably will explode soon!"

Vicki and Joseph approached the big, hairy guy shouting profanities to the group and claiming someone had damaged his vehicle.

Joseph grabbed his arm and calmed the situation somewhat by saying, "Maybe I can help. What is all the anger about?"

The tough guy shouted, "What's it to you, you red-skinned bastard, and who are those two idiots with you?"

Someone in the crowd shouted, "He's just trying to start a racial riot over his jalopy that wouldn't startand grabbed us one by one and threatened to fight us with that chain you see on the ground!

Vicki was getting impatient, and Gerry was hanging back.

Joseph said, "let me take a look at your car, maybe it's a loose cable on your battery."

The tough guy took a swing at Joseph and picked up the chain and began flailing it into the crowd.

Joseph snapped into action, giving a powerfulright to the jaw of the brute. He fell to the ground, the chain landing across his face!

Meanwhile, Vicki had spoken to the group and told them,"I think the big guy is in trouble now! Someone call the police department, and we'll see if the cable is loose on the jalopy. Okay?"

The police came quickly and was satisfied. The thug was disturbing the peace, and they took him away.

A quick look under the hood of the jalopy, and sure enough, the cable was off of the battery, and no tampering was evident.

The crowd slowly dispersed, and all was quiet.

The Angel Flight threesomehad hamburgers and called a taxi to take them to DoubleTree.They talked about the incident and the day in general. They decided to wear their uniforms for tomorrow's tourist sights. Goodnight. See you in the morning."

Gerry looked at Vicki and said, "I can't realize you care for me.I love youand promise to always be there for you even though I cannot handle violence and crime. I sincerely believe, God works His wonders in mysterious ways."

They fell asleep in each other's arms.

CHAPTER 59

The crew arose on a rainy day in Omaha. They met in the breakfast room and enjoyed the continental breakfast once again.

"Good morning, they all said in unison!"

Gerry commented, "I think this would be a good evening to go to a steakhouse for a someNebraska raisedbeef. Do you agree?"

"Absolutely," said Vicki

"Sounds like aplan," agreed Joseph.

Dr, Ward greeted them at the Med Center and gave an update of the case."Union Pacific Railroad officials have data on the cause of the train wreck as well as the Asian container company and the status of the two gentlemen that were severely injured. I was the one who had the sorrowful task of telling them all of the death of the older man, but I was thankful that I could say the young man is recovering quite well."

Vicki spoke, "I am happy to hear that contact has been made, and the young man will recover. I will call Mike, our CEO at Angel Flight headquarters, and explain thesituationas it stands now."

Dr. Ward continued, " The men were on the train with their own container company to observe and see first hand how their containers were transported across the United States. Mr. Luau Chin was President of Chin and Chan Container Company of China. Mr. Luiu Chin was the Vice President, and they were father and son. The company is well established in China and has beenshipping to the U.S. for several years.

There were, of course, other container companies involved in the wreck, and the many settlements will be complicated and under legal scrutiny. I understand the Angel Flight policy has no billing or charges for services provided to anyone, wealthy or not. It has certainly been a privilege to meet you and know of your exceptional plan in the philanthropic arena and the opportunitiesit affords to all those inclined to share in charity programs.The young man will be able to talk to you tomorrow. Thank you for coming."

"I will call Mike and give him the story," said Vicki. "You guys search for a point of interest to visit this afternoon."

Chapter 60

"Hello, Heather, this is Vicki. Is Mike there? I have a story to tell."

"Yes, here's Mike."

"Hi, Mike. We've had a lot going on and will tell you the highlights now and file a formal report when I get back to the office. The two injured men were severely injured. They were Chinese father and son, and sadly the father did not survive, but the doctor tells me the son should be able to talk to us tomorrow. His recovery is promising. They are owners of one of the container companies that were on the freight train that ran off the rails and had a violent wreck. Nothing has been said yet about the cause of the train leaving the track. I suppose it will take a long term investigation to solve that problem. We are finding interesting things to see and do in Omaha. We will tell those stories when we get home. Say 'hello' to everyone back there. I think we will head home tomorrow."

"Okay, thanks for the update, Vicki. Bye for now."

"See you soon, Mike. Bye."

"Hey, guys! Did you find somewhere for us to visit?"

"Yes," Gerry said. "The Union Pacific Railroad Headquarters isjust downtown. The Union Pacific Railroad Museum is across the river in Council Bluffs, Iowa. I think it would be fun to have lunch in Council Bluffs, visit the UP Museum, then come back to UP Headquarters in Omaha and finish our stay here with a good steak. We can ask the taxi driver what steakhouse he likes. Okay?

Vicki said, " Sounds like a plan to me, how about you, Joseph?"

Joseph said, "Sure, sounds good to me."

Vicki called the taxi service, and they were soon looking at the Missouri River again on their way to Duncan's Café on Main Street in Council Bluffs, Iowa.

"Welcome, here is a table for you. Here is our menu, I'll be back in a moment."

The Angel Flight trio was comfortable and viewing the menu with interest. They were also aware that the patrons in the café were unusually attracted to the attractive three who were stunning in their Angel Flight uniforms.

They all ordered soup and salad, keeping in mind the steak dinner they will have later. The helpful and attractive waitress returned promptly with their orders.She asked them, "what service are your uniforms?"

Vicki explained," I am the pilot of a Gulf-Stream plane named Angel Flight Six. Our headquarters is in The Dalles, Oregon. We transport victims of extreme urgency to a hospital having state of the art technology and personnel."

The crowd was all attentive, and the waitress complimented them. What brought you here?" she asked.

Gerry continued Vicki's explanation," I am the Medic on this mission. Two men were injured,and we transported them to Nebraska Med Centeryesterday with life or death injuries. We have the planes equipped as complete Medivac units to provide comprehensive hospital care for injured or severely ill patients.

Joseph said, " I am the copilot. We were dispatched to a tragic train wreck east of Ogden. The train went off the track and tipped over. It was a violent crash, and two Asian men were severely injured. Those are the men being cared for at Nebraska Med Center.

Gerry asked her about the UP Museum. She directed them; it's walking distance from here,just straight west to South 6th street, a couple of blocks. It's an old library building with a flight of stairs to the main entrance and, of course, UP Museum sign on the building. It will be well worth your time to visit. We appreciate your mission and are glad to know you are out there. Thank you for telling us your story, and we do hope the injured men recover."

"You are very welcome. We do like to talk about Angel Flight Sevices to people we meet in our travels."

They all highly rated their lunch and said their good-byes.The brief conversation about the train wreck, Angel Flight services,and the medical missionheld the employees and diners in great attention. Goodbyes were many, and the trio went out the door,walking toward the old library building!

The waitress called to them. "Just a minute, folks. When we heard of the generosity of your Angel Flight Service company, we hurriedly passed the hat for donations for you. Please accept this envelope for you to remember your visit with us. Thank you for what you do, and God keep you safe on your flight home."

"Thank you. We will remember you."

They entered the old building and, at first glanceinside, were enamored by the historical and visual reality of the place.They were amazed by the exhibits showing actual furniture of the passenger trains and dining room facilities, even an engine cab set up to actually be a realistic experience of engineering the train as it goes down the track. Videos of natural fields, mountains, forests, depots, and towns go by as you take the simple controls of the train's levers, handles, cords etc. Many posters and signs displayed the years of events and statues of Abraham Lincoln, and General Dodge and other scenes were perfect in predicting the activities of the era.

Vicki said," wasn't that amazing? "

"Yes," said Gerry. "I'm glad we took the opportunity to visit."

Joseph said, "I will remember this visit forever. It was wonderful!"

It was time to leave this excellent museum and go to Omaha and the Union Pacific Railroad headquarters building.

Gerry called the taxi, and again they crossed the muddy Missouri River and stepped out of the cab facing a vast steel and glass building.

"WOW!" Said Gerry.

" How beautiful," said Vicki.

Joseph just stared in awe!

Inside they studied the timeline of the Union Pacific from 1862 when the new charter was signed by Abraham Lincoln,and every two to four years, some major event, purchase, addition, invention, celebration,and other historical events happened until 2012, the last on the list. This was the 150th anniversaryof the Union Pacific Railroad.

Gerry called his buddies attention to a statement under the picture of the magnificent steel and glass structure that stated this building was the largest singlecorporate office building in the State of Nebraska.

Joseph stated, "Today has been most educational and enjoyable despite the rain! I can't wait to order that steak. Do you think we should call our taxi and find a good steakhouse before it gets any later?"

"By all means," Vicki said.

Vicki asked the driver, "We are in Omaha for the first time and hear the steakhouses have earned thelabel for the most delicious steaks anywhere, and theyare cooked to an individual's own choice, and the taste is incomparable to any other meat. Is this right?"

"That's right." The driver said.

"OK, We want you to take us to the steakhouse you think is the best in the city. We are going to have a Nebraska steak on our last night here."

The driver took them to Angelo's.

The steaks were as delicious as anticipated,and the time went by quickly as they oohed and aahed over the excellent meal. It was a rather noisy corner with the conversation of the day's experiences and visits and expressed pleasure.One of the other guests in the restaurant began to take an interest and asked what brought them to Omaha. Angel Flight crews are always ready to advertise their mission. When an opportunity like this comes around,they are happy to keep the conversation going. This evening developed into an unforgettable happening. Everyone was friendly and delighted at thishappening!

Someone said, "I hate to be a party pooper, but I have to get up early to go to work tomorrow. I have enjoyed this evening,and it will remain in my memory for a long time. Thank you and goodnight, friends."

Joseph called the cab, and soon they were in their rooms and PJ's and sleeping peacefully.

Chapter 61

The skies were clear this morning.

"Good morning all," Vicki said.

"Good morning, Vicki," Joseph said. "Yesterday was a good day. It is always good to return home too."

Gerry was having coffee and looking adoringly at Vicki.

Will we all go to the hospital, or shall I go to Eppley and check Angel Flight Six for takeoff later?"

Vicki said, "To keep our policy of staying with the victim until protection is secure, we must all go. I am eager to find ifLuiu is out of danger and has been in touch with any family members."

"Gerry, please call our taxi, and I'll call the hospital."

"Dr. Ward? This is Vicki Parks calling for the status of Luiu Chin."

"Yes, Miss Parks. Mr. Chin is recovering quickly. He had a restful night and will be able to talk to you today."

"Thank you, doctor. We will be there shortly."

Joseph said, "I am so grateful to be a part of the Angel Flight fleet and be accepted by the folks in The Dalles and to be a crew member with the two of you. I am counting my blessings. I hope we find Mr. Chin in good spirits today.

Gerry said, "It's too bad his father did not survive; such a tragedy to happen when they are such a long way from home and family.

"Yes," Vicki said, "The doctor was pleased with his recovery so far. I'm sure he will give us his ok to question Luiu. We need to complete the data for this mission.Oh, here we are!"

"Hello, Dr. Ward," Vicki reached to shake his hand.

"Yes. I believe I remember Gerry and Joseph, is that right?"

"That's right, doctor." Gerry and Joseph responded almost at the same time.

"Here is our patient, Mr. Luiu Chin, Vice President of Chin and Chang Container Company of Hong Kong, China. Mr. Chin, Luiu, he wants us to call him, meet your Angel Flight crew that transported you and your dear,departed Father to our hospital just three days ago. This is Vicki, the pilot, Joseph, the co-pilot, and Gerry the Medic."

Luiu responded in almost perfect English, "I am happy to meet you all.I want to know everything about your business of mercy flights. I amvery impressedwith what the people here have been telling me about this terrible train wreck we had."

Vicki said, "Thank you, Luiu. We are glad to see you are recovering quickly and so sorry your father did not survive.Joseph and I piloted the plane, and Gerry took medical care of you and your father. It was a massive wreck, and the Union Pacific will have a long and challenging job investigating the cause of the derailment and the legal issues of you and your father's injuries.We wish you well!"

"I want to know about the expenses involved in this extra-ordinary business of mercy flights. Will you explain the procedure to me, please?"

Angel Flight Services was founded six years ago when Mike returned home as an ex-Navy Pilot. Mike Murphy and Mike Murphy, Sr. formed a partnership with the concept of providingurgent medical emergency transports of victims to hospitals equipped to treat life-threatening injuries and illnesses. There is a network system of information to allow any place in the USAto contact us for immediate dispatch to collect and deliver the victim of an accident or illness.

"Yes, Miss Parks. That explains the operations, I want to know the financial process."

This is Mike's and his father's business, and they have vowed to make it free of charge to anybody, wealthy or impoverished. No exceptions.

However, to finance a sizeable philanthropic endeavor as Angel Flight, it is necessary to receive donations, large or small. This practice has been successful so far, and there is no reason to think otherwise. People are generous and compassionate in this country, especially where life and death matters are involved.

"Thank you again, Miss Parks. You have given me precisely the answer I needed to determine the payment I will gladly give to Angel Flight. You may call it a donation. You may also be interested to know I have been in touch with my Company in China.They have agreed with my decision to donate to Angel Flight Services the amount of USD 500,000 for the honorable and efficientmanner in which I was indeed rescued. My father would feel the same. I hand you my check with gratitude and goodwill. Thank you."

Vicki, Gerry, and Joseph all shook Luiu's hand and expressed their sincere gratitude and best wishes for him and his family and business.

Small conversations of goodbyes, well wishes, and values, health, families, ended withDr. Wardalso present during the meaningful gathering.

The crew walked down the halls of thehospital in silent thanksgiving for the positive outcomeof this mission. Mr. Luiu, Sr. was at peace in Heaven.

CHAPTER 62

They passed by the hospital coffee shop.

Joseph said, "Would anyone like to have coffee while we wait for the taxi. I'll call for it."

"Yes, thank you, and one for Gerry," said Vicki. "We'll get our luggage and check out of DoubleTree,after our coffee, and go directly to Eppley. I'll radio Mike from there and tell him we're leaving Omaha.

They arrived at Eppley Airport, and the security guardwas at his post.

Vicki said, "I am the pilot of Angel Flight Six. There are just three crew members altogether. We will be returning to The Dalles, Oregon. Please notify the hanger that we will be waiting to perform our preflight tasks, checklists and flight plans as soon as the plane is ready.Thank you."

" Gerry. I'm going to call Mike on this phone instead of from the plane radio. When the hangar calls that the plane is ready for us, we will be able to takeoff without any unfinished business. Right? Where is Joseph?"

"He went to get some snacks for us. He won't be too long."

The hangar called the desk clerk, and she announced to the crew,"Your plane is ready.You are to go totheir office first to pay fees and check out. Have a good flight."

Vicki called to Joseph, "would you make the walk-around check, and Gerry will get a weather report. I will do the flight plan, and we'll be ready to take our seats and complete the checklists covering the control panel and gauges."

Joseph took his copilot seat and said to Vicki, "Walk-around checklist complete, no problems."

Gerryreported, "weather in Western Nebraska shows cloudy and possible thunderstorms moving in from the West.

"Okay, here we go. Fasten your seatbelts, last stop The Dalles, Oregon.

Vicki guided the plane out of the hangar toward the tarmac.She keyed to the Control Tower.

"Control Tower here.Over."

"Angel Flight Six, ready for departure. Over."

"You will taxi to Runway 34. You will be 10th in line. Over"

Angel Flight Six. Roger. Over and out."

The plane finally came to the takeoff moment on Runway 34.

The pure white Medivac Gulf Stream, was an impressive sight against the vivid blue sky. The crew was happy to be in the air at last. Their conversation over the plains of Nebraska was about the success of their mission, even though Mr, Luau did not survive, his son was pleased with Angel Flight Service. They all were eager to share their tourism stories with folks back home.

Vicki said, "Gerry, did you say storms were brewing on the Western border of Nebraska. I see thunderheads straight ahead! Get on the radio and get an update on the weather in this area.

"Okay." Gerry listened to the weather report with a keen ear. Thunderstorms are severe in Eastern Wyoming and wind stronger further West."Looks like wemight be meeting some turbulence soon."

"We have some turbulence. It's going to get stronger, be sure the equipment is secure and strap your seatbelts tightly." Vicki said.

Fifteen minutes later, Joseph said. "We're in a violent thunderstorm now. Heavy thunder, lightning, and wind will make a rough ride. Hang on to your hat!"

Joseph said, "How much longer do you suppose this storm is going to be violent?"

"No way to judge until later," Gerry said.

Vickisaid to Joseph, "I'm glad there are two of us pilots. It would be almost too much for one pilot on a massive plane like our Gulf Stream to have the staminato managecontrol when turbulence and wind conditions are so violent.What is ordinarily slight physical effort becomesstrenuous. We are doing fine, and we will be out of it sooner or later. Ihave hadthe experience once, how about you, Joseph?"

"Same here. Once at school."

"I'm going to check the weather for Utah and Oregon,"Gerry said.

"All clear the other side of Ogden and to the coast! Good news! I think it has calmed down."

"We have come through the storm without incident.Thank you guys, for another job 'well done'"

"I'll retake control, Jeffrey. We're close to The Dalles already. That last hour was calm. We can be proud of our mission in every way."

Vicki keyed to The Dalles Control Tower.

"Air Contol at The Dalles, come in,"

"Angel Flight Six, requesting landing instructions. Over."

"You are two miles out. Make your approach to land on runway 64. Welcome home. Over."

"Approaching to land on runway 64. Over and out."

Vicki brought the big plane to a smooth landing and felt the electric thrill and knew she had made a perfect landing. Her crewmates congratulated her." They were home!

Chapter 63

Mike was the first to welcome them home, Heather was the second.

He said, "Hi, guys. So good to see you safe and sound. I knew about the storm in Utah, but I didn't realizehow much danger there might be. Come into my office. We'll get the report out of the way, thenyou can go home get some rest. I will listen as the report you file here will be almost word for word the story. Don't be surprisedthat you will be requested byeverybody in town, to tell sooner or later.

It was a long, tragic, exciting, and fun report. Mike was humbled by the $500,000 check Mr. Luiu had given Angel Flight Services and grateful for the Duncan Café consideration as well.

"It's time for us all to go home and have a good, long rest.

Vicki drove into her driveway, "Mama, we're so glad you are home. We missed you very much."

Mrs. Parks said, "Vicki, I am so proud of you. We are happy and want to hear your story, but you rest now.

Gerry's children gave him a warm homecoming, and Joseph went to his lodging.

It had been a short time ago that a remarkable event took place at Mike and Susan's ranch. In fact, it was the next morning when Vicki was called to pilot Angel Flight Six to Ogden, Utah, for this mission of mercy. Gerry was with her.

Mike said goodnight to his beloved Susan, and all in this friendly town was blessed and at peace.

The cougar screamed, thewolf howled, the owl hooted, and the Columbia River gurgled and splashed its way to the Pacific Ocean under the magnificent Mt Hood, as it will be forever!